THE
MASTER PLAN
A TOMMY O' LEARY MYSTERY

PETER GIANNOTTI

Outskirts Press, Inc.
Denver, Colorado

The Master Plan
A Tommy O'Leary Mystery
All Rights Reserved.
Copyright © 2010 Peter Giannotti
v3.0

Cover Photo © 2010 photos.com. All rights reserved - used with permission.

Outskirts Press, Inc.
http://www.outskirtspress.com

ISBN: 978-1-4327-5936-0

Outskirts Press and the "OP" logo are trademarks belonging to Outskirts Press, Inc.

PRINTED IN THE UNITED STATES OF AMERICA

DEDICATION

For Tierney
You are the answer to my prayers

Chapter 1

New Haven, 8:05 PM

Dr. Edgar Green exited the side door of his run-down office building in the Fair Haven section of the city. This, his place of employment for the better part of three decades, had fallen into disrepair in recent years. But Edgar, the parsimonious fellow that he was, saw no need for any updates. Structurally the building was sound. So what if it looked a little bit weathered? It gave it a little character, right?

After all, the people who came to his building were not interested in architecture. Well, they might have been in their spare time, but that was certainly the last thing they thought about when they came to pay him a visit. No, they had other things on their minds. They didn't care how it looked, so why should he? And even if they did care, it didn't matter to the building's owner. It was paid for. That's all he cared about.

The building was originally home to a textile factory constructed around 1900. However, some time during the 1960's it was converted into commercial office space. Connecticut's unfriendly business environment and the cold winters prompted the owner to pack up his business and relocate to South Carolina. Edgar picked it up for a song some ten years later.

The structure was a mixture of red brick and stucco; its peeling wooden windows were covered with iron bars. At the building's front entrance hung a steel door. A closer examination of the door revealed a number of indentations -- bullet holes. A protester had pulled a gun on Edgar in 1999, but he had managed to close the front door before the man could get off two shots. To the right of the door, a faded brass sign was visible. It read "The New Haven Reproductive Clinic."

The staff parking area where Edgar currently stood was flanked by a chain linked fence topped with razor wire. You couldn't take any chances in this day and age, he reminded himself. Due to the nature of his business, Edgar had received an interesting nickname, "Edgar Green the Baby Killing Machine," and his fair share of threats over the years. So rather than having to contend with possible assailants in the parking lot, he enclosed it to protect himself and his staff. Truthfully, Edgar didn't really care about his staff. His only concern was himself. But if it made the peons who worked for him feel safe enough to come to work everyday, that was an added bonus.

Edgar locked the door to the clinic, pretended to arm the security system, and began the short walk to his car. It's true that Edgar valued security, but he placed a far greater value on the almighty dollar. He had the security system installed around the time he received his first death threat, but discontinued the system monitoring a few months later. It was a waste of money he told himself. After all, he still had the security company signs around his property and the keypads were in plain sight. In his infinite wisdom, he figured this would be enough to frustrate would-be intruders.

Despite the security fence, he looked around the parking area to make sure he was alone. Nothing caught his attention. Had he looked beyond the fence, he might have noticed a blue van parked just up the street. The occupant of the van certainly saw Edgar. He had become quite familiar with Edgar over the last several months. "Oh Edgar," he said to himself, "you are so predictable. You almost make it too easy."

Yes, he was predictable, and for Edgar, this predictability would be his downfall. Like most people, Edgar got up at the same time everyday. In his case, the magic hour was 6:00 am. And after rolling out of bed, he began his morning ritual by retrieving the *New Haven Register* and the *New York Times* from his front stoop. He read them cover to cover while consuming generous helpings of coffee, eggs and breakfast meats. More often than not, he'd spill half his breakfast all over the papers, but he didn't care. Occasionally he would shower before work, but not today.

He dressed himself in a white shirt, black tie, black shoes and a crumpled brown suit that had not seen the inside of a dry cleaner in years. He gazed in the mirror and half-heartedly fixed his tie. Edgar was not a good looking man, far from it. And the years had not been kind. His grey-brown hair had been thinning for as far back as he could remember. He did his best to comb his hair over to cover up his receding hairline and ever-expanding bald spot, but to no avail. He stood at about 5'5" and weighed in at 210 pounds, most of which seemed to settle around his midsection. Truth be told, Edgar had the physique of a pear. His face was lined, wrinkled and puffy from a lifetime of heavy drinking; his eyes, bloodshot. His hands were filthy, his nails, untrimmed. They looked more like the hands of a ditch digger than a doctor. God only knew what was under his nails.

Pleased with his appearance or simply accepting the fact that he could do little to improve how he looked, Edgar left his bedroom and proceeded down the hallway. He descended the basement staircase and made his way into the adjacent garage. He climbed into his late model *BMW*, turned on the ignition, hit the garage door opener and was off down the driveway tossing gravel in his wake. All the while, the man in the blue van sat patiently, watching and waiting. His time would come, and that time would be tonight.

Edgar lived just a short drive from the clinic in the suburb of Woodbridge. His residence was a 'modest' Tudor style home; 15,000 square feet to be exact. Calling his home 'modest' was Edgar's idea of a joke. When he made his first million, he bought the house and he'd lived there ever since. He had no intention of ever moving. He was the king, and this was his castle. He liked the fact that he didn't have to drive very far to work. Like most Americans, he despised commuting. Aside from his daily commute, Edgar traveled very little. He was quite content with his existence, but that had not always been the case.

Edgar was born in New Haven in 1947 to Rabbi Daniel Green and his wife, Rebecca. He was the youngest of their three children. Edgar was what one might call the black sheep of the Green family. His older brother David followed in the footsteps of their father and became an Orthodox Rabbi. He married his high school sweetheart, Esther Goldberg. His sister married the local kosher butcher, Saul Rosen, after getting her degree from Boston University. They each had three kids. Edgar on the other hand chose another path. He never married, and he couldn't stand kids.

From a very early age, it was apparent that Edgar had a mind of his own. Instead of engrossing himself in his studies or his faith like his older siblings, Edgar preferred the pastimes of drinking beer and smoking pot with his friends. If you looked up self-centered in the dictionary, it would be no surprise to see his picture there in the margin. That's just the way he was, that's the way he had always been.

Edgar was about as different from his father as any child could be. Rabbi Green was generous to a fault. He and his wife gave much to their congregation and to the community at-large. They would take in people who were down on their luck and give them food and a place to stay until they were able to get back on their feet.

Edgar on the other hand was about as selfish as a person could be. He had nothing but contempt for the people his parents helped. He couldn't understand why his parents went out of their way for total strangers. In his mind his parents were suckers.

And just as his parents put God first in their lives, Edgar was a devout atheist. The last taste of religion Edgar had was his bar mitzvah. He had not set foot in a house of worship since that day, and didn't care to ever again. As far as he was concerned, there was no supreme being that governed all. Each man was a god in his own right who had to stake out his dominion in this world, just as he had. How naive his parents were to believe in some fictitious man in the sky. As a younger man he was so embarrassed by his father's chosen profession that when people asked what his father did for a living, he simply replied that he was dead. In Edgar's mind, his father and mother died long before their physical deaths.

Edgar made the seven mile commute in short order and pulled into the clinic's parking lot at five minutes to 8:00, just like every other day. You could set your watch by Edgar's schedule. The man in the blue van did just that.

The clinic didn't open until 9:00, but Edgar was not one to arrive at the last minute. He had lots of things to do before his day of medical "procedures" began. He was always the first to arrive and the last to leave, and he liked it that way. And as much as he enjoyed operating, he really enjoyed the moments when he was left all alone. He couldn't stand making small talk with his employees. He really had nothing in common with them except for the work. He didn't care about their families; he didn't want to know about their life stories and he wasn't interested in their hopes and dreams. They worked together -- period. The only times he didn't have to make chit chat was when he was alone or operating.

Edgar plopped himself down at his desk and dove into a large pile of paperwork. He looked over the clinic's income statement for the first part of the year. Yes, he thought, it will be a good year indeed. Despite an industry-wide decline in reproductive surgeries over the last decade, Edgar had seen a sharp increase in his own revenue during the same period of time. This increase was due in large part to a new market he had tapped.

About five years ago Edgar stumbled upon a new anti-aging craze. Rich men and woman the world over were injecting embryonic stem cells into their faces in an effort to reduce the signs of aging. And although it had not yet caught on here in the United States, as it was currently illegal, the international demand was staggering. The only obstacle was supply. That's where Edgar came in. He had plenty to go around.

In the old days, the "leftovers" from his procedures, as he affectionately called them, were picked up by a medical waste disposal company once or twice a week, and he paid a large premium for this service. With his new venture, Edgar was able to sell these same leftovers, making a huge profit in the process. He had a lucrative practice compared to many of his contemporaries and he could have made a great deal of money selling only his "leftovers," but

Edgar had an even bigger prize in mind. Anticipating the increasing demand, Edgar added embryonic wholesaler to his business's bottom line. He charged dramatically lower prices than all other medical waste disposal companies, and he put his competition out of business virtually overnight. It was a gold mine. On average he made about $1,000 per aborted fetus. And the people who were administering the treatments charged another $7,000, of which Edgar got a cut. Life was good for Edgar Green. Unfortunately for him, it would be short-lived.

Edgar's day at the clinic was pretty routine. He performed a large number of procedures, but all in all it was uneventful. After the day's last surgery, he sat down in the clinic's kitchen and poured himself some coffee. He was tired. He had not been this tired in a long while. It reminded him of his days in medical school when he got little or no sleep for days on end.

Edgar barely squeaked by during his undergraduate years at Southern Connecticut State University, but in the end, he graduated with a degree in biology. Despite his mediocre grades and a low score on his entrance boards, he was determined to attend medical school. After being rejected by just about every medical school program in the continental United States, Edgar was finally accepted to a small school in northern Mexico. It was cheap, the climate was warm and, well, they were the only school that would take him.

He dove into his studies at the University of Northern Mexico like he did everything else in his life, half-assed. But in seven years, he managed to graduate and eventually settled back east in New Haven. Edgar emerged from med school even more arrogant than when he entered. So it came as a big surprise to him that job offers were not as plentiful as his female conquests during his med school days. Undeterred, Edgar came up with another plan of attack. Several years earlier, the judges on the highest court in the land made abortion in the United States a so-called Constitutional right. After a little research, Edgar discovered only one other clinic in the State of Connecticut. Why not open a clinic of his own, he mused? He had learned the procedure in med school. Why not put that training to good use? Thanks to some well invested gambling winnings, he was able to buy the old factory building a few months later, and he never looked back.

Edgar opened the driver's side door, and threw his battered briefcase on the passenger's seat. Unlike most businessmen, Edgar didn't carry work related materials in his briefcase. Instead, he used it to carry cash, when necessary, and his personal supply of smut magazines. In his downtime at the clinic, he enjoyed perusing the magazines, even in front of his female employees. Edgar had no shame.

Safely in the car, Edgar turned the ignition on and headed towards the nearby gate. A motion detector responded to the presence of the car, and the fence slowly rolled back. Edgar took a right out of the parking lot and headed west toward his favorite watering hole, Liam McGuire's.

Liam McGuire's was a dive in every sense of the word, and Edgar loved it. He was a regular and had been for as far back as could remember. Unlike most bars in Connecticut, Liam McGuire's was a smoke friendly environment. And like many of Liam's patrons, Edgar could not have a cocktail without lighting up.

When the state smoking ban went into effect several years ago, Liam, the bar's owner and namesake, had an ingenious idea, why not turn the bar into a private club? In its infinite wisdom, the Connecticut state legislature exempted the Indian casinos and private clubs from the statewide smoking ban. So Liam, the entrepreneur that he was, capitalized on this loophole by turning his establishment into Liam McGuire's Irish American Club. To keep up the charade, he made each person who entered his establishment for the first time sign the membership book and pay a membership fee of $5.00. He even gave out membership cards. In reality, the five dollar fee was applied as a credit to the new members tab at the end of the night. It was a win-win for everyone.

Edgar pulled into his usual parking spot a few doors down from the bar. He didn't like to park too close to the front door. For years he parked just curbside of the entrance, but his car had been showered one too many times with the urine and vomit of Liam's patrons. Edgar had to admit, he even pissed on his own car once or twice. Also, no one else liked to park where he did, so he figured his car was less likely to be dinged. He locked the car, and hobbled to the front door.

As if on cue, the man in the blue van pulled up behind Edgar's car and put the vehicle into park. He knew just how long Edgar would be inside, one hour. The man had a number of things to attend to before Edgar stumbled back to his car, so the one hour would suit him just fine. Preparation was the man's middle name and this mission was no exception. He pushed aside the burlap curtain that separated the cab of the van from the cargo bay, flipped over an empty milk crate, sat down and finalized his preparations for the evening.

"I hope you enjoy yourself this evening Edgar, because it will be your last. It's time for you to come face to face with that imaginary man in the sky your parents spoke off. With any luck he will show you more compassion than you deserve, but I hope not."

Despite the nature of this evening's undertaking, the man in the blue van was a person of faith. There were plenty of nuts in the world who killed in the name of God and religion, but he was not one of them. Not in the least. In fact, he was quite certain that the God he worshiped was quite disappointed with his actions, but he had made up his mind long ago and there was no turning back.

Chapter 2

Edgar sat down at the bar. He preferred the bar for no other reason than it was the fastest place to get a drink. There were waitresses, but trying to get drinks from them just wasn't worth the effort. When he came to McGuire's first and foremost it was about drinking. Sure he picked up an occasional piece of ass, but his main goal was to tie one on. He was in no mood to wait for his liquor. Nick the bartender brought Edgar the usual, *Dewar's* straight up. He could never understand why people added mixers to their booze. What was the point? He downed the drink in one quick gulp, nodded a thank you to Nick and headed for the john.

The bathroom was filthy, but what would one expect from a bar of this caliber? The floor was covered with toilet paper, pubic hair and cigarette butts; the walls awash with graffiti. There was only one toilet, but no door to the stall that enclosed the porcelain receptacle. Adjacent to the stall was a long trough for those who only needed to urinate. Edgar sidled up to the trough just as he'd done many times before. It took him a little while to get nature to take its course, but eventually he took care of business. "Damn enlarged prostate," he muttered. Getting older didn't bother Edgar. Pissing every twenty minutes did. Despite the bathroom's shortcomings, it did have a working sink, soap and even paper towels. Edgar looked in the cracked mirror, fixed his hair, but did not avail himself of the hand washing facilities. He never did.

By the time he got back to the bar, Nick had already poured him another drink. Of all the people he knew, Edgar treated Nick the best. Nick didn't bother Edgar and he never talked to Edgar unless Edgar engaged him first. And most importantly, he always kept Edgar's glass full. Edgar tipped him graciously for it. Nick was as close to a friend as Edgar had. Sure, they didn't see each socially and for the life of him, he couldn't say where Nick lived, but of all the people Edgar dealt with on a daily basis, Nick was at the top of his list.

Edgar took a sip of drink number two, and headed for the juke-box. McGuire's had a great song selection and Edgar usually spent a good five dollars on songs every time he came for a visit. The staff joked that between the money Edgar spent on booze and the juke-box, Liam put his oldest son through college.

Edgar chose a few of his favorite songs. Despite his advancing years, Edgar liked to think that he was still hip. His choice of music was always very eclectic. He picked "Rhinestone Cowboy," by Glenn Campbell, "Wasted Years," by Iron Maiden, and "It's the End of the World as we Know it," by REM. However, unbeknownst to Edgar, this evening would be anything but fine.

He returned to the bar and picked up a nearby racing sheet. Not only could you get your fill of cigarettes and alcohol at McGuire's, you could place your bets with Liam as well. Edgar enjoyed playing the ponies, and he was quite good. There were plenty of off-track betting places in the area, but Edgar preferred to sit on his favorite stool while picking the races for the following day. Despite an impressive winning streak over the last month, Edgar's picks for today's races all tanked. There's always tomorrow, he thought.

While Edgar lit up a *Winston* and made his choices for the following day's races, the man in the blue van finished his final preparations. From his black bag, he removed a small envelope containing a yellowish powder. He then produced a vial containing a clear liquid. He poured the contents of the envelope into the vial, and waited for it to dissolve. After a few minutes he inserted a syringe into the vial and extracted the cloudy liquid. This will be plenty, he thought. Sodium thiopentone is a fast- acting barbiturate. Within fifteen to thirty seconds of being administered, his "patient" would lose consciousness rather quickly, and wouldn't come around for a good ten minutes. That would be just enough time to get Edgar back to his beloved clinic.

Next, the man produced two pairs of plastic restraints; one for Edgar's hands and one for his feet. It was very unlikely that Edgar would regain consciousness before they made it to the clinic, but the man wasn't about to take any chances. Edgar would be hard enough to maneuver as it was. It would be even worse if he put up a fight. The man put the restraints in his jacket pocket along with the re-capped syringe, and waited.

By this time Edgar had been inside for approximately 20 minutes. As much as he enjoyed spending time at McGuire's, he was not one to linger too long. Well, unless there was a lady involved, and tonight pickings were slim indeed. By the time he placed his bets with Liam, he'd finished off drink number two.

Nick, true to form, had his next drink all ready to go. In a gesture of gratitude, he thanked Nick for the drink by plopping down a $20.00 dollar bill on the bar. As fast as the bill hit the bar, Nick had it in his breast pocket. He nodded thanks to Edgar and went to the cooler to change the *Guinness* keg that just kicked.

As Edgar took the first sip of his drink, the beginning bars to

"Rhinestone Cowboy" filtered through the bar. And although he had a terrible singing voice, he sang along. The regulars paid no attention. They knew Edgar's routine as well as the man in the van. There were a few snickers from a couple of Yale students, but it was nothing Edgar hadn't heard before. He reminded himself that he could buy and sell anyone in this bar. So if they wanted to laugh, fine. He didn't give a shit what they thought.

Nick returned from the back with a bowl of stew and a basket of brown bread and placed them on the bar in front of Edgar. Occasionally Edgar would have some shepherd's pie or a traditional Irish breakfast to mix things up, but tonight it would be his favorite. Liam made the stew fresh every Wednesday, and he'd always save a bowl for Edgar.

Edgar stuffed a paper napkin into his collar; he liberally buttered up a slice of brown bread and used it to scoop up a healthy portion of the lamb, *Guinness,* and potato mixture. Damn that was good, he thought. He repeated this ritual until both the basket and the bowl were empty. Satisfied, he let out a large belch, and hopped off the stool for the bathroom. Nick cleared away the remnants of the meal and dumped them in a bus tray under the bar.

By this time Edgar was starting to feel the effects of the alcohol. The stew helped to slow the process down a bit, but Edgar knew that he could have only one more drink before he headed home. He was a seasoned drinker, but even he had his limits. He pushed opened the door to the bathroom and nearly knocked over one of the Yale students who mocked his singing earlier in the night. The guy laughed as he met Edgar eye to eye.

"Screw yourself you piece of shit," Edgar mumbled.

"You first, fat man," the kid replied as he walked out the door.

"You little punk; you're lucky I don't beat the shit out of you."

The kid just shook his head.

Edgar hadn't been in a fight in years, but he was pretty sure he could kick the crap out of that kid. Fucking Yalies. They treated you like shit unless they needed something from you. Oh, he'd seen his fair share in the clinic over the years. You could tell a Yalie from a mile away. He kept a little journal of all the men and woman who walked through his door. There were more Yalies than he could count. His little journal had come in handy over the years. The patients called it blackmail, he called it a part of doing business. He wouldn't be surprised to see that little prick and his girlfriend in his clinic in the not-too-distant future. He could just picture the look on his face.

Edgar couldn't stand the youth of today. They were so arrogant. In his day you were taught to respect your elders. Come to think of it, he never respected his elders either, but that wasn't the point. He had accomplished much in his 60 plus years. He deserved the respect of that kid and all the little weasels like him.

Edgar finished up in the bathroom a little faster than he did on his first trip, and made a quick exit back to the bar. Once you break the seal, it just doesn't stop, he reflected angrily. On the way back to his stool, he stopped to play a quick game of *Golden Tee*. He wouldn't be caught dead on a golf course, but he did like to engage in a game of video golf from time to time. What was the point of "real" golf? Sure you could drink while you played, but what fun was it lugging a fifty pound bag around for a couple of hours while chasing a little ball? Nick brought over another drink, and Edgar proceeded to play nine holes.

He wrapped up his game after dumping in $8.00, and finished the last of his *Dewar's*. It was time to go home. Early to bed, early to rise, makes a man healthy, wealthy and wise, he said to himself.

It had certainly been the case for him. He was wealthy and wise. However, the jury was still out on the healthy part.

Edgar settled up his tab with Nick and threw him another $20.00 for the effort. He waved to Liam who was down at the other end of the bar, and headed out the front door. The humid air caught him off guard. The air conditioning had been so nice in the bar that he had forgotten just how hot it was outside. He grabbed a soiled handkerchief from his inside pocket and dabbed it across his forehead. As he neared his car, he noticed the blue van. That's odd, he thought. No one else usually parks this far away from the bar.

He unlocked and opened the door in one, fluid motion. He eased himself onto the seat and closed the door, but before he could insert the key into the ignition, a gloved hand covered his face and pulled his head backwards. Edgar reached up with both of his hands to remove the hand from his face, but the man's grip was too strong. This was not good, Edgar thought. As he struggled, he tried to look in the mirror for a glimpse of his assailant, but all he could see was darkness. The man reached around with the syringe, and jammed it into Edgar's neck. He continued to struggle, but little by little any will to resist subsided. Within fifteen seconds, Edgar was out.

Chapter 3

New Haven, 9:25 PM

Edgar stopped struggling and the man released his grip. The man had only a small window of time before Edgar regained consciousness. Luckily, it was only a short ride to Edgar's clinic, and even though he still had to drag Edgar's obese body into the van, there was plenty of time to get the doctor ready for surgery.

There was a risk in using the van instead of use Edgar's car, but the man felt the risk was worth it. He grabbed Edgar's slumped body under each arm, and dragged him to the side door of the van. With one hand he held Edgar, with the other, he opened the door. He lifted Edgar's lifeless body, and rolled it into the van. He then placed the plastic restraints on Edgar's feet and hands. Without missing a beat, he closed the front door of Edgar's car and hopped behind the wheel of the van. He threw the vehicle into gear, made a U-turn and was on his way. It had taken him approximately 48 seconds to render Edgar unconscious and load him into the van.

It had been easy to catch Edgar off guard, the man thought. Edgar was too cocky for his own good. Despite all of his misdoings, Edgar thought himself invincible. He never thought his past deeds would come back to haunt him. That was the nature of the narcissist; the world revolves around you, and you are its master.

However Edgar inadvertently relinquished his master status as soon as he sat down in his car. To make things even easier, the man had entered Edgar's home two weeks prior, and made duplicate keys of Edgar's home, clinic, and automobiles. He also obtained the necessary frequencies for Edgar's garage door opener and for the gate at the clinic. As luck would have it, both had the same frequencies.

The van approached the clinic and the man pressed the button on his newly purchased door opener. Within seconds the gate slid open. As the van cleared the fence he pressed the button a second time and the gate closed behind him. So far so good, he thought. He pulled the van around the left side of the building and brought it to a stop around the corner. It was the perfect spot. There was just enough space to accommodate the van between the building and the fence, and there were no lights to reveal its position. After making sure he was not being watched, the man opened the rear of the van. Edgar lay there like a sack of potatoes. He pulled Edgar to the edge of the door, and lifted him into a fireman's carry position. Edgar would have been heavy for the average man, but not the man in the blue van. He lifted the abortion doctor with great ease. He carried Edgar the short distance to the side entrance of the clinic, and the man produced a key. He opened the door, not worrying about the alarm system. He knew the alarm was inoperative.

Edgar's clinic had two operating rooms. The man chose the larger of the two to place his patient. He positioned Edgar face down on the operating table with Edgar's head hung slightly off one side. From his bag, he produced a knife, several polyprolene straps and two pairs of metal shackles. He began by cutting the plastic restraints he had placed on Edgar in the van. Next, he placed the shackles on each of Edgar's hands and feet, securing them beneath the table. He then took the straps, and one by one he placed them over Edgar's lifelessly body, starting with his neck and ending with his ankles. He pulled the straps under the table and buckled them together. He then tested each of the straps to make sure they were secure; they were. Edgar was helpless.

The effects of the *Sodium Thiopentone* were rapidly wearing off. The return of consciousness came to Edgar almost as fast as the drug had plunged him into darkness. Edgar slowly opened his eyes and craned his neck. He tried to focus, but the bright overhead lights made even this small task difficult. Little by the little the room finally came into focus. Although he had never viewed the room from his current position, he was quite familiar with his surroundings. He was in Operating Room Number 2.

Shit, he thought, I must have had quite a time last night.

It wasn't unheard of for Edgar to get so drunk that he didn't make it home. The clinic was much closer to Liam McGuire's than his house, so occasionally he ended up crashing at the clinic. However, this was the first time he ever ended up in one of the operating rooms. Usually he slept on the old couch in his office, but there was a first time for everything.

Oh well, he thought, shit happens.

Finally able to muster the strength, Edgar attempted to lift himself from the table. As hard as he tried, he could not move. He realized he was strapped down. "What the fuck," he muttered. "Is this someone's idea of a sick joke? Liam, Nick, what the hell is going on?"

The last two people he remembered speaking to last night were Nick and Liam. It had to be them. They must be busting my balls, he thought.

"Hey guys, come on, will you let me go already? Enough is enough. You made your fucking point. Ha ha ha. I'm all for jokes, but this one isn't funny. Let me up or I swear to God, I'll beat the living shit out of the both of you. Liam, Nick!"

"It's funny that you mention God, Edgar. I didn't think you believed in the Almighty."

The man's voice was soft, almost soothing. Edgar heard the voice, but he could not see where it was coming from. He did know one thing, it wasn't Nick or Liam. The voice was too refined to have come out of Nick's mouth, and it certainly didn't have the Irish brogue Liam was famous for.

The velvety voice continued, "Edgar, you have been a bad boy. And you know what happens to bad boys? They get punished of course. Sure, some people argue that many bad deeds go unpunished. I tend to disagree. On the surface, that might appear to be true. I will concede that many people escape punishment in this world. However, I firmly believe that those same people get what is coming to them in the next."

Edgar was confused. Who was this guy and what bad deed did this asshole think he committed?

The man edged closer to the operating table a little at a time while continuing to speak. "Edgar, your life has consisted of nothing but death and destruction. And I think it is fair to say that when you finally leave this earth, no one will miss you. This world will be a far better place without you in it."

He was finally in Edgar's line of sight. The man leaned in closer so Edgar could see his face. His eyes widened and fear washed over his body, his bowels loosened. He knew exactly who this man was. This was no joke. This was very bad.

"Wait, stop. You don't have to do this. We can work something out, I swear. I'm sorry, I never meant for any of that to happen. You've got to believe me. I was only doing my job."

Edgar wasn't sure what the man was going to do, but he knew it was going to be bad.

"Come now Edgar, the Germans tried that excuse. It didn't work at Nuremberg, and it will not work here."

"Please, give me a chance to explain. I don't deserve this. What can I do to make you change your mind? There must be something? I've got money, plenty of money. There's a safe inside the walk-in cooler. Take whatever you want, but please, just let me be."

"Edgar, I am well aware of your safe. I know everything there is to know about you. In fact, I probably know you better than you know yourself. I could pilfer your treasure at any time, but I am not a thief. No, I have a different agenda. Mine is to avenge a past wrong. You had your chance to make things right, but you chose a different path. Do you have any final words?"

Edgar screamed. "You son of a bitch, please, please don't do this. Please, oh God, please stop. You don't have to do this."

"On the contrary Edgar, this is exactly what I must do.'

Edgar continued to scream and struggle. The man walked slowly across the room to a small metal cabinet. Inside were the tools of Edgar's trade: scalpels, clamps, you name it. The instruments of death were aplenty. He removed an oversized pair of scissors and a surgical mallet. Next, he retrieved a high powered surgical suction unit from the opposite side of the room. He wheeled the unit across the cold tile floor to the head of the operating table.

"Edgar, you have always been a big fan of the partial birth abortion. I figured it was a fitting tribute to end your life in a similar fashion."

Edgar screamed, "No, God no. You can't do this. Help, please God, help."

Tired of Edgar's screaming, the man again walked across the

room, but even slower this time. He removed a roll of white surgical tape from the cabinet. He ripped off two pieces and placed them over Edgar's mouth. He picked up the scissors with his left hand and the mallet with his right. A small smile graced his face.

"Sweet dreams Edgar."

The man raised his right hand above his head, and with all the force he could muster, he slammed the mallet into the base of Edgar's skull, shattering it into hundreds of tiny pieces. Edgar's body began to twist and convulse, the table shook violently. Undeterred, the man placed the mallet onto a nearby surgical tray and from that same tray he removed a towel. He placed the towel over Edgar's head. He then switched the scissors to his right hand. He lifted the scissors in an arc above his head and came down with such force that scissors exited Edgar's head by way of his left eye socket. Blood quickly covered the towel. Leaving the scissors imbedded in Edgar's head, the man stepped back and grabbed another towel, placing it over Edgar's head. He then grabbed the hose from the suction unit and jammed it under the towels into the exposed brain cavity and turned the unit on. Truthfully, he did not expect to retrieve much in they way of brain matter from old Edgar's head, but the machine did add a nice effect. Edgar's body continued to convulse for another minute or so, and finally, it ceased to move at all.

The man grabbed his bag, doused the lights and quickly exited the room. In no time the floor would be covered in Edgar's blood. He certainly didn't want to get any on himself. He did have one other thing to attend to before he left. He closed the door to Operating Room Number 2, proceeded down the dimly lit corridor, and rounded a corner to the right. Straight ahead lay a stainless steel walk-in refrigerator. This was the place where Edgar kept his most valued possessions: his money and the aborted fetuses of countless innocent souls. The idea of walking into the cooler made the man sick to his stomach, but there was something he needed to do. He said a prayer for Edgar's victims, and stepped inside. The light automatically came on and illuminated the temporary tomb. The man felt a chill, but it wasn't from the cold air escaping the cooler. Edgar had installed his safe in the walk-in because he figured it was the last place a person would look for his valuables. And even if they did venture inside, the surroundings would likely turn them away in short order.

The man stepped to the left, and at eye level he removed a plastic container from the top shelf. Behind the container was a steel door with a combination lock. He placed the container on the opposing shelf, and removed a small crowbar from his bag. He could have opened the lock with ease, but that was not his goal. Using the crowbar, the man half-heartedly attempted to open the safe, or rather, used the crowbar to make it look like he was trying to open the safe. Satisfied with his window dressing, the man placed the crowbar back in his bag, and quickly made his way to the building's side door.

The man peered outside the door, and seeing nothing unusual, walked to where he had parked the van. It was just as he'd left it. The man had been a little concerned about his vehicle. Edgar's clinic was in a very undesirable part of town. Car thefts were very common. Fair Haven was where he picked up the van in the first place, and that's where he'd leave it as well. He hit the button on the door opener and by the time he approached the gate, it was wide open. He hit the button one last time, and took a right out of the lot. He drove one half mile, and pulled into the parking lot of an abandoned warehouse. It was sad, he thought. When he was a kid, Fair Haven bustled with industry. Now, it was only a shell of its former self. He opened the rear doors of the van, and removed a long wooden plank. Next, he wheeled down a motorcycle, a *Suzuki DRZ 400SM*. He removed his outer clothing to reveal a set of leathers. He took off his shoes and replaced them with boots, and he grabbed a matching helmet from inside the van, and he secured it on his head. He threw the clothes and shoes into the back of the van, along with the wooden plank, and closed the doors. He slung his bag over his shoulder, mounted the bike, started it up, and raced out of the parking lot. When he was about five hundred yards away, he unzipped his breast pocket and removed a small remote control. He turned the unit on with one hand, and with the same hand, he pressed the two small black buttons just below the power switch. Within seconds, the van exploded and burst into flames. The man turned off the unit and placed it back where he had found it and re-zipped the pocket. As the man looked back, flames consumed the van. A few miles away, Edgar's beloved *BMW* also burst into flames. Car fires were not unheard of in this part of town, so the man didn't think anyone would give them much notice. Not until they found Edgar's body anyway. And by that time, he would be long gone.

Chapter 4

Joanna Carpenter arrived at The New Haven Reproductive Clinic at 8:27. Not too bad she thought. Joanna was paid hourly so she only hurt herself when she was late. She typically arrived anywhere between 8:30 and 9:30, but sometimes it was a little later. Her boss only gave her a hard time if she wandered in after 10:00. Luckily, she hadn't been in after 10:00 in a long while. She remembered the last time vividly. Edgar nearly shit himself; he was so pissed. Her old boyfriend Bobby had come to town unexpectedly for a visit the day before, and they partied well into the night. They didn't end up getting back to her place until 5:00am. How on earth was she expected to get to work on time that day?

This morning, on the other hand, she was able to drag herself out of bed with little difficulty. For once, she went to bed at a reasonable hour. Most nights she would stay up and watch old movies until she could no longer keep her eyes open. Last night's TV listings were pretty lame, so she decided to turn in early.

Joanna had worked at the clinic for two years now, and she was lucky to have the job. Early in her "nursing" career, she was arrested for "borrowing" pills at a nearby hospital. (Truthfully, she never obtained her nursing degree.) Man, she had been wild in those days, she thought. Now, she stuck strictly to the bottle, booze that is. Occasionally, she'd do a little Ecstasy, but that was as far as she'd go. When she applied to the clinic, Edgar overlooked both of her indiscretions. He could have cared less. She did what she was told, and because of her sordid past, he paid her less than he would have paid a fully qualified nurse. This was fine with Joanna. She couldn't stand Edgar, the sexist pig that he was. But a job was a job. After a few more years of keeping her nose clean and getting enough credits to graduate, she would start looking for a new position. But for now, she was happy to have a steady paycheck. Edgar had given her a key about a year ago; he parted with it like a starving man parts with his last morsel of food. To her recollection, she had only used the key one other time. On that particular day, Edgar had to go see his dentist, something about a broken crown. He called her at home early in the morning and told her to drag her ass into work and open up the clinic because he was going to be late. Fearing for her job, she did as she was told. She hadn't had occasion to use the key since. But today, she didn't see Edgar's car, so she would probably have to let herself in.

She fumbled through her well-worn purse looking for the key. Damn, where did I put it, she asked herself? She didn't keep the key on her key ring because she hardly used it. As it was, she had as many keys as a janitor on her ring already, so why add another? She ran back to her car, and rifled through her ash tray. And there it was. She walked back to the door and inserted the key. Yep, she found the right one. She entered the side door, and got ready to begin her day.

Edgar usually made the first pot of coffee each morning, but to-day it was her turn. Twice in a lifetime was no big deal, she reasoned. She threw her belongings into her locker in the staff office, (Edgar had his own office, everyone else shared an old walk-in closet), and walked to the lounge to get the coffee going. She grabbed a filter, placed it into the basket and loaded it up with a French Vanilla; her favorite. She filled the pot to the rim from the Poland Spring dispenser, and poured the contents into the coffee maker. She hit brew and began the task of opening the clinic.

First, she turned on all the lights and made sure the air conditioning was at an acceptable level. Edgar was so cheap that he would go all day without turning up the AC just to save a buck. And as if the heat was not bad enough, the warm temperatures seemed to accentuate Edgar's horrible body odor. If she had to wager, she'd bet that Edgar bathed maybe once a week, if that. She set the thermostat at a comfortable level and went from room to room making sure everything was stocked and tidy. She peeked into Operating Room Number 1 and noticed it was low on linens. She made the short walk to the storage closet, removed the necessary items and put them in their respective places. Satisfied that everything was all set in Room 1, she headed next door to Operating Room Number 2. Unlike Room 1, Room 2 was used less frequently, but she had to check it nevertheless. Occasionally they would have two surgeries going at the same time, but more often Edgar would spend most of his day in Room 1. She opened the door, but before she could lift up her eyes, she noticed a strange sound. Was that the surgical pump, she thought? As the sound registered in her head, she noticed something on the floor: blood. She had seen plenty of blood on operating room floors, but never this much and never congealed. That's odd, she thought. Edgar didn't perform any surgeries in here yesterday, and even if he did, the cleaning crew was usually in around 6:00 pm, and they had the place all shined up before Edgar left for the evening. Before she could complete that thought in her head, she noticed the body lying face down on the operating table.

"What the hell?" she muttered.

The body lay exactly as the man left it. Blood had soaked through the second towel as well, and it stuck to Edgar like a maroon hood. Joanna stepped closer to get a better look. There was no movement from the body. She spotted the scissors protruding from the person's head.

"What on earth happened here?" she asked herself out loud.

The face was covered with a bloody towel, but something seemed familiar: the brown suit, the cheap shoes and the pear-shaped body. Edgar. Suddenly she was overcome with fear. And her body began to tense.

"Oh my God," she screamed. "Help! Somebody help!"

She ran out the door, tripping over herself to get away from the gruesome scene she had just witnessed. The nearest phone was at reception. She grabbed the phone out of the cradle and frantically dialed 911. She was nearly hyperventilating.

"911, please hold," the operator said.

"No! You can't do that," she shouted. "Oh please God, get back on this line. I don't know what to do. Please help me," she mumbled. "My boss is dead. Come on, pick up, pick up damn it."

"Thank you for holding, what is your emergency?"

"I, ah, I came into work ten minutes ago, and I found my boss. He's dead!"

"Are you sure he's dead ma'am, did you check to see if he was breathing or if he had any vital signs?"

"Yes, I am sure, damn it. He is dead, I repeat, dead. I am a nurse, and I know dead. The room is covered in blood. Please send someone over here right now. I need help. Oh, please help me."

"Ma'am it's going to be alright. Police and emergency response will be dispatched immediately. What is your location?"

Joanna relayed the clinic's address to the operator in frantic, clipped tones.

"Would you like me to stay on the line, ma'am?"

"No, just tell them to hurry!"

"They'll go as fast as they can ma'am. You have a nice day."

A Nice day? Was this woman for real? She sounded more like a customer service rep with the *Pottery Barn* than a 911 operator. What was this world coming to? Joanna sat down on one of the metal chairs in the reception area. The steel was cold against her pale skin. Ok, pull your self together Joanna, she thought. The authorities will be here soon enough. She couldn't believe this was happening. Why did bad luck always seem to follow her around? She shook her head. "Where the hell am I going to find a new job on such short notice," she said to herself? "Damn you Edgar, why the hell did you go and get yourself killed? Couldn't you have at least waited 'til I got a new job? Shit!"

Officer Johnny Sabian sat in his patrol car and took a healthy bite of his *Egg McMuffin*. Thank God for *Mickey D's*, he thought. He put the sandwich down on the passenger's seat, and grabbed his third hash brown of the morning. He dipped it in the giant pile of ketchup on his *Egg McMuffin* wrapper, and polished it off in two bites. He then picked up his coffee; black with three sugars. As he prepared to take a swig, his radio came to life. Startled by the sudden noise, he spilled the black liquid all over his pants. "Son of bitch," he screamed.

"This is dispatch; we've got a 10-54 at 277 Front Street. Are there any patrol cars in the vicinity?"

"Shit, I am right there," he replied to himself. "I guess the rest of my breakfast will have to wait."

He responded, "Dispatch, this is Car 220, I'm en route, with an ETA of three minutes, 10-4."

"Thank you, car 220. Dispatch out."

"What was 10-54 again?" he wondered. Johnny had graduated from the academy less than six months ago, but for the life of him he couldn't remember what a 10-54 was. He was quite sure he'd find out soon enough. He finished the last of sandwich, and he threw his cruiser into gear.

"10-54, here I come. Damn it. Maybe I should have spent as many hours on the books as I did on the firing range. Here goes nothing," he said.

Johnny pulled up in front of the clinic four minutes later. He had driven by this building countless times, but had never really given it a second look. Most of the buildings in this part of town had seen better days. This building was no exception.

He couldn't get into the parking area due to the chain-link fence, so he parked his cruiser in the street. He immediately exited the car and bolted straight for the front door. He read the sign as he walked up the steps.

"Abortion clinic, great," he remarked sarcastically.

He rapped on the door three times and waited for a response. He reached for the door handle, but the door was locked. Just as he released his grip, the door swung open. Standing there was a blond haired woman, probably in her late twenties, although from the look of her, she had probably lived a hard life; if she didn't look out, she'd age awfully fast, he thought.

"It's about time you guys got here. My boss is laying dead in the operating room!"

A 10-54, he remembered, was a possible dead body. He knew it would eventually come back to him. At least it wasn't some crazy guy wielding a shotgun. He'd had one of those last week, and that was an experience he didn't feel like reliving anytime soon. It had taken a week for his ears to stop ringing from the sound of the gun.

Despite the circumstances, he remained ever courteous. "Alright ma'am, please lead the way." "Ok, follow me."

Johnny stepped inside and closed the door behind him. If it was a murder, he wanted to protect himself and this woman from the assailant if they decided to return to the scene. Johnny followed Joanna past the reception desk and down the narrow corridor to where she claimed to have found the body. She stopped outside one of the closed doors, and waited for Johnny to catch up. She motioned to the door.

"I came in about fifteen minutes ago, and this is what I found."

Not knowing what to expect inside, Johnny instructed the woman to step back. He then drew his weapon. Better safe than sorry. He grabbed and twisted the door knob with his left hand while steadying the gun with his right. Slowly he pushed the door open. The first thing he heard was the hum of the pump. The light was dim in the room, but he didn't want to turn on anymore lights just yet. He held his gun out in front of him and methodically swept the room from right to left. All clear, he thought. Thank God.

He holstered his weapon and his eyes were drawn to the table in the middle of the room. From the door, it was hard to make out the shape on the table. But the closer he got, the clearer the picture became. He saw the blood on the floor and just above, the blood soaked head with the scissors sticking out. "Oh man, that's a dead body alright," he said to himself. He had never seen a dead body up close. Well that wasn't entirely true. He'd seen a "cleaned up" body in the funeral home setting, but never a body that had been subjected to this type of trauma.

The metallic odor of blood wafted into his nostrils. "Man, it smells funny in here," he remarked.

Suddenly he felt his stomach tighten. Oh shit, he thought. Not wanting to contaminate the crime scene, he raced to the door and stuck his head out into the hall, nearly knocking Joanna down in the process. He tried to turn his head away from the woman, but it was too late; out came his breakfast. It hit the woman in the face and chest. She nearly fell down from the force of the vomit.

"I am so sorry," Johnny remarked. "The scene just caught me off guard, I guess."

The woman stood up, and walked a few steps to a nearby storage closet. She grabbed a towel and used it to clean herself up.

"First dead body, huh?"

"What?"

"I said first dead body?"

"Well, yeah. How'd you know?"

"The same thing happened to me when I saw my first one. Don't feel bad honey."

He laughed. "Maybe I shouldn't have had that third hash brown after all."

She looked down at the front of her shirt. "Maybe not," she replied.

Despite the circumstances, they both had a good laugh. When the laughter subsided, Johnny reached for the radio handset attached to his to lapel and pressed the send button.

"Dispatch, this is Officer Sabian. I'm at the Front Street location.

There is a dead body, I repeat, there is a dead body. It has suffered severe head trauma. And it doesn't appear to be accidental or self-inflicted. Send in the cavalry; this is certain to be an interesting one. Sabian out."

"Copy that Officer Sabian. Dispatch out."

Johnny redrew his weapon.

"Ma'am, is there a safe place for you to hole up while I take a look around?"

"Yes there is; and the name's Joanna. Calling me ma'am makes me feel like an old lady."

"Sorry, old habits die hard. Joanna it is; where to?"

"The staff has a small office that we share. I could wait in there while you look around."

"That would be perfect."

Joanna walked to the office with Johnny in tow. He opened the door and had a look around.

"When you said the room was small, you weren't kidding. Good luck trying to hide in here"

"You're telling me."

"When I come back, I'll knock three times, so you know it's me, Ok?"

"Ok. Be careful."

"Will do."

Johnny closed the door; he heard the click of the lock as he walked away. From the look of the body and the crime scene, it was very unlikely the killer was around. The guy had obviously been dead for awhile if the congealed blood on the floor was any indication. However, with killers, one never knew. If a person was capable of taking another person's life, they were capable of just about anything.

Johnny went room to room, closet to closet, but found nothing. When he had finished his sweep, he returned to retrieve Joanna, and wait for the re-enforcements. It was going to be a long day, he thought, and man I'm hungry.

Chapter 5

Peggy Baldwin strolled out the front door of her spacious bungalow and took a seat in one of the Adirondack chairs on her covered porch. She placed her cup of chai tea on the matching end table and took in her surroundings. What a beautiful day, she thought as she looked around the scenic New England campus. "It will be the perfect day for a kayak ride," she remarked under her breath.

Peggy was in her mid-forties, but looked ten years younger. She credited her youthful appearance to her daily fitness regimen. Each day began with an hour's worth of kayaking, weather permitting. (In the winter, she substituted her kayaking with a swim in the academy's Olympic size pool.) In the early evening, she'd usually run five to ten miles. Peggy was slim with long brown hair and brown eyes; her skin, a soft alabaster.

Peggy was the current Head Mistress at the prestigious Middlesex Academy where she'd been employed for over 20 years; first as a teacher and for the last eight years, as the academy's Head Mistress. She still taught an occasional class, but running the academy she called home took up most of her time these days. Despite the long hours, she couldn't think of any place she'd rather be. Although she despised the

United States, deep down she knew she wouldn't have this charmed existence anywhere else in the world.

Just as her idol John Dewey re-shaped public education in the United States in the early part of the last century, Peggy was using her position as Head Mistress to reshape this small yet influential private institution. Middlesex had been quite conservative when she arrived, but thanks to her diligence, that was no longer the case. Early on in her career, she kept her opinions to herself and said very little. She didn't want to reveal too much of herself to her colleagues. Her approach was much like that of her other idol, Justice Ruth Bader Ginsburg. Upon confirmation to the Supreme Court, Justice Ginsburg likewise kept a low profile, but all the while she was waiting to implement her progressive agenda through her court decisions. Ginsburg held little regard for the law. Her goal was to destroy the country from within. The advances for the progressive cause had been staggering during Ginsburg's tenure. Peggy's approach was similar, albeit on a smaller scale. But she was doing her part to further the progressive movement nevertheless. Truth be told, she was a Marxist. However, the moniker "progressive" had a more acceptable connotation. This was fine with her. She knew what she was and what she stood for. The name to her was irrelevant.

Peggy's parents had instilled this ideology in her from a very early age, and every waking moment since that time, she thought of new ways to press the agenda. Middlesex Academy had been the perfect place to disseminate her propaganda. For years, her fellow travelers had been turning America's public school system and secondary education institutions into progressive indoctrination centers. However, they had not been as successful with many of the private elementary and high schools. Those racist white men were still running the show at the majority of those schools. Sure, there were liberal schools where the progressive ideology was espoused, but the progressives had a harder time trying to crack the more well-known and traditional private institutions. Unlike public schools where boards of education wielded large amounts of influence, the curriculum at Middlesex was formulated primarily by the instructors. This freedom allowed Peggy to slowly introduce her political views into the subject matter she was charged to teach. Little by little, she began to notice a change in her students: they were abandoning long held beliefs in exchange for her progressive ideology. The faith-filled were turning their backs on organized religion; the America lovers were becoming skeptical, and in some instances, outright antithetical of the place of their birth; the pro-lifers were embracing 'reproductive rights.' It was marvelous to behold. She never dreamed how easy it could be. The key to her success was guilt, plain and simple. She made these rich, white, largely Christian, conservative kids feel guilty for what they had. And once she got them to despise themselves and their status in life, the rest was relatively simple; she replaced their beliefs with a "kinder," "gentler" way of thinking. And her students loved her. After all, she was the "cool" "young" teacher; yet another arrow in her quiver. The girls wanted to be like her, and the boys were in love with her. She used every tool at her disposal.

From a very young age she attended summer camp in the Pocono Mountains. On its face, the camp was typical in many ways; there were arts and crafts, water sports, hiking, horse back riding, you name it. But beneath the surface, there was a more sinister agenda at play: Marxist indoctrination. For the kids, this part of camp life became as common place as archery; it was ingrained in their personalities. And this indoctrination manifested itself in many ways. For instance, Peggy learned to use her sexuality as a way of furthering her cause during these years. It served her well at Middlesex. Some of the boys were the hardest to convert to her way of thinking, so she used her body to bring them around. Very few could resist her charms.

Peggy finished up her tea, and left the empty cup on the table. She'd retrieve it when she returned. She descended the three steps in the middle of the porch, and turned left toward her driveway. She pressed a button on her key ring and the doors to her *Toyota Prius* unlocked instantaneously. As she did this, she headed for the large shed behind her house and to the right. It looked like a little barn. She opened the double doors, and removed her kayak: a *Wilderness Systems Tempest 165*. It was a little more kayak than she needed for today's outing, but she just loved the way it cut through the open water. She left the doors ajar; the campus was very safe, so she wasn't worried about anyone stealing her belongings. After all, she had created a place of trust with her students. Little did they know that trusting her was the worst mistake they'd made in their young lives.

She carried the kayak to the side of her car and hoisted it into the cradle of the kayak carrier. She fastened the straps and was ready to go. While opening the driver's side door Peggy hesitated and quickly headed back into the house. "I almost forgot," she muttered. Peggy retrieved a little waterproof bag from one of her kitchen drawers. "How unfortunate that would have been, she giggled to herself." Now that she had her bag of pot, she was all ready to go.

One of the reasons she enjoyed kayaking so much was that it gave her a great workout. The other was the tranquility she experienced after her workouts. She would light up a joint and then float around, becoming one with nature, oblivious to the rest of the world. She got her first taste of kayaking and swimming during her days in the Poconos. These activities were as much a part of her as Marxism. When she looked back, she couldn't have envisioned a better childhood. The kids that came to Middlesex were not as lucky. But she would do all she could to make them see the light.

She drove the short distance down her driveway to Campus Way. When she started at Middlesex, this road had been named after one of those dreadful founding fathers. She fixed that in short order once she occupied the seat of power. Eventually she would have the road renamed for a true patriot, but for now it would have to wait. She had achieved her success at Middlesex because she implemented her views in small doses. Gradualism was the key. It was the main reason the progressive movement had come so far. Change didn't happen overnight. Rather, true change had to be achieved slowly, gradually. Too much change too soon draws attention. When you are trying to convert the world to your way of thinking, they last thing you want is its inhabitants be aware of your plans. For her part, Peggy stared her quest by banishing any positive mention of the Founding Fathers and their idea of liberty. How passé, she thought. After all, the masses weren't equipped to look after themselves. They needed others; they needed a government to provide for them. And that government consisted of people like her. Smart people who knew what was truly in the peoples' best interest. They couldn't be expected to figure it all out on their own.

Next, she replaced the nation's history with a dumb-down version of events. And in doing so she painted the founders as villains instead of saviors. Their memories forever tarnished in the eyes of the unsuspecting students. Pretty soon the name George Washington brought only contempt; and the name Abraham Lincoln, ridicule.

Campus Way snaked its way through the picturesque hamlet,

eventually delivering Peggy onto Route 81. She took a left out of the campus and headed South on Route 81 toward Clinton. In two miles, she entered a traffic circle; she took the third Exit: Route 80. She followed Route 80 for several miles and took a right at the blinking light onto Route 145. Messerschmidt Pond was little over a mile on the left. She pulled into the dirt lot and parked among the trees. The lot was encircled by trees on all sides, most of which were pines. There were a handful of maples as well. The only visible gaps in the trees consisted of the entrance and the path leading to the boat launch. She put the car in park, and readied herself for her workout.

It was a hot day, so she dressed in a pair of blue canvas shorts with a gingham bikini top. She wore a Che Guevera t-shirt over her bikini top. Maybe she'd rename Campus Way for him, she thought. Che Guevera Avenue sure had a nice ring to it, she thought. She threw on her sunglasses, and began the small task of removing the kayak from the roof rack. As she reached up, she had to laugh, her bumper stickers were funny, she thought. Leftist propaganda covered the rear of her vehicle. She had the kayak off and by her side in only a few moments. She opened the hatchback and grabbed her paddle; it came apart for easy storage and she was off to the launch.

At one time the launch had been used for larger boats, but this had changed in recent years. The state wanted to preserve the natural beauty of the pond, and larger boats did not facilitate this goal. She carried the kayak the small distance to the boat launch and placed it on the ground by the edge of the water. Hers was the only car in the lot, so she got a spot only a few yards from the launch. She walked back to her car and picked up her paddle. Now she was ready. She had a life jacket, but she seldom used it. She was an expert swimmer and the bulky jacket took away from the overall experience. Barefooted, she waded into the water, pulling the kayak along until she reached a proper depth. The water was quite shallow where she stood, so she had to wade out quite far. The last thing she wanted was to scrape the bottom of her prized possession on the pond's rocky floor. When the water depth was to her liking, she climbed into the kayak. Moments later, she broke the water's surface with her paddle and was off, propelling herself and her small craft through the majestic pond. She would do five laps before she was done. For the first lap, she would warm up; for the remainder of the time, she would push herself and her body to its limit. At the end a small reward awaited her.

Just as the man had come to know Dr. Edgar Green "The Baby Killing Machine," so too did he know Peggy Baldwin. Compared to Edgar, killing Peggy would be quite easy, and more satisfying. After all, she was the one who set the events in motion that brought the man to this point in time. If he were to kill only one person, it would be her. And despite Edgar's arrogance, the "good doctor" had taken safety precautions in his every day life. After all he had been shot at and had received more death threats than he could count. Peggy on the other had convinced herself that she was safe in her little cocoon called Middlesex Academy. The man had to agree with Peggy on that point; Middlesex Academy would be a more difficult place to eliminate her. That's why he chose an alternate location to send Peggy into the netherworld. The trick to killing, in the man's experience, was planning and surprise. He was quite sure that Peggy was oblivious to her death sentence. Unlike Edgar, the man would make this one look like an accident. He did not want to draw too much attention to Peggy's death; an accidental drowning would make for a nice end to her sordid life.

The man rode his motorcycle today. It had served him well in the past and he thought it perfect for today's events. Plus, he had to admit, it was a nice day for a ride. He didn't get out riding as much as he'd liked to, so he was pleased he could use his bike today. In addition, the motorcycle helmet was the perfect disguise. There were very few instances where he could cover his face entirely without drawing attention to himself. The motorcycle gave him the anonymity his task required.

He followed Route 145 from the south, took a right just before the south west corner of the pond, and headed east. He turned left onto an unused access road that emptied out on the far side of the pond. There was a barrier that prevented larger vehicles from entering the road, but there was more than enough space to accommodate his motorcycle. There was quite a bit of overgrowth and the road was littered with bumps and potholes, but that suited the man and the bike perfectly. It was unlikely that anyone would venture down here by chance. He continued down the road until he came to a small clearing. From his reconnaissance, he knew the pond was only about twenty yards away. He dismounted the bike and walked it into a small patch of bushes. He turned the bike around so that it was facing the way he'd come. The spot was perfect to conceal the bike, but access was easy should he need to retrieve it in short order. He opened up his saddlebags and removed several items: a mask, a snorkel, a pair of fins and *a Spare Air 300 system*. The man was quite good at holding his breath for extended periods of time. However, he wasn't as young as he used to be, he reflected. The *Spare Air* would be plenty of air if he needed it. He proceeded to remove his helmet and outer clothing. Instead of the traditional leathers, he wore a nylon jacket with matching pants. They breathed better than the leathers, and they were easier to get on and off. And instead of boots, he wore a pair of high top sneakers. Underneath his riding clothes, he sported a spring wetsuit; on his leg, a diving knife. He put his riding clothes into the saddle bags, and covered his motor-cycle with several branches from a nearby tree. He picked up his gear and began his short walk toward the pond.

Peggy finally hit her stride. Her warm-up lap went fine, but her second lap was a disappointment. For some reason, she had trouble focusing. Maybe it was tonight's big ceremony, she thought. By the time she started lap number three, she was back on track. She want-ed to finish her workout in a timely fashion. After all, she had big plans later in the day and didn't want to be late. Plus, she still had to buy an outfit; so much to do, so little time. The United States Civil Liberties Association was hosting its annual awards ceremo-ny tonight in New York City, and Peggy was receiving an award. She was ecstatic. For years she had poured her support and money into the civil rights group whose main, yet hidden purpose was to spread the Marxist agenda. Truthfully, she poured a great deal of money from Middlesex Academy coffers into the group. She had siphoned off tons of money during her tenure and had given quite generously to progressive causes. From environmental and animal rights groups, to political action committees, she did all she could to help her Progressive brothers and sisters. There was supposed to be checks and balances when it came to the school's finances. However, she fixed that issue when she hired one of her friends from her days in the Poconos as the school's comptroller. With the two of them overseeing the money, the possibilities for their cause, financially speaking, were endless. She had to laugh; if the American people only knew what went on in the backrooms in Washington and the country as a whole, there would be a revolt. Currently, there were eight members of the Senate and twenty-two members of the house who had attended her camp or similar summer camps in the Poconos. Not to mention the judiciary. She had lost count as to how many federal judges were on the progressive bandwagon. Many of them would be at the ceremony tonight, and they would be there to honor her. It would be a night to remember.

As Peggy paddled her way around the pond, the man slipped into the water; he barely made a ripple. He had grown up close to the shore and had spent many days splashing around Long Island Sound. He even became a lifeguard when he was a teenager. During those years, he rescued at least two dozen people from drowning. Today however, he would have to forget everything he had learned during his lifeguard training. Instead of saving a life in the water, today he would be ending one. The man moved effortlessly through the murky water. He knew the woman would paddle to the small island in the center of the pond after her final lap. She would retreat into the woods for several minutes and smoke her beloved marijuana. That was more than enough time to get into place.

The pond's surface from his current position to the small island was covered with hundreds of lily pads. What beauty, he reflected. The lily pads were the perfect camouflage for his approach. Not only would the water aid in concealing his position, so too would the expanse of lily pads. He continued to advance slowly, stealthily, the only thing visible was the top of his snorkel, and even that was almost impossible to make out.

The woman finished her fifth and final lap and turned her kayak toward the island in the middle of the pond. Just as she used the first lap to warm up, the slow, leisurely ride to the island was her way of cooling down. The man lifted his head a few inches out of the water. In two minutes, the woman came into sight. Perfect, he thought. As Peggy made her approach, the man eased himself below the surface. He was about fifteen yards from the island and she was coming directly toward him. However, he knew she would turn, and land the kayak long before she got close to him. As if on cue, Peggy turned the kayak again, and slowly coasted to the shore. She climbed out of the kayak, and walked the boat the last few yards, being careful not to scrape the bottom. She chose this side of the island because there was a tiny beach. The rest of the island was covered with trees and brush. And although it was ideal for concealing her during her smoke break, the trees made it difficult to enter the island on any other side.

She placed the paddle into the kayak, leaned over and retrieved her waterproof bag. "Come to mama," she uttered. Unknowingly, she turned her back on the man, just as she turned her back on someone in need all those years ago. She walked up the little beach, pushing dozens of branches aside to make a little path to the center of the island. After a few steps, she disappeared from sight. She settled down on a large, flat rock. This was the place she always sat. It was her little sanctuary, her church alter. She put the bag on her lap, and undid the tiny zipper. She removed an *Altoids* tin, and opened the lid. Inside were two perfectly rolled joints and a *Bic* lighter. She placed one of the cigarettes in her mouth and brought the *Bic* lighter up and touched the yellow flame to the thin paper. She inhaled deeply, and toasted herself: "to Peggy Baldwin, queen of the progressive movement. If only I could find my king. Maybe tonight," she giggled as she exhaled the grey smoke from her lungs.

The man closed in on the beach. Peggy's kayak was half in the water, half on the beach. He grabbed the stern of the kayak with his right hand, and slowly backed away from the island. In a minute, the boat was floating in the middle of the pond. Peggy made little effort to secure the kayak on the beach, so she wouldn't be surprised if it drifted away. The second day the man had observed her, that very thing happened when she retreated for her pot break. When she returned to the shore to find her kayak had drifted away, she dove in and swam out to retrieve it. That small chain of events gave him the idea for today's plan. He steadied the boat from underneath. It was unlikely that she would see him from the tiny island, but he didn't want to take any chances.

Peggy finished up the last of her joint, and tossed the roach into the woods. By now, there was probably a pretty big pile in there, she thought. She placed the lighter back into the tin, and inserted the tin into the waterproof bag. She zipped it up and began the short walk to the beach. As she broke through the trees and stepped onto the coarse sand, she noticed her kayak was gone.

"Damn it," she spoke through gritted teeth.

She stepped closer to the water and caught a glimpse of the kayak some thirty yards away.

"Shit! Why did this have to happen today?"

Angry, but undeterred, Peggy took a few steps, and dove into the cloudy water. She was a great swimmer, but swimming through the lily pads grossed her out. Who knows what lurks beneath them? She thought.

Despite her reservations, she had little choice. She was either going to swim to her kayak, or wait for it to float back. She was pretty certain option number two wasn't happening anytime soon, if ever, so she pressed on to the middle of the pond.

Through his mask, the man could see Peggy coming his way.

She was about ten yards out. He reached down and around, and felt for the *Spare Air* unit attached to his belt at the small of his back. He located the mouthpiece and inserted it into his mouth. Better safe than sorry, he thought. Peggy closed the distance in about ten seconds. As she reached her hand out of the water to grab the kayak, the man wrapped his arms around both of Peggy's legs, pulling her underwater. She flailed and twisted, but the man would not let go. His grip was tight, his determination unrelenting.

Peggy began to panic. She could only hold her breath so long. As it was, she didn't take a good breath because she was coming out of the water, not going in. Think Peggy, think. All of the sudden, Peggy went limp. She stopped resisting. Maybe he'll think I'm dead, she thought.

On the contrary, the man did not loosen his grip. If anything, his grip was even tighter. The man was not taking any chances. He would not let go of her until he knew she was dead. By his count, only thirty seconds had lapsed. He was going to hold onto her for at least five minutes. The world record for holding one's breath was fifteen minutes, fifty eight seconds. He was certain she wouldn't last that long, but he knew it was very unlikely that she would succumb within thirty seconds.

What is up with this guy? Who is he and why is he doing this, she cried. I am supposed to receive an award tonight for all I've done, why me? Feigning unconsciousness didn't help, so she started to struggle again. Her lungs were burning and felt like they were going to burst, but she was determined to hold out as long as possible. She would survive. She had to survive to further her cause. She had to have kids and pass her ideology onto them. Our movement will not prevail without offspring, that's what she was told. At one minute and forty seven seconds, she couldn't hold her breath any longer. She let out the last of her air, and tried to force herself to keep her mouth closed. But it was no use. By two minutes she was inhaling large amounts of the cloudy water. By two minutes thirty seconds, she stopped struggling, this time for good. Undeterred, the man maintained his grip. He glanced down at the diving watch on his right hand; he could barely see it since his arm was wrapped around her legs, but it was clear enough: he still had two and a half minutes to go. By the time five minutes arrived, it was clear that Peggy was dead. He only wished he could have looked her in the eye when he killed her. But it was not to be. Of all the people he had on his "to do" list, he knew he would receive the greatest amount of satisfaction from this one. How many children had she contaminated over the years? He thought. He could only imagine. She wouldn't hurt anyone, anymore.

He released her lifeless body. Another accidental drowning, that's what the authorities would say. He swam to the spot where he had entered the water. He lifted his head slightly, and peered around; No one in sight. He was confident that he was all alone. He crawled out of the water on his belly, and entered the woods without making a sound. Once he was among the trees, he removed his gear; first the fins, and then the goggles, snorkel and Spare Air unit. He sprinted to his bike, and opened the saddle bags. He removed his shoes and clothes, and replaced them with his diving gear. He dressed quickly. Lastly, he put his helmet on and pushed his motorcycle out of its hiding spot into the clearing. He hopped on and started the bike and quickly retraced his route. He was back on Route 145 and heading south in under two minutes. The time was 10:47.

Chapter 6

Clinton, 11:01 AM.

Tommy O'Leary nearly fell out of bed when his cell phone rang. He turned off the ringer on his land line the night before, but forgot to silence his mobile phone.

"Shit, I knew I forgot something," he mumbled.

The shades in his small bedroom were all drawn, so he didn't know what time it was. It certainly felt early. He had an alarm clock, but it had broken a few weeks ago. OK, he smashed it with his service piece. Tommy was not a morning person.

He was a detective with the New Haven Police Department. Yeah, an Irish cop. Go figure, he often remarked. He knew it was a cliché and he'd heard every Irish cop joke ever written. He'd even made up a few jokes himself. After all, the Irish were great storytellers and Tommy was true to his heritage. He loved his job, and a cop was all he ever wanted to be. Yes, he dabbled with a few other jobs in his younger years, but his ultimate goal was to be a man in blue. These days he didn't sport the uniform too frequently, but he was a man in blue tried and true.

Tommy was currently on vacation, and enjoying every minute of it. Although he loved the job, he was tired of the scumbags he encountered everyday. And he'd met plenty over the years. Tommy had arrested so many that he couldn't go anywhere in New Haven without seeing one. Whether he was going out to dinner or for a pint, he bumped into many of the wonderful people he'd arrested. It made life pretty miserable at times. Technically he was supposed to live within twenty miles of New Haven, but he spent most of his free time at his cottage on the beach in Clinton. He kept an apartment in New Haven to make it "official," but spent very little time there. Why bother? He thought.

After a long stretch without any time off, almost a year to be exact, he took a well deserved break from the madness. Today was the last day of his vacation and he was going to make the best of it. The last two weeks had been wonderful, and with any luck, today would be the same. Although that damn phone going off didn't start the day of on the right foot. He looked on the bright side; he had to get up eventually, and there's no use wasting a day off. He'd take a nap later to make up for the lost snooze time.

He climbed out of bed and nearly tripped over a mountain of dirty laundry in the middle of the floor. Note to self: do laundry. After regaining his balance, he walked to his dresser and picked up his cell. He recognized the number right away. It was work. Damn it. They must be knee deep in shit to be calling me on the last day of my vacation, he thought. He'd call them back, but he needed some coffee first. They'd understand. Tommy was great at his job, but punctuality was one of his lesser traits. He headed into the tiny galley kitchen, and went straight for the fridge. He stored his coffee in there so it would stay fresher longer, or so "they" said. He didn't know who "they" were, but if it prolonged the life of his favorite beverage, why not give it a try? (OK, *Guinness* was his favorite beverage, but why split hairs). Oddly enough, he consumed so much coffee that it probably didn't matter where he stored it. As it was, he'd opened this bag three days ago and it was almost gone. He preferred a good dark roast to those sissy flavored coffees, and he drank it black. What good was coffee if you had to load it up with cream, sugar and artificial flavors? You might as well be drinking hot chocolate or *Ovaltine*. No thanks.

He dumped a generous amount of French Roast into the filter and picked up the coffee maker and placed it in the sink. He positioned it under the faucet and let the cold water flow. Why fill the pot and then dump it in to the maker? You're only wasting time. The coffee maker filled quickly and he transferred it back to the counter, wiping off any excess on the sides. He hit the brew button, walked into the living room and turned on his stereo. A little *Oasis* should do the trick, he thought. He popped in *The Masterplan* and hit play. The opening chords to *Acquiesce* rang out.

What could the boss need me for so damn early? As he walked back the kitchen, he noticed the time on the stove. OK, maybe it wasn't so early after all; my bad. He poured some coffee into his blue Michael Savage mug, and opened the fridge to retrieve a pizza box. There were few slices leftover from last night's dinner, so why not indulge? He thought. He grabbed the box and his mug and headed for the slider. He opened the door and positioned himself down at the bistro table on his tiny deck. "Great view," he remarked sarcastically. It's true he lived on the beach, but he had a few houses blocking his view of the water. "Son of Bitch," he muttered. Absent a hurricane or a wrecking ball, he'd have to live with the obstruction. At least he had beach rights. The bastard who blocked his view bought up three of the surrounding houses. He wanted to buy Tommy's place but Tommy told him to go screw himself. He wasn't selling. The guy wanted to put up some McMansion. He hated assholes like that. They thought they could buy anything.

Well, they couldn't buy him. His grandfather had left him the cottage and there was no way he was going to sell it to some prick who used the place only on weekends.

He finished up the pizza and coffee and headed back to the kitchen for a refill. This would be the second of many cups that Tommy would consume today. He took a swig and lifted the kitchen phone out of its cradle. He knew the number by heart. Margie Hilbert picked up after the second ring. She'd been the Lieutenant's secretary for as long as he could remember.

"Lieutenant Canapino's office, who may I ask it calling?"

"Margie. It's Tommy."

"Well if it isn't the long lost detective? How goes that vacation of yours?"

"Great. Well it was great until a few minutes ago. What's Tony want with me? I thought you guys were going to leave me alone for two weeks. Isn't that the whole idea behind vacations?"

"Tommy, don't shoot the messenger, but we've got a dead body that needs some attention. Tony said you're next in the murder rotation."

"Can't it wait until tomorrow? I am quite certain that our dead person will still be dead twenty four hours from now. On top of that, I have a nice leisurely day of watching TV and drinking cheap domestic beer planned."

"Sounds like fun. I wish I could join you. Say, why don't you ever invite me over, Tommy? We could have a lot of fun together"

"I don't know, maybe because you're married and older than my mother."

"You're such a charmer, Tommy. I'll transfer you to Tony. Good luck. I'm sure he'll understand," she replied sarcastically.

"Thanks. Something tells me I'm going to need it."

"This is Lt. Canapino."

"Thomas Patrick O'Leary reporting for duty, sir."

"It took you long enough to get back to me."

"Tony, I'm on vacation, or did you forget?"

"Tommy, you know cops don't take vacations. It's not in our blood. Accountants take vacations; lawyers take vacations. Cops are always on the job. Besides, today was your last day off anyway. I'm sure you were bored after a day or two away. I know you. You've been probably pacing around that tiny cottage of yours trying to figure out what the hell to do with yourself. I'll bet you're just itching to come back and round up some bad guys."

"That depends."

"On what?"

"On whether you ask me nicely."

"You're such an ass. What time can you get here?"

"Tomorrow."

"No seriously."

"Seriously, tomorrow."

"Do I have to drive out there and drag your sorry ass back to New Haven?"

"How's 1:00 sound?"

"Not as good as 12:00, but OK. Why don't you head directly to the crime scene? It might save you a little time."

"Fair enough. Where I am going?"

"277 Front Street. Fair Haven."

"Great."

"I hate to break it to you, but murders don't always happen in the nice part of town."

"You're telling me. I don't think I ever investigated a murder scene in the nice part of town. The people who kill each other in the nice part of town dispose of their bodies in the not-so-nice part of town. So any way you look at it, you're going to end up in the shitty part of town."

"Are you through?"

"I guess."

"Check in with me when you're done. This one looks to be a little special. It's no garden variety kill. There might be wider implications."

"What do you mean?"

"You'll find out soon enough. I don't want to put any ideas in your head. We need a fresh set of eyes, and seeing that you've been off for a few weeks, you're just the man for the job."

"Whatever you say, you're the boss."

"The people of New Haven are your boss. I'm just the guy who busts your balls on their behalf."

"You have such a way with words, Tony. You ever thought about writing greeting cards? You'd have quite a future."

"Thanks for the kind words. I'm getting a little misty."

"Anytime; I'll be in with my preliminary assessment as soon as possible."

"Happy trails kid."

"You too. O'Leary out."

He hung up the phone. That was weird. It was unlike Tony to be so vague. He could blab for hours, and that was just with his hands. What on earth happened at 277 Front Street? There was only one way to find out.

Tommy jumped into the shower. He was in and out in two minutes. That must be some kind of record, he thought. He brushed his teeth and applied the very last of his deodorant. Note to self: get some deodorant that works this time; stay away from the cheap stuff. He found some not-so-wrinkled clothes on his easy chair, threw them on, and headed for his car, but not before pouring the rest of the coffee into a giant travel mug.

Tommy was six foot one, and a lean one hundred and eighty pounds. God had blessed him with a fast metabolism. He could eat anything and never gained an ounce. He had dark brown hair and, despite his Irish heritage, he had a far darker complexion than his pasty white parents. He climbed behind the wheel of his *1966 Pontiac GTO* and was on his way. He loved the GTO, and couldn't think of better company car. Two years ago he'd busted a drug dealer. What a scumbag he was. Nice car though. Anyway, thanks to the RICO statutes, they were able to seize the car. At about the same time, Tommy's other car had been demolished in a high speed chase. Don't ask. Tony told him to take it temporarily. That was two years ago, and Tony hadn't asked for it back yet. The drug dealer wasn't very pleased, but Tommy couldn't be happier.

He headed down the causeway, and turned left at the end onto Route 1. He banged a right onto to Route 145 and followed it all the way to the entrance ramp for Route 95 South. He'd be on the scene in about twenty five minutes, traffic permitting.

John Lee Tucker grabbed his fishing pole, tackle box, and net from his garage, and loaded them into the back of his vintage *Ford* pick-up truck. He just loved the truck. He'd restored it himself and couldn't be more pleased. It took him five long years, but it was a true labor of love. It reminded him of the truck his grandfather had when he was a kid. It brought back many fond memories. He only wished his grandfather was alive to see it.

John Lee spent the last thirty five years serving the country he loved in the United States Navy. Two months ago, he finally re-tired. It was a hard decision, but he knew he couldn't stay in the Navy forever. Occasionally he might do some work for the govern-ment on a contract basis, but he wasn't about to work full-time ever again. Life was too short, and he had much to do in his retirement years. And today was all about fishing. His wife Agnes was going antiquing; she'd be at it all day. So he was going to use the free time he had to reel in a few fish, if he was lucky. And even if he didn't catch anything, he didn't care. He just enjoyed being outdoors. He felt closer to God when he spent time outdoors, so he did it ev-ery chance he got. As a submariner in the Navy, he didn't see the outdoors for months at a time, unless you count looking through a periscope. But that just wasn't the same. So he relished all the outdoor time he had now.

He ended his time in the Navy stationed in nearby Groton. He and Agnes loved the area so much that they decided to stay. John Lee grew up in Tupelo, Mississippi, so Connecticut seemed like a world away. But it was a world they both came to love. John Lee joined the Navy right out of high school. Like most young men, he wasn't sure what he wanted to do with his life. His dad had been a cotton farmer, but John Lee knew that life on the farm wasn't for him. It was backbreaking work, and Tupelo was pretty damn hot in the summer. If all else failed, he knew he could come back. But as it turned out, the Navy was the perfect fit for John Lee. And although he visited home every chance he got, he never became a farmer.

He walked back into his Cape Cod style home. It had been built in the late seventeen hundreds. He and Agnes had been out for a drive one day and they just stumbled upon it. As it turned out, the house was in their price range, and the location was per-fect. Chester was a great little town. It was just meant to be. John Lee retrieved a small cooler and a folding chair from his kitchen. In the cooler he had two sandwiches and a six pack of beer. He probably wouldn't finish all the beer, but he'd have one to offer a fellow fisherman if the occasion arose. He opened the door and headed for the truck. That was everything. And even if he forgot something, it was a short drive to his house. He put the rest of his supplies into the bed of the truck, and climbed in. There was no AC, so he rolled down the windows to let in some fresh air. He turned the ignition; she started on the first try. Damn I'm good, he thought. In a few short minutes he was off to catch some fish. He really hoped to land a trout or two. He had found a great recipe for stuffed trout online, and Agnes said she'd make it if he managed to catch one. The last few attempts had been unsuccessful, but he had a feeling he was going to reel in the big one today; it was his time.

John Lee reached over and opened the glove box. The factory stereo was still in the dash, but he'd added a CD player for his favorite tunes. Although he enjoyed the talk radio stations on the AM dial, good music was scarce. He pressed play and Elvis echoed through cab. Yet another success story from Tupelo, he reflected.

Messerschmidt Pond was one of many small fishing holes in the area, and lucky for John Lee it was only several miles from home. Also, it was the one place where he'd had the best luck lately. Hopefully his luck would return today. He pulled his truck to the side of the road and turned off the engine. Unlike most of the fisherman who frequented Messerschmidt Pond, he avoided parking down by the boat launch. All the activity going on down there spooked the fish. He preferred the opposite end of the pond near the small dam; he usually found a quiet little spot. He looked around and saw only one other person. That suited him fine. He didn't want too many other folks out there going after the same fish.

It took him two trips to retrieve all of his gear. He opened his folding chair, lifted the cooler lid and removed a beer. He grabbed his trusty rod. He'd already had his favorite lure on the pole; *a Magnum Stinger Spoon*. He cast the line and began to slowly reel it in. "Let the games begin," he said to himself.

Chapter 7

Tommy made the trip to Fair Haven in twenty minutes; traffic was light, his foot heavy. The only trouble spot was at the Frontage Road exit. As luck would have it, that was Tommy's exit. He looked around at the road construction and shook his head. "Morons," he uttered to no one in particular. They'd been working on this project for years. He didn't think they'd ever finish. People thought cops had job security. That might be true, unless of course you were on the take. But at this rate Tommy would be retiring before these idiots were done with this project. He waved to the cop who was directing traffic and continued on towards his destination.

He turned right onto Front Street and followed it for about a mile. To his right was the Quinnipiac River. He remembered pulling a body out of the river when he was a rookie. Oh the good old days. Caught up in the nostalgia, he lost track of the street numbers. Although it didn't really matter; there was no mistaking a crime scene. Just look for the circus. And there it was: there were police cars, an ambulance, two news vans and lots of yellow police tape. The only thing missing was the big top. He parked across the street, and walked towards the front entrance, ducking under police tape along the way. An eager young officer was the only obstacle in his path.

Rookies; he loved messing with them. The rookie spoke first.

"Can I help you sir?"

"Yeah, I heard there was a dead body inside. I've never seen one up close. Do you think I could have a peek?"

"Sir, this is a crime scene, and I am not at liberty to discuss what's inside. Please step away. Thank you."

"Jeez, I drove all this way. Can't I have just a little look? I won't tell anyone."

"Sir, if you don't leave now I will be forced to arrest you."

"Arrest me? For asking questions? What ever happened to the first amendment?"

"Sir…"

OK, he had his fun. Tommy pulled out his badge. The rookie's expression rapidly changed.

"Uh."

"Don't worry about it kiddo; just messing with you. You're doing a great job. You never want to let anyone near the crime scene. That's rule number one. There are plenty of reporters who'll do anything to weasel their way in. That's the last thing you want happening. You don't, under any circumstances, ever want to contaminate a crime scene. Got it?"

"Yes sir."

"Call me Tommy. Keep up the good work."

"Thanks Tommy."

"Don't mention it. What's your name?"

"Sabian, Johnny Sabian."

"Officer Sabian, where might I find this body I've heard so much about?"

"Go past reception, and head down the hallway on the other side. You can't miss it. Don't mind the smell."

"What smell?"

"I might have thrown up a little in there."

Tommy laughed.

"That bad, huh?"

"I think I cleaned it all up, but who knows. Most of it hit one of the nurses. On the bright side, I managed to make it to the hallway before I blew chunks. Never contaminate the crime scene, right?"

"You're a fast learner, Johnny. Thanks."

Tommy walked past Officer Sabian and through the front door, but not before noticing the small sign to the right: The New Haven Reproductive Clinic.

Reproductive Clinic my ass; this was an abortion mill, plain and simple. What happened here, he wondered?

There were many people milling about, but none paid him much attention. Since he made it past the centurion at gate, they probably figured he was alright. Plus, they all had jobs to do, just like him. As he moved on, he saw some familiar faces; he got a few waves. Tommy's attire was a little informal for the occasion, but he didn't care. It was his last day of vacation, and even though he was working, he was going to be comfortable.

He walked down the narrow hallway and noticed a red headed woman whom he didn't recognize and the department's crime scene photographer, Eddie Kron, coming out of a room on the left. They didn't see him. This must be the place. He called to Eddie.

"Eddie, please tell me you're not here messing up my crime scene again?"

Eddie turned around and smiled. He knew that voice anywhere.

"Man, they'll put any lowlife on a murder case these days. What's this department coming too? I hope to God I don't get bumped off in New Haven. They'd probably never find the killer."

Tommy laughed. He walked towards Eddie and stuck out his hand. Eddie grabbed it, and gave it a good pump.

"Good to see you my friend."

"You too, Eddie."

"Where you been? I haven't seen you in weeks."

"Vacation."

"Vacation, are you shitting me? We've got criminals coming out of our ears, and you're off sitting on your ass."

"Tell me about it. If it makes you feel any better, Tony cut my vacation short for this little party."

He took in Tommy's attire: a Hawaiian shirt and matching shorts.

"If I didn't know better, I'd swear you were heading to a freakin' luau."

"Very funny; I actually stole this shirt from your closet."

"I wouldn't be caught dead wearing a shirt like that."

"Come on, you know you like it. Your wife said I could borrow it."

"I'll bet."

"So, what have we got in there?"

"White male, early sixties, very dead."

"Dead. I thought I was here for a party. Damn."

"Tommy, I've never seen one like this."

"My friend, there is a first time for everything in this business, you know that."

"Maybe so, but this one is really deranged. Come take a look."

Eddie led Tommy into Operating Room Number 2. The medical examiner was fast at work. He looked up as Tommy entered the room, a small smile creasing his otherwise serious face.

"Where's the luau Detective? How come I didn't get an invite? You know how much I love roasted pig."

Tommy laughed.

Dr. Michael Patel had been Connecticut's Chief Medical Examiner for fifteen years. He was in his early forties, but looked like a teenager. His straight hair was jet black, and his complexion a dark mocha. Unlike his predecessors, he still visited crime scenes on a regular basis. He could have spent his days concentrating on administrative matters, but that just wasn't in his make up. He was a doctor, not a paper pusher. Tommy and he had become good friends in the last several years due to an ever increasing murder rate in the city.

"Doctor, I never knew you were so witty."

Dr. Patel extended his gloved hand. Tommy winced.

"You think I am going to shake that? I'd rather roll around in pile of cow shit. It would probably be cleaner."

Doctor Patel laughed. He knew Tommy wouldn't shake his hand while he was conducting an exam. Tommy suffered from Obsessive Compulsive Disorder. One of the disorder's manifestations was an overwhelming need to wash one's hands. In Tommy's case, he felt a compulsive need to wash his hands after shaking hands with others. He avoided shaking hands with Dr. Patel all together while he was examining a body. Doctor Patel understood, but he liked to tease Tommy about it from time to time.

"Tommy, isn't it time you saw someone about your aversion to handshaking? It's quite rude."

"Thanks for the advice, Doc. Yours is the only hand I won't shake. But I'll take it under advisement."

Tommy avoided looking at the body on the table until now. Cops and medical examiners alike used humor as a defense mechanism.

Tommy was no different. Time to get down to business, he thought.

"Your thoughts, doctor."

"White male, with severe head trauma; the lower part of the skull has been crushed, most likely with this."

He produced a large mallet in an evidence bag and handed it to Tommy.

"In addition, the head was pierced with a large set of surgical shears. This is not conjecture. I removed the shears just before you arrived."

He motioned to a nearby table. The oversized scissors were sitting in an evidence bag. Another bag contained what looked like a bloody towel. Tommy shook his head.

"The victim was most likely tied up before he was killed. There is little or no trauma to the body except for the obvious injuries to the head. My guess is that he was unconscious when he was tied up. It is unclear whether he was conscious when the injuries were inflicted, but I find it hard to believe that he would have let the assailant tie him to the table without putting up a fight."

Tommy interrupted. "Time of death?"

"Based on my cursory examination of the body and the internal temperature of the victim, I'd say between nine and eleven. But I'll have a better idea once I open him up."

"Anything else?"

"There was one other thing."

He motioned to his right. A surgical pump was in plain view.

"When I first came into the operating room, this pump was running. And this tube was placed inside the victim's cranium."

"What's the pumps significance?"

"Do you know what they use these machines for detective?"

"To remove excess blood during surgery; to give the doctor a better view of the area he is operating on."

"Smaller pumps, yes, but not this type of pump. It's too large for that purpose. This particular pump is used specifically for abortion procedures. Are you familiar with the term partial birth abortion?"

"Yes, of course."

"What the doctor does, and I use the term 'doctor' loosely, he delivers a late term baby, and while it's still in the birth canal, he punctures its head with a pair of scissors, crushing the skull. Next, he uses this type of pump to suck out the brains of the dead fetus. He then removes what's left, and disposes of it. It's dreadful. During medical school, a number of my instructors taught this and other abortion 'procedures.' We were all supposed to participate. I told them in no uncertain terms to screw themselves. It is barbaric. I didn't go to medical school to take human lives. It goes against everything I was raised to believe."

Tommy understood the pump's significance. The person who did this mimicked the partial birth procedure. Tony was right; this was no garden variety murder. If the killer had wanted this man dead, he could have picked far easier methods. The killer was trying to make a point, and he certainly succeeded. But what point was he trying to convey?

"Doctor, I couldn't agree with you more. Any person who performs this type of procedure is a monster. Unfortunately for us, we have to find the people who kill monsters as well as the people who kill angels."

"Detective, I'm just about through here. Would you mind helping me untie him?"

Tommy's face turned a pale white.

Doctor Patel laughed. "I didn't think so. I'll call you with any updates. We can do lunch at Sitar."

"Sounds good to me doctor. On that note, I must be going. I do have a luau to attend. I'll have a mai tai in your honor."

"Please do. Aloha Tommy"

"Aloha right back at you doc."

Tommy and Eddie walked back into the hall. The mystery woman was patiently waiting for Eddie. Her name was Susan Kendall. She was five foot four with auburn hair and pearl white skin; her eyes were the color of slate. And she had a smile unlike Tommy had ever seen. It managed to light up the otherwise dingy hallway. Eddie made the introductions.

"Detective Susan Kendall, I'd like you to meet Detective Thomas O'Leary."

She stuck out her hand.

"Please to meet you detective."

"The pleasure is all mine, Detective Kendall."

"Please, call me Susan."

"Susan it is."

Shit, she has a stronger grip than old Eddie, Tommy reflected.

Eddie continued. "Susan just joined us a week ago."

"I was working as an investigator for the State Police, but it seemed like you local boys were having all the fun."

"Well I hate to disappoint you, but life on the New Haven PD is pretty boring. It's nothing like you see in our brochures. I told them we might run into some truth in advertising issues if they didn't update them."

Susan laughed. "I guess it's too late now."

"Don't say I didn't warn you."

"Fair enough, Mr. Ho."

"Mr. Ho?"

"Yeah, Mr. Ho, Mr. Don Ho; isn't that who you are imitating?"

"Very funny. Everyone's a comedian these days."

"I do try."

"Anyway, I was wondering if you might get me up to speed on our little situation here. Tony dragged me off of vacation, so I am a little behind today. Not to mention, I have only had a few cups of coffee today and don't function on all cylinders until I've had a pot."

She laughed. "I'd be glad to. And I sure know what you mean about the coffee. Anyway, as far as the crime scene goes, it looks pretty clean. The nurse who found the body stated that the room was hardly ever used. In addition, the likely murder weapons are all standard equipment found in this type of clinic. In other words..."

"In other words, the killer probably used whatever was at his disposal."

"Correct. The nurse did not have a chance to take an inventory. However, we can go through the room with her once Dr. Patel removes Dr. Green's body. Also, it's my guess that the only items the killer brought with him were the implements he used to secure the victim to the table. Those instruments are not typically found in this type of facility."

"So, we have a positive ID on our victim?"

"Yes. The nurse said she is quite certain the victim is the clinic's owner, Dr. Edgar Green."

"The Baby Killing Machine?"

"Yes, he is known by that name in certain circles I'm afraid. And based on the victim's build, his clothing, and the wallet we removed from his back pocket, we are quite certain it's Dr. Green. We'll have Ms. Carpenter take a look at his face before Dr. Patel removes the remains, but at this point it looks to be a formality."

"Is there anything else about the crime scene that stands out or looks out of place?"

"Ms. Carpenter, the nurse, stated that aside from Operating Room Number 2, everything looks pretty normal. There was no forced entry. Either Dr. Green let the assailant in, or the door was unlocked. The building was spotless, except for the immediate crime scene. Each night a cleaning crew comes in around 6:00. They usually wrap up about 7:00. They did their job quite well last night. We're scouring the place for prints, but I am not very hopeful. We do know that the killing took place, at the very least, after the cleaning crew left."

"Dr. Patel confirmed as much."

"Yes. The only thing that stuck out in Ms. Carpenter's mind was the absence of Dr. Green's car in the lot."

"Maybe he rode his bike."

"Detective."

"He might have," Tommy joked.

"Did you see how large the victim was? I'm pretty certain he wasn't riding a bike anywhere."

"I know, I was just kidding. I can be funny too Susan. OK, let's put an APB out on his car. Maybe our killer used it to get away. If we're lucky, it might still be in his possession; although I'm not getting my hopes up. At the very least we might be able to get some prints or something that might help us out."

"I'll get the make and model from Ms. Carpenter."

"That would be great, thank you."

"Detective, you seem convinced it's a man."

"Well, considering the size of our victim, as you expertly pointed out, I think it's unlikely a woman could have done this; unless we are dealing with some female power-lifter. Dr. Patel thinks the victim was probably unconscious when he was tied up. That seems to be a pretty good assumption. If that's true, our killer would have had to have lifted Dr. Green up and placed him on the table. I don't know very many men, let alone women, who could have done that."

"Could it have been more than one person?"

"That's a possibility as well. However, considering the nature of the crime, I'd say it's unlikely."

"What do you mean?"

"I don't know; it's a hunch I guess. The dead body to me re-sembled a work of art; a disgusting work of art, mind you, but a work of art nevertheless. I find it hard to believe that more than one person could come together and envision this style of killing. Is it possible? Sure. But in my mind, the killer is a loner who killed the good doctor in a horrific manner as a way of making a point. My best guess is that the killer is a pro-life zealot who wants to show the true horror of the abortion procedure. At least that's where I think we should start looking."

Susan responded.

"I think the radical pro-life movement is the logical place to start as well. According to Ms. Carpenter, Dr. Green received death threats on a pretty regular basis. I called down to the station, and we have a number of files dedicated to the many people who threat-ened Dr. Green over the years. There's even one gentleman who actually shot at Dr. Green sometime ago. Lucky for Dr. Green, he missed. But who knows, he might have hit the mark this time."

"What do you say we start with him?"

"I'll find out his current residence."

"That's great. I want to look around some more. How about we regroup back at the station, and go and pay this gentleman a visit?"

"Detective, you read my mind."

"I knew those mind reading classes would eventually come in handy."

Chapter 8

Westbrook 1:15

John Lee had a pretty uneventful morning of fishing. He caught a couple of sunfish, but he had yet to land anything truly edible. Sunfish were pretty boney, and although Agnes was a great cook, he suspected she'd be able to do little with a couple of sunnies, so he threw them back.

He opened his fourth beer of the day and took a bite of his second sandwich; roast beef and cheese. Agnes made the roast beef fresh the night before. There was nothing better than a good roast beef sandwich, he thought. Maybe sticking some roast beef on the hook would help; it couldn't hurt. I like it; maybe the fish will like it too. John Lee laughed. I might go through the entire six-pack after all, he reflected.

Despite not catching anything, John Lee was enjoying himself. The sun was shining brightly on his shaved head. The dark hue of his skin allowed him to stay in the sun for long periods of time without getting burned, and he loved it. Truthfully, he couldn't have asked for nicer day to be out fishing. The only thing he lacked was fish.

John Lee opened his tackle box in search of a different lure. He had a large assortment. Maybe that was the problem. He grabbed *a Blue Minnow.* He caught a few big fish with this one; why not give it a try? He removed the old lure and replaced it with the minnow. He gave it a good cast and began reeling it in; nothing. He recast; this time out a little farther. Finally, he felt a little tug on the line. Now we're talkin'. He turned the reel a few more revolutions, stopped and waited. The fish did not respond. That was odd, he thought. John Lee pulled back on the rod, and took in a little more line. The fish must be quite large; his rod was bending a considerable amount, he deduced. As he continued to reel it in, the rod bent more and more, yet he didn't seem to be making any headway. He wanted to get this fish, but he didn't want to break his rod in the process. He reeled some more, but whatever it was, it wasn't pulling away nor did it move in his direction. Maybe it wasn't a fish after all.

At this point, he didn't have very much line out, so he decided to grab his net and wade into the water. Whatever it was, it was only a short distance from shore. He hoped it wasn't an old tire. He reeled in one of those when he was a kid. At the time, he thought it was a giant catfish. To his dismay, it was a giant *Goodyear.* People will throw anything in the water, he remembered.

He placed the rod on the ground, and picked up the net with his right hand. With his left hand, he grabbed the fishing line and followed it into the water. Luckily he wore his waders today. He originally thought it would be too hot, but decided to wear them anyway. He'd waded into this water many times in the past, so he knew it was not very deep.

He walked until he bumped into a very large object with his right knee; at this point he was chest deep. He reached down into the water and felt around for the obstruction. He gasped when he realized what it was; it was no fish, it was a body.

He quickly threw his net onto the shore and concentrated on pulling the body from the water. He reached down with both hands and grabbed hold of the feet. The legs were smooth; it must be a woman he thought, although these days, who knows? "Here goes nothing," he muttered to himself. John Lee backed up slowly and pulled with all his might. He was only about ten feet from the shore. He covered the short distance in no time. He placed her lifeless body on the sand, face up; her brown hair matted to her face and neck. John Lee let out a sigh. What a waste, he thought.

John Lee looked around. He knew he had to call the police, but had no phone. When he retired from the Navy, he also retired his cell phone. For once, he wished he still had the damn thing. He noticed one other fisherman a short distance away. With any luck, he'd have a phone. He ran to the truck as best he could in his waders, and opened the driver's side door. He pulled back the seat, and grabbed a plaid blanket that he and Agnes used for picnics. He closed the door in a hurry and ran back to the body. He covered the woman from head to toe with the blanket, and headed to see the other fisherman.

The pond had numerous inlets, and the other fisherman had positioned himself at inlet in front of John Lee and to his left. John Lee could see the man from where he'd been standing, but the man had his back to John Lee. Once again, John Lee ran as fast as the waders allowed. He reached the man's position in a few minutes. As he got closer, he noticed the man was quite old. His hair was thin and wispy, his face like leather. The elderly man greeted him warmly.

"How are you making out today my friend? Catch anything? I've had a little luck, but nothing to write home about. I did reel in an old tire."

The man motioned to his left. John Lee wished he was the one who caught the tire this time. John Lee answered the kindly gentleman.

"As a matter of fact I did catch something. I was wondering, do you have a phone I might borrow?"

"Yes, of course. When you get to be my age, it's a good idea to have a phone nearby just in case, if you now what I mean. That must be quite a fish. Are you going to call one of your buddies and rub it in? That's what I'd do. In the old days we used the telegraph," the man chuckled.

"Actually, I need it to call the police. My big catch was a dead body."

"I can't say that I've ever landed me a dead body, but the day isn't over yet. Sorry, bad joke; there's something about gallows humor that just makes me laugh. The older you get, the more you have to live with death. I figure, why not joke about it? Since for me, it's probably just around the corner."

"Don't worry about the joke. You said you have a phone?"

"Oh yes, my young fellow, I know I put it somewhere."

The man started by searching his pockets, but had no luck.

"I'll never get used to these new fangled devices. When I was a kid, shit we didn't even have a phone in our house. Life was sure peaceful those days."

Next, the man reached into a small duffle bag. He removed several items before locating the phone. He handed it to John Lee.

"Here you go."

"Much obliged."

"Don't mention it."

The man continued to fish as if nothing had happened. I guess when you got to be his age, death was a more likely occurrence than catching a fish, he reflected.

John Lee dried off his hands as best he could and flipped open the phone. He dialed 911 and pushed send. At least the old guy kept the thing charged.

"911, what is your emergency?"

"I am at the northeast end of Messerschmidt Pond in Westbrook, off Route 145. I was fishing when I discovered a body in the water. From the condition of the body, I'd say it's pretty recent. Please send someone right away."

"Can I have your name sir?"

"Tucker, John Lee Tucker."

"Thank you Mr. Tucker. Do you have a number you can be reached at?"

"I'm not sure. I borrowed this phone from another fisherman."

"Please stay on the line Mr. Tucker. I have to put you on hold for a few seconds."

"Yes, ma'am."

A minute or two passed. To John Lee, it felt like an eternity.

"Mr. Tucker, are you still there?"

"Yes."

"The State Police are en route."

"Tell them to look for the green antique *Ford* truck. The woman's body is located between the truck and the pond."

"Copy that Mr. Tucker. Thank you for your help."

John Lee closed the phone. Maybe he was in shock; or maybe it was the beer. He didn't know. He hadn't seen a body in the water in a long while; although he certainly would never forget the last time. It was about ten years ago. His boat, that is his submarine, had been on a routine training exercise in the North Atlantic, just off the Maine coast, when one of the missile hatches started leaking. Several crew members did their best to fix the leak, but in a matter of minutes, the entire forward torpedo room was flooded. All of the crew members working in that part of the sub, except for one, escaped before sealing the compartment. The one person who did not get out in time perished. It was truly a sad day for John Lee. As the captain, every man on that boat was his responsibility. When they got back to Groton and opened the hatch, John Lee was there. They were able to reseal the missile compartment from the outside, but when they opened the torpedo room door, water flooded the neighboring compartment. John Lee watched as they recovered the body of the fallen sailor while standing knee deep in water. He personally went and broke the news to the man's family; he figured it was the least he could do. He would never forget that young man's face. He owed it to the man for the sacrifice he'd made. Petty Officer First Class Lionel Thomas, may you rest in peace.

Tommy finished up at the crime scene in an hour. However, after meeting Susan Kendall, police work was the last thing on his mind. Although he'd been thorough in his investigation, he couldn't stop thinking of her. He'd never worked a case with a woman before. OK, he'd never worked a case with a *beautiful* woman before. There were plenty of police women who could probably kick the shit out of him, but Susan didn't seem to be one of them. This was bad. He always followed the old rule of not dating one's co-workers. And it had served him well. But now he was tempted to cast that credo aside. Maybe things with Susan could be different, he thought. He'd never felt this way about someone, let alone a partner. In any case, romance would have to wait. He had a murder to solve.

He gathered his notes, said his goodbyes and headed back to the station. It was a short drive, and luckily he didn't pass any construction projects on the way. One a day was plenty, just like the vitamin, he thought.

He couldn't find a spot, so he pulled the car onto the sidewalk in front of the station. Tony would give him flak, but he didn't care. He had to put the car somewhere and he wasn't about to look for an open meter. Susan was digging up the whereabouts of the guy who tried to off Dr. Green; with any luck he would still be in the Nutmeg State and they would be leaving in a short while to go pay him a visit anyway.

Tommy walked to his cubicle and plopped himself down on his ancient chair. He looked around. What a mess, he thought. He was in such a hurry to leave for vacation he neglected to tidy up before making his exit. Note to self: clean cubicle; it looks like shit. He removed a few pieces of paper from atop his keyboard, and started hammering away at the keys. In about ten minutes he'd produced his preliminary report for Tony, and saved it to his hard drive. He then e-mailed it to his boss, but not before printing out two copies for himself. He figured he and Susan could compare notes on the car ride. As he grabbed the pages from his printer, his phone rang.

"This is O'Leary."

"Hey Tommy, this is Walker from towing. I think we might have found that *BMW* you were looking for."

"What do you mean, think?"

"Well, it looks like a *BMW*, she was found a short drive from the crime scene; unfortunately she's a little bit charred."

"How charred are we talking about?"

"I wouldn't expect to find any useful evidence if that's what you mean."

"Any luck with the VIN."

"Not yet, but I'm confident we'll find at least one component part with the VIN on it. It's just a matter of time."

"Where did you say the car was found again?"

"You know where Liam McGuire's is?"

"What Irishman worth his salt within twenty miles of this city doesn't know where Liam McGuire's is?"

"Good point. It was parked just up the street from there. The funny thing is we also found a van that was torched as well."

"And that's unusual in that part of town?"

"If you'd asked me a few years ago, I'd say no. But these days, gas is so damn expensive, people are more likely to siphon it out than use it to set a car on fire."

"You're right about that."

"It might just be a coincidence, but I'm not one to believe in coincidences."

"Where was the van found?"

"The van was even closer to the crime scene; about a half a mile away in the parking lot of an old abandoned warehouse."

"What's the address of the warehouse?"

He jotted it down on one of the copies of his report.

"Thanks Walker. I don't suppose anyone saw anything?"

"No such luck. I'll give you a call when I confirm the VIN. On the bright side, there were no dead bodies in either vehicle."

"Thank heaven for little favors."

"You said it. Talk to you later."

"Lucky me; thanks Walker."

"Anytime."

So much for finding our killer cruising around town in his new BMW; Tommy wasn't surprised. Doctor Green's killer was methodical. He would not be a person who left things to chance, hence the torched car or cars. However, Tommy wasn't sure where the van played into the picture. In any case, he couldn't rule out its significance. Maybe Susan was right, there might have been more than one person who did the good doctor in. It wouldn't be the first time.

Tommy wasn't sure where to find Susan, so he decided to pay Tony a visit and ask him. Also, he had to give Tony shit for not telling him about New Haven's newest detective, so why wait? Most of the floor that Tommy occupied contained rows and rows of cubicles, but due to Tony's station in life, he scored himself an office. It wasn't pretty, but it was an office nevertheless. From time to time Tommy would nap on Tony's couch when he was out of the office. There would be no naps today. The blinds were drawn and the door was closed. Tommy knocked three times.

"Come in," was Tony's response.

Tommy turned the knob, and opened the door. Tony had the phone to his ear. He motioned for Tommy to sit down with his free hand. He then held up his right index finger, and mouthed the phrase "one minute."

Instead of sitting down, Tommy walked to the closet to the right of Tony's desk. He pulled open the accordion door, revealing a tiny fridge. He opened the door and grabbed a *Diet Coke*. There were a few beers as well, but Tommy didn't want to press his luck. He closed the door with a little kick. There were two leather chairs. One was ripped. Tommy picked the non-ripped one and sat down facing Tony's desk. He cracked open his *Coke,* took a big sip and waited for his boss to finish his call. It took him five minutes to wrap things up.

"Sorry Tommy, it was the mayor."

"Wow, royalty. What did he want?"

"As it turns out, the late Dr. Green was a big contributor to the mayor's campaigns."

Tommy couldn't stand the mayor. "It Doesn't surprise me. Dr. Green seems like the kind of lowlife who'd give money to get that dipshit re-elected."

"Anyway, he wanted to know if we had any leads, and to make sure that we make this case a priority."

"Word travels fast in this town."

"You're telling me."

"The mayor is such an asshole. Does he think we sit around with our thumbs up our butts all day? I'll tell you, that guy and his policies are a huge part of the crime problem in this town. It's bad enough that we have to deal with the home grown criminals, but now that he's turned New Haven into a sanctuary city, we have to deal with every Tom, Dick and Julio that crosses the Rio Grande. That guy needs a good kick in the pants if you ask me."

"Tommy, I couldn't agree with you more. Just do your job, and this case will be a distant memory in no time."

"If we're lucky, maybe it'll be an illegal alien. That would put our esteemed mayor in quite the awkward position. After all, they only come here to work."

"Yeah, yeah, yeah; I know. Just solve this thing, so we can move on, capice?"

"Yeah I understand. That's easy for you to say. Not only am I chasing bad guys, but my wonderful boss decides to assign a gorgeous woman to be my side kick."

"Actually, you're her side kick."

"Very funny; is there a reason you failed to mention Susan Kendall when last we spoke?"

"I know how much you hate working with a partner, so I figured it was better left unsaid. Don't hate me," he said with a crooked smile.

"Tony, how could I hate you?" he replied sarcastically.

"So true."

"I'm just having a little trouble concentrating, that's all."

"I see where that might be a problem, but look on the bright side…"

"What bright side?"

"You could be working with Hank again."

Hank was Tommy's former partner. One day while chasing a suspect, Hank nearly ran Tommy over with his police cruiser.

"Good point. So, where might I locate the newest member of New Haven's finest?"

"She's downstairs in Kyle's old cube."

"Thanks chief."

"Not yet, but trying."

"Just think, if you get the chief's job, you and the mayor will fast become best buddies. It's a win win situation if you ask me."

"I didn't ask you."

"I know, but if you did."

"Tommy, do you have something for me?"

"Oh, right."

Tommy threw fifty cents onto his desk.

"Here's the money for the *Coke.*"

"Not that you idiot, I meant the prelim on Dr. Green's murder."

"Don't you ever check your e-mail? I sent it to you about fifteen minutes ago."

"What's e-mail again?"

Tony was an old school cop. He hated computers even if they were part of the job. Back in his day you carried your gun, cuffs and a notepad. Cops these days relied too much on technology and he hated it.

"I'll unload it and get back to you."

"Don't you mean download?"

"Whatever. Let me know how your meeting with Lester Bell goes."

"Who's Lester Bell?"

"He's the nice gentleman who took a shot at Dr. Green several years ago."

"She found him?"

"He wasn't too hard to track down. He's living up in Uncasville."

"What's he an Indian?"

"No, he's an inmate up at Corrigan."

"Shit, I guess that makes it a little harder for him to be our killer."

"I agree, but he's the best lead we have so far. If he didn't have a hand in it, he might know who did. Use that charm of yours, and you might get lucky."

"I know I haven't had a date in a while, but I have yet to resort to consorting with male prisoners."

"If it helps catch a killer, I'll turn a blind eye."

"You are a sick man."

"I have to be to put up with your shenanigans."

"I'll call you on the way back from Uncasville. Do you mind if I play the ponies while I am up there?"

"What do you think?"

"Maybe next time."

"Happy trails; tell your girlfriend I said hi."

"Will do."

Chapter 9

Tommy walked downstairs to meet Susan, but not before stopping in the bathroom to relieve himself. It was about an hour to Uncasville, and he didn't feel like holding it the entire way. He washed and dried his hands and used the paper towel to open the door. He tossed the towel in a nearby trash can and headed into the maze of cubicles. He located her cube, but Susan was no where to be found. Great, he thought. With any luck she already solved the case and I can go back on vacation. Susan snuck up behind Tommy and spoke into his ear.

"Well, well, look who decided to pay me a visit."

Tommy was startled, but happy to see her.

"I was wondering if I might borrow a cup of sugar. I am making a bundt cake and I seem to have run out."

She smiled. "You're a funny guy, detective. I'm fresh out of sugar, but I could spare a little Equal, if you're game."

Tommy smiled back.

"Tony might have mentioned that you tracked down one Lester Bell."

"Yes I did. Are you still up for a little road trip?"

"Always."

"Let me just a grab a few things."

"Take your time. I've got all day," he replied.

Susan grabbed a couple of files and stuffed them into a leather messenger bag. She opened the bottom right desk drawer and pulled out her gun and slipped it into its holster at the small of her back. She then put on a blue cardigan sweater and slung the bag over her shoulder.

"All set; my car or yours?"

"I'll drive if you don't mind."

"Not at all. I'm used to being chauffeured around."

Tommy extended his arm in the direction of the exit, and bowed slightly. "Your chariot awaits."

Susan followed Tommy out a side door and onto the sidewalk. The first thing she noticed was the GTO illegally parked.

"What arrogant jerk parked on the sidewalk? I wish I had a ticket book; I'd write them up in a flash."

Tommy smiled at Susan. "That arrogant jerk would be me. I hope you don't mind going for a ride with someone who'd park on the sidewalk. If you'd like, you can give me a ticket when we get back."

Susan was embarrassed, but didn't show it. The steely look remained on her face. She grabbed the door handle and pulled.

"I might take you up on that."

They both laughed.

Tommy headed up the ramp and merged onto Interstate 95 North. Despite the construction, they cleared the Frontage Road area with little or no problem. Tommy turned on the radio, but couldn't find a decent station.

"Mind if I try?"

"Please do."

As she fiddled with the dial, she continued talking to Tommy.

"So, how does a lowly detective afford such a fancy car?"

"Can you keep a secret?"

"Of course."

"I'm on the take."

"You better watch your step mister; I spent two years in IAD at the state police. I'll nail you to the wall if you don't watch yourself."

"I'm sure you would. Actually, this car belonged to a fellow by the name of Pedro Gianito."

"The drug trafficker?"

"One and the same; I told you I was on the take. He gave it to me in lieu of my monthly hush money payment."

"Very funny."

"Anyway, I was on the drug rotation at the time, and we were fortunate enough to catch Pedro and his three amigos with fifty pounds of heroin. Needless to say, Mr. Gianito was driving this lovely car at the time, so we seized it. And the rest, as they say, is history."

"Good story. You think you can get me one of these? I'd like to upgrade from my Honda."

"I'll see what I can do. There is a van that recently came into our possession. How do you feel about driving a stylish van?"

"If it's got a waterbed in the back and a funky mural on the side, sign me up!"

"I'll have to check on that, but I agree, if it doesn't have a waterbed, it isn't really a van."

"So true."

"What do you think our tack should be with Mr. Bell?"

"Mr. who?"

"Mr. Bell."

"How about we break out the rubber hoses and give him a good beating. Isn't that what you old guys did to get people to talk back before electricity?"

"Ouch, that hurt. How old do you think I am?"

"Forty-four?"

"Try again."

"Forty?"

"And you call yourself a detective? Try thirty-six."

"Wow, judging by the look of you, I'd say you had a few more miles on the chassis than that."

For the first time in his life, Tommy was speechless.

"Just kidding detective; I was told to give you the business any chance I got. I was just following orders."

"Tony. Some friend he is. Speaking of age, how old might you be?"

"Detective, don't you know it's rude to ask a lady her age?"

Tommy nodded.

"If you must know, this lady doesn't care. I'm twenty-nine."

"And you're calling me old?"

"Maybe if you took a little better care of yourself people wouldn't mistake you for someone with an AARP membership," she playfully replied.

"I can see that I'm not going to win this one. Am I?"

"Probably not; we'll chalk up one for me in the win column, shall we?"

"Fair enough."

Susan pulled a file out of her leather bag and began reviewing it contents before she continued. "Now back to Lester. Considering Mr. Bell received no visitors in the last eighteen months, I'm sure he'll jump at the chance to talk. He's the kind of criminal who likes to brag about his exploits. Most cons will proclaim their innocence to anyone who will listen, but not our Mr. Bell; he's a bragger. In his own twisted way, he thinks he's doing God's work. So shooting at Edgar Green "the Baby Killing Machine" is alright in his eyes."

"Likewise, he's certain to feel a kinship with the person who ultimately finished the job he set out to do."

"I agree."

"Religious fanatics are funny that way. I just don't understand them. I think what Dr. Green did for a living is deplorable, but I know my God wouldn't want me to pop a cap in his backside. That's not how He works."

"Vengeance is mine, says the Lord."

"So true Detective Kendall."

"That's what twelve years of Catholic school will get you."

"Me too. Well eight anyway. Then my folks sent my off to Middlesex Academy for the high school years."

"I can't picture you at an uppity place like that."

"What, I'm not sophisticated enough for such an institution?"

"No, I don't see you as pretentious enough."

"But I'm religious enough for the Catholic schools?"

"Funny, I didn't peg you as the religious type, either."

"Really? In my experience, the closer one gets to the great beyond, the closer they come to their Creator. After all, I have one foot in the grave, so it's a logical conclusion that I'd be a churchgoer."

"Touché, detective."

"We'll chalk that up as a one for me in the win column."

"OK, one to one."

"One to one it is."

"Speaking of faith, I have a confession. I'm really thirty-one."

Tommy laughed.

"You're a pretty good liar."

"Why thank you."

"As far as Lester goes, I agree that we should let him talk and see where he takes us. He probably has nothing to do with the murder, but he might unwittingly point us in the right direction. And if that doesn't work, I guess we can try the rubber hoses."

John Lee waited around until the police and the paramedics finished up. His shoulders hung abnormally low, his head throbbed. What a strange day, he thought. The police had asked him questions, and he answered as best he could. He wished he could have been more helpful, but the truth was, he hadn't noticed anything until he'd reeled in the body. The trooper in charge gave John Lee his card and told him to call if he thought of anything else that might be helpful. He couldn't think of anything.

The police found an empty kayak not too far from his location. They asked if he'd seen any kayakers in the immediate area, but he had not. They surmised the kayak belonged to the dead woman. Upon further investigation, they also located an empty car parked in the lot off of Route 145. They checked with all of the people who were in and around the pond at the time, but the vehicle did not belong to any of them. The woman had no identification on her, but a check of the abandoned automobile registration revealed the car belonged to one Margaret Baldwin of Killingworth. Several of the kayakers recognized the car, and their description of the woman who drove it matched the victim. They said she was an avid kayaker who spent most mornings there. None of them ever got to know her, but they would say hello to her when they saw her on the pond or at the boat launch. It at least gave the police a place to start.

John Lee packed up his gear, and headed for his truck. Not only did he not catch any fish, he reeled in a horrible memory that he'd be unable to shake for years to come. Maybe fishing wasn't for him after all. Maybe I'll take up stamp collecting, he thought. When's the last time somebody stumbled upon a body while stamp collecting?

He drove the short distance to his beloved home. Agnes was there to greet him as she always did. She hugged and kissed him. John Lee needed that.

"Did you catch anything, love?"

"Just a dead body."

"John Lee why can't you just say you didn't catch anything? Why do you have to always make up these ridiculous stories?"

John Lee wished it was a story. Despite his horrible find, he smiled. She always made him smile. He knew she was right. In the past when he'd had no luck fishing, he did make up stories about the one that got away. He wouldn't be doing that again. He'd tell her the whole story tonight, but for now he'd keep it to himself. He didn't want to ruin her jovial mood.

"I caught a couple of sun fish, but I threw them back."

"You ever thought of taking up a different hobby? We can always buy fish at the market."

"It's funny you mention that. I was thinking the same thing. Maybe we can find a hobby that we can do together."

"On second thought, maybe fishing isn't so bad after all."

They both laughed.

The man grabbed a manila envelope from the passenger's seat of his car with his gloved hand, and rolled down the driver's side window. He slipped the envelope into the mailbox and drove away before anyone knew he was there.

The letter was addressed to the *News editor* of *The New Haven Register*. The man was no fan of *the Register*. In his mind, it was a left leaning rag one step above the tabloids. With that said, might be an unlikely ally in his plan. Due to their left leaning policies, they were sure to print his letter. *The Register* despised anything religious. They would print anything that would cast the faithful in a negative light. And his letter would point the finger away from himself and in the direction of a religious zealot. He hated to use religion in this way, but there was always a chance he might be discovered, so a little misdirection never hurt. The only thing that mattered was to finish what he had started, and he was halfway there.

Chapter 10

The Corrigan-Radgowski Correctional Center is located off Route 395 in Uncasville. The level four, high security facility is home to some of Connecticut's most notorious criminals, among them, Lester Bell. It houses approximately fifteen hundred inmates. Lester was transferred to the facility from Somers in late 2003 after a series of "incidents" with his fellow inmates. In other words, Lester didn't play well with others.

Since arriving at Corrigan, Lester has spent the majority of his time in a four by eight foot cell. He has a toilet, a sink and a small transistor radio. There are two bunks, but Lester currently has the place to himself. He occupies his time by reading the Bible and preaching to anyone who will listen. Not many people do. Occasionally he'll listen to his radio, but unfortunately, reception is pretty lousy in his part of the prison.

Lester was sitting on his bunk when he heard his name called. He was wearing an orange jumpsuit too big for his narrow frame. His gray hair was long and unkempt. He stood at 5'8". However he was a habitual sloucher, so he looked much shorter than his actual height.

"Bell, you've got visitors."

It was Jamal Robinson, the captain of the guards.

"I thought I could only have visitors on Tuesdays, Thursdays and Saturdays," he replied.

"We've decided to make an exception in this particular case because you're such a model con."

Lester knew he was full of it. He was no model prisoner. The department of corrections sent their trouble makers to Corrigan.

Something must be up. He bookmarked his page and placed the Bible on his bunk.

"In that case, let me freshen up. I can't be accepting visitors looking like this."

"Drag your ass out of this cell right now or I'll send your friends on their merry way."

Lester knew better than to press his luck with Robinson. Unlike some of the other guards he had occasion to meet, Robinson did not take any shit.

"Since you put it that way, where to?"

Robinson removed a set of keys from his pocket and inserted one into the lock of Lester's cell door. He turned the key and pulled the door open. He motioned Lester to come forward. To Captain Robinson's right were two other guards. Working in concert, the two placed shackles on Lester's hands and feet; a chain linked both sets of shackles together. When they finished, one guard stood on either side of Lester. Captain Robinson slammed and locked the door.

Lester's cell was located on the second tier of a two tier block. The four men, led by Captain Robinson, descended a metal staircase and approached the first of two doors leading out of the cell block. Robinson signaled to the guard behind the bullet proof window to open the inner door; a buzzer sounded and Robinson pulled the door open. Once all four men were inside and the inner door was shut, the man behind the glass hit another button, and a second buzzer rang out. Robinson pulled on the outer door and the two guards with Lester in tow, followed.

The foursome walked down a series of corridors before ending up at another set of double doors. They repeated the same routine as before and found themselves in the hallway leading to the Contact Visiting Area. Captain Robinson pulled out his keys and used them to unlock a door on his right. He opened the door and stood aside while the guards escorted Lester into the visiting area.

Lester hadn't had any visitors in a very long time. He was beginning to think the outside world had forgotten about him. He looked around the large room. There were two rows of long tables, with chairs on either side. At the far end was a mural of the State House in Hartford. There were several windows, all covered with steel mesh. The floor was an off-white tile, shined to perfection. The inmates really knew how to clean. He saw only two people; a man and a woman. He had never laid eyes on them before in his life. Something told him they were cops.

The two guards escorted Lester to the table on the right where the man and woman were seated. Captain Robinson made the introductions.

"Detectives O'Leary and Kendall, this is Lester Bell. Mr. Bell, these are Detectives O'Leary and Kendall. They have a few questions to ask you."

Lester responded first. He held his shackled hands and with a slight smile, addressed his visitors.

"Well, I'd shake your hands, but as you can see, I'm a little tied up at the moment."

Lester's attempt at humor fell on deaf ears.

One of the guards pulled out a chair and motioned for Lester to sit down. There were eye bolts every three feet on the prisoner's side of the table. The guard secured Lester's shackled hands to the eye bolt directly in front of him and stepped back from the table.

Satisfied that Lester wasn't going anywhere, Detective O'Leary spoke up.

"Thank you captain, I think we can take it from here."

"As you wish detective; if you need us, we'll be right outside."

"Will do."

Captain Robinson and his deputy guards exited the room through the same door they had entered.

Tommy pulled in his chair and folded his hands in front of him on the table. He then took a deep breath. "So Lester, can I call you Lester?" Tommy inquired.

"Please do."

"We know you're a busy man, but we were wondering if you could spare a little time to talk about an old friend of yours."

"Who might that old friend be, detective?"

It was Susan's turn to talk.

"Dr. Edgar Green."

"Oh, don't you mean Dr. Edgar Green the Baby Killing Machine?"

Susan continued.

"Yes. We understand that you and Dr. Green are acquaintances."

"Yes, the good doctor and I go way back."

"That's what we wanted to talk to you about. How is it that you and Dr. Green, excuse me, Dr. Green the Baby Killing Machine became acquainted?"

"Well, I came to know Jesus Christ as my personal savior in late 1999. Up until that point, I'd led a life of true debauchery. I must admit, I am quite ashamed of they way I was. At my darkest hour, a friend gave me a Bible and it changed my life forever. I subsequently joined a nearby church, and through the guiding hand of my pastor, I started an outreach ministry staging vigils at the local abortion facilities. It just so happens, that Dr. Green owned and operated one such facility."

"I see," replied Tommy. "Please continue."

"On this particular day, I was standing in front of Dr. Green's clinic, when the baby killer himself walked outside to pay me a visit. It had been pouring all morning long, and I was the only who showed up. He called me every name in the book. Not the good book, mind you. And at that moment, it dawned on me; God had caused it to rain for a reason. He knew I would be the only one to show up this day. Also, he knew what a coward Edgar Green was. Edgar never came out to confront protesters. He was gutless. I knew what I had to do. I had to stop this man, this killer, from harming any more children. I reached into my coat pocket and removed a twenty-two caliber pistol. As I released the safety and cocked the hammer, Dr. Green ran for the door. And unfortunately for me, he was able to close the door before I got off my shots. It was a sad day. I came so close to sending him to hell where he belongs."

Tommy interrupted the prisoner. "Lester, we thought you'd like to know, Dr. Green was killed last night at his clinic."

Lester took a moment to let it sink in; he looked surprised. This was the first he'd heard of it. Suddenly, a smile creased his wrinkled face.

"That's the best news I've heard in a long while. Thank you, detective O'Leary. Although, I can't imagine you and the lovely detective Kendall came all the way down here just to break the news; there's got to be more to it than that."

Susan jumped in.

"Mr. Bell."

"Lester, please."

"Lester, is there any chance you had something to do with this?"

"Detective, you give me way too much credit. I'm behind bars, or have you forgotten? As I said before, I missed my opportunity to kill Dr. Green once before. However, I would, excuse me, would have taken the opportunity to finish the job, but I never got the chance."

"Mr. Bell, Lester, it's not unheard of for incarcerated individuals to order hits outside prison walls. Maybe you sent someone to take care of some unfinished business."

"You must be kidding."

O'Leary thought it was time for a little bad cop.

"Lester, cut the shit. We know you had something to do with this. Look at you; because of your failed attempt on Dr. Green, you'll spend at least another ten years as a guest of the state, if you're lucky."

"I am a martyr, detective, and I would gladly stay here for another fifty years serving my Lord."

"A martyr; please, spare me."

"An eye for an eye, a tooth for a tooth; I was doing God's work and for that I will accept the consequences, detective."

"Is that right?"

"Detective, maybe if you accepted Jesus Christ as your personal savior, you'd understand where I am coming from."

Tommy answered him, not with his own words, but with the words of God himself: *"But to you who hear what I say, love your enemies, do good to those who hate you, bless those who curse you, pray for those who mistreat you. To the person who strikes you on one cheek, offer the other one as well..."*

"Luke 6:27-29. I know the passage well, detective; although I am surprised you do."

"Eight years of Catholic school will do that to you."

"So you're Catholic?" That's too bad. You do realize that you're not really a Christian despite what that fellow in Rome says? On the bright side detective, it's never too late to embrace the Lord."

"Yes, I've heard that before."

"Maybe you can quote God's word. However, the Devil can quote scripture for his own purposes as well. I'm talking about living your life for God."

"Just like you?"

"That's right, just like me."

"Say Lester, who's the founder your church?"

"The Reverend Jefferson T. Sawgrass."

"Isn't he that guy on TV?"

"Indeed he is."

"Those are some great polyester suits he wears. I'd love to find out where he shops. Any ideas?"

"Are you mocking the Rev. Jefferson T. Sawgrass?"

"Not at all Lester. I don't mock, I point out facts. Let me tell you a fact that may come as a surprise to you."

"I'm all ears."

"The founder of my church was Jesus Christ himself. Now if you want to trust the televangelist with the polyester suits over the Son of God, you go right ahead. But remember this, if you had a hand in killing Dr. Green, you will spend the rest of your days behind bars and the Rev. Polyester Suit Man will not be able to help you."

Lester was taken back, but attempted to stand his ground.

"*Blessed are you when they insult you and persecute you and utter every kind of evil against you because of me,*" he spat maniacally. "Are you familiar with that verse detective?"

"Yes, it's Matthew 5:11. If you think you're being persecuted because of God, you're sadly mistaken. You tried to kill a man. That's why you're in prison. Yes, Dr. Green was the lowest of the low, but that doesn't give you the right to kill him."

"I didn't kill him, I told you that! But I am sure I'm not alone in wanting him dead."

Feeling a little left out, Susan re-entered the conversation. Time for a little good cop, she thought.

"At least we're in agreement on that. Lester, look at it this way, Dr. Green will no longer be able to hurt any more children. That's what you wanted after all. We just want to know who killed him. Is that so hard? Please tell us what you know. It's a win-win situation for everyone."

"Detective, as I stated before, I had nothing to do with this and I don't know who did. But if you find the guy who killed Edgar, tell him thanks from me."

Lester attempted to stand up, but the shackles limited his movement and held him in place.

"Guard, get me out of here," he called.

As if on cue, Captain Robinson and his men re-entered the room.

"So Mr. Bell, had enough?"

"Captain, they thought my appearance was shabby. I told you to let me freshen up."

Robinson had to laugh. If anything Bell was funny. Bell continued by saying goodbye.

"Detective Kendall, any time you want to pay me a visit, my door is always open."

He nodded in Tommy's direction.

"Detective O'Leary."

Captain Robinson and his men started escorting Lester away.

"Thanks again, Captain."

"Anytime Detective O'Leary."

"Oh, Captain, could you do me a little favor?"

"Name it."

"You've got an inmate by the name of Pedro Gianito, right?"

"Yeah, he's over in C Block."

"Can you give him a message from me?"

"Sure thing."

"Tell him Detective O'Leary loves the car. He'll know what you mean."

"Sure thing. Detective Kendall, it was very nice meeting you."

"The pleasure was all mine, Captain."

Tommy and Susan sat in silence for a few minutes before making their exit from the Visitor's Area. They were escorted by a friendly guard who recommended some great restaurants in the area if they were hungry. They were not or so they said. They stopped briefly to sign out and retrieve their guns; they thanked the guard and the rest of the staff for their assistance. As they walked out the front door of the facility, Susan was the first one to speak.

"If that wasn't a waste of time, I don't know what is."

"You really think it was a waste?" Tommy replied.

"Well it's obvious that Lester had nothing to do with it."

"I agree. He was genuinely surprised to hear that Edgar had met his maker."

"Either that, or he's a great actor, but I really doubt it."

"Who knows, maybe he became a thespian while behind bars."

"I guess weirder things have happened behind prison walls."

"You're telling me. But don't worry, I think we learned plenty."

"Is that right? Would you care to elaborate, detective?"

Tommy turned on the charm. "For you Susan, anything."

"Well, what are you waiting for? I'm growing older by the minute."

"Yes, and you're fast approaching me."

"Not quite, but good try."

"Let's start driving and then we can go over what we learned today."

"As you wish."

The two walked across the parking area and Tommy unlocked the doors to the GTO starting on Susan's side. Susan was about to get into the passenger's side door when she had a thought.

"Say detective, you mind if I drive?"

The look on Tommy's face was priceless. It was the look of a spoiled child who was asked to share his favorite toy.

"I don't know Susan. Why don't you ask me for my first born while you're at it?"

"Man, you are a selfish jerk."

"What?"

"Just giving you the business. I figured it was worth a try."

"Since you put it that way, here you go."

Tommy tossed her the keys and walked around to the passenger's side of the car. Susan slid across the hood of the GTO *Dukes of Hazzard* style and jumped behind the wheel. She jammed the key into the ignition, turned it forward and threw the car into drive.

"And away we go!" she screamed.

Tommy laughed.

"First time driving a car, detective?"

"You'd think so, huh? So tell me, what did we learn today?"

Susan swerved to miss a family of wild turkeys crossing the road.

"Just watch the road and I'll tell you."

"It's a deal."

She continued driving, and within five minutes, they were back on Route 395 heading towards New Haven.

"So detective, what have you got for me," she said.

"First, I think we can both agree that Lester had no hand in Dr. Green's killing. I'm sure he would have liked to have been involved, but he was, shall we say, preoccupied."

"Tell me something we don't know."

"Man, you're tough. I was getting to that."

"I just wanted to make sure you didn't forget. Dementia is a huge problem with men your age. Please continue."

"If you're going to be like that, I'll keep my observations to myself."

"I'm sorry. It won't happen again… for another few minutes anyway."

"It's also pretty likely that he doesn't know who did do it. From Lester's own account, he went after Dr. Green by himself. He never mentioned anyone else. No shadowy network of would-be killers. I'm sure Lester would have turned a dime on someone else if it would have saved him a few years in the big house. Despite what he says about accepting his martyrdom, I think he's full of crap. Needless to say, I find it unlikely that he had any co-conspirators."

"And you got all this from our brief conversation; astonishing."

"Would you mind, I am not done."

"Sorry."

"The important thing I took away was this: our killer is not at all like Mr. Bell. Lester carried around that little peashooter hoping to get a chance to shoot the good doctor, presumably. And as luck would have it, he finally got his opportunity. My guess is that he was as surprised as anyone that Dr. Green showed his face on that particular day. He said it himself: Dr. Green seldom exited the front door of the clinic. Could you blame him? So when he finally came out and started giving Lester some shit, Lester was caught off guard. So by the time he drew his weapon, Dr. Green had found sanctuary in his little clinic. Our killer didn't wait for an opportunity. He made his own opportunity.

Second, Lester's attempt on the Dr. Green's life was an emotional response more than anything else. You saw how he reacted when I started pushing his buttons; he couldn't control himself. Our killer on the other hand is all about control. Let's look at his method. He had to subdue the doctor. That takes time, and planning. In addition, someone like Lester who plants himself in front of the building might have some idea of the doctor's comings and goings. Our killer on the other hand knew Dr. Green's moves probably as well as the good doctor himself. Next, our killer didn't use some clumsy method to kill the doctor. He brought certain necessary items with him; the rest he knew would be at his disposal. The best murder weapon is the one that belongs to the victim. It can't be traced back to the killer."

"So what you're saying is…"

"What I'm saying is, maybe we don't know who are killer is. However, we know who he is not. He's not an emotional, religious fanatic. He is methodical and precise, and my guess is we haven't seen the last of him."

"Why do you say that?"

"He put a lot of thought into this. My guess is that he has some more he wants to show us before he's through."

"What leads you to that conclusion?"

"It's a hunch. But the last time I had hunch like this one, I was right on the money."

"What were you right about?"

"The next partner they assigned to me would be a big pain in the ass."

"I resent that."

"I had a hunch you'd say that too."

"Very funny."

"What do you say we regroup and meet at my place around eight?"

"Like for a date?"

Tommy was caught off guard by that, but kept his cool. "I've never dated a partner of mine."

"Well maybe that's because all of your partners have been men."

"You're a funny lady."

"How about this; you drop me off at my car and I'll meet you at 8:30. I'll see if there have been any updates and I'll bring the paperwork along with me. How does that sound?"

"It sounds pretty good. Don't you want the address?"

"I'm a detective, I'll figure it out."

"Just so you know, I don't live in the city."

"Maybe giving me your address isn't such a bad idea after all."

Chapter 11

Tommy and Susan arrived at the station at 6:30. Susan forgot where she parked her car, so they ended up driving around for ten minutes until they found her Honda Civic. Tommy gave her his address and they re-confirmed dinner for eight thirty. He agreed to take care of the food if she'd pick up some wine.

He headed back to Clinton, first stopping at Star Fish Market to get some scallops, and next at Gator Creek Farm to pick up some fresh vegetables. He gathered his purchases and headed back to the beach to get things started. He marinated the scallops in a mixture of garlic, olive oil, fresh ginger and soy sauce, and stuck them in the fridge. He cut up the fresh eggplant, zucchini, squash and red onion, and put them aside for grilling later on. Next, he cubed some day old bread, avocado, grape tomatoes and tossed them with a vinaigrette, and put it in the refrigerator along with the scallops. He figured he could get away with some instant couscous for a starch. He had a few boxes in the cupboard above his sink.

Despite his OCD, Tommy's place was a mess. He'd meant to tidy up over the last two weeks, but kept putting it off. He grabbed all the empty beer cans and miscellaneous debris, and discarded it in the trash can outside his back door. Next, he tackled the problem that was his dirty clothes. Being a beach resident had it benefits.

However, he couldn't do laundry at his house because of septic problems. Usually he'd visit his folks and do it there, but he'd neglected to pay them a visit since he'd been on vacation. More than likely he'd have to go to the laundromat, a prospect that sent chills up his spine. For the time being he decided to throw the dirty clothes into the trunk of his car, figuring he'd come up with a solution by the time he needed something clean to wear. He gave the bathroom a quick once over as well.

Satisfied with his cleaning job, he put a call into Dr. Patel, but his assistant said he had left for the day. He left a message. Tommy hoped to catch up with him in the morning and with any luck learn something that might shed some light on his killer.

Tommy was stepping out of the shower, when the doorbell rang. He quickly dried off, wrapped the towel around himself and ran to the front door. He opened the door with one hand, while holding the towel at his waist with the other; Susan was standing there with a bottle of cabernet and a smile.

"I know I'm a little early, but originally you said 8:00, so I figured you probably wouldn't mind."

Tommy lied. "I don't mind."

She gave Tommy a good once over and nervously touched her face.

"Although, if I knew it was going to be this casual, I would have dressed down."

Tommy purposely played with his towel. For a moment it looked like it might fall. This seemed to catch her attention. He then drew her eyes back to his face.

"I have a few more towels in the hall closet. Be my guest."

"Maybe after a few drinks," she joked. "I just can't resist a man in a towel."

Susan had her auburn hair pulled back. She had on a khaki mini skirt and a white cotton blouse; on her feet a pair of sandals. She wore just the right amount of make up.

Tommy continued. "Please, come on in. As you can see, I'm in the middle of getting ready. However, I'm a fast dresser. Just give me a few minutes."

"Take all the time you need, I'm not going anywhere."

"By the way, there's a cork screw in the drawer next to the fridge and there are wine glasses somewhere. I'm sure you'll find them. After all, you are a detective."

"Thanks for the vote of confidence."

"What are partners for?"

Tommy walked down the short hallway and out of sight while Susan opened cabinet doors in search of some glasses. After two tries, she found the right cupboard. She pulled out two burgundy glasses and set them down on the counter. She opened the drawer, as instructed, and retrieved the wine opener. She removed the cork, poured herself a generous glass of the cabernet and took a sip.

She decided to walk around and explore the place Tommy called home. It was small, but she had to admit to herself, it was quaint. Most of the men she knew cared little about the furnishings in their dwellings. If they had a Lazy Boy chair and a plasma-screen TV, all was well in the world. Tommy on the other hand seemed to have a flare for decorating. The place had a country feel with nautical accents. It was sensitive, yet masculine. She nodded her head in approval. She really liked it.

She found Tommy's CD collection and thumbed through the catalogue. She picked one she liked, put it in the CD player and pressed play. In a few seconds Ella Fitzgerald echoed through the house. She loved Ella's voice. To Susan, it was the closest thing to God singing she'd ever heard. When she was a kid, her grandmother exposed her to Ella. While other kids were listening to the teen sensations of the day, she listened to Ella and her contemporaries. She made herself comfortable on an oversized chair and waited for Tommy to return. True to his word, Tommy was ready in only five minutes.

"Thanks for pouring me a glass," was the first thing out of his mouth.

"I'm sorry. If it makes you feel better, I did put out a glass for you."

Tommy walked into the kitchen and picked up the bottle and the lone glass and joined Susan in the living room. He sat down on the couch and poured himself a healthy glass as well. He raised his glass in the air.

"What should we drink to?"

"How about, to new friends?"

"Is that all you've got?"

"Uh, I'm not very good at these things."

"Just kidding; to new friends is perfect."

"To new friends…"

"…and to catching a killer."

"Cheers."

"This is a great cab. It's nice and dry. I'm not big on fruity reds."

"You can say that again. So what's on the menu for this evening Chef O'Leary, if you don't mind me asking?"

"Actually, I do mind," he replied playfully. I want it to be surprise."

"I do like surprises, detective."

"Please, call me Tommy."

"For some reason I find that difficult to do. In my mind, 'Tommy' is little kid's name."

"Well, plenty of people tell me I act like a five year old, so I'd say the name is fitting."

"OK, you win; Tommy it is."

"Now that we sorted that one out, I put a call in to Dr. Patel's office when I got home, but he'd already left for the evening."

"The nerve of that guy going home and spending time with his family," she replied.

"I agree." Tommy took a big swig of his wine and added sarcastically: "Look at us, it's after 8:00 pm and we are still hard at work."

Susan laughed. "You are so right. After spending so much time trying to find my car, I bagged going back into the station. I checked in with forensics and they had nothing to report on the evidence they collected as of yet. However, they did say they found one interesting tidbit at the scene. It seems Dr. Death, that's what they're calling him, had a safe in his walk-in refrigerator; whoever sent him into the great beyond tried to open it before making their exit."

"A robbery?" Tommy shook his head back and forth. "It doesn't add up. I can't imagine our killer going to such great lengths to cover up a theft."

"Is it possible that the killer tried to convince Dr. Green to open the safe, and when he failed to comply, killed him to cover it up?"

"Anything is possible."

"It wouldn't be unheard of for a thief to cover his tracks with a murder."

"I agree, but our man seems to be a better killer than a thief."

"You can't be good at everything, Tommy."

"So true, but I do try," he replied. "Was forensics able to get the safe open?"

"Unfortunately, no."

"Well then, I think that should be our first stop tomorrow morning."

"I concur; whatever's in that safe might hold the key to this case."

"We should be so lucky, but at the very least it might open another door for us."

"It's certainly worth looking into."

"Maybe Dr. Green left a note identifying the person or persons who might do him harm."

"And maybe our killer will walk in tomorrow and confess."

"I've seen it happen before."

"Maybe you should lay off the vino, Tommy."

"Maybe you're right," he joked. What do you say to me getting dinner started?"

"Now that's a great idea; I'm starved. Can I do anything to help?"

"You can top off my wine and open another bottle. There's a wine rack in the hall closet. Pick out something to go with scallops if you wouldn't mind."

"Did you say scallops?"

"Yeah."

"I hate to be the bearer of bad news, but I'm allergic to all shellfish."

"You must be kidding."

"Actually I am."

"Very funny detective Kendall; although I did have some frozen fish fillets as a backup."

"I'll eat anything, but I prefer the scallops, thanks."

"Scallops it is."

Tommy headed into the kitchen to start dinner, while Susan riffled through the hall closet. She had to laugh. The closet was filled with wine. There were a couple of towels, but the wine far outweighed the linens. It wasn't hard to figure out Tommy's priorities. A small wine cooler sat on the closet floor; it held twenty bottles. Above the wine cooler were pine racks, filled with dozens of bottles of every variety. She considered her options, and decided on a red zinfandel. With any luck she'd be able to sample a few more before the night was over, she thought to herself. Susan closed the door and walked back into the living room. Tommy was nowhere to be found.

"Hello," she called out. "Tommy, are you there?"

Tommy opened the slider and stepped back inside.

"Were you looking for me, detective?"

"As a matter of fact, I was; just wondering about the ETA on dinner."

"I just put some veggies on the grill. They should take about ten minutes or so; the scallops won't take long at all. I'd say we should be ready to eat in fifteen minutes tops."

"Great."

"Would you care to join me out on the deck while I finish up dinner? If we hurry, we'll be able to catch the tail end of a beautiful sunset."

"How can I pass up an invitation like that? Let me just grab the wine opener."

Tommy walked outside and took up his position at the grill; he was flipping a piece of eggplant when Susan stepped onto the deck.

She fixed her gaze on the bistro table. There were two place settings as well as a pair of candles. She was pleased. It looked great. She almost felt like she was on a date. A pair of speakers hung on the exterior wall of the cottage, so Ella could serenade them outside as well.

"You certainly pulled out all of the stops Tommy."

"What can I say? Police work and food are my passions. As far as I'm concerned, there's no use in doing either half-assed."

"A man after my own heart."

He pulled out a chair. "Please have a seat, Detective Kendall."

"Why thank you."

"If you lean back in your chair ever so slightly, you might be able to get a glimpse of the Sound. It's just past the home of the neighbor from hell."

Susan gave it a try, but just couldn't get the right angle.

"I'm just not seeing it."

"How about this, we can head down to the water after we eat."

"Sound-s good to me; no pun intended."

"You're a real comedian, Susan."

"OK, bad joke. It happens to the best of us."

Tommy removed the vegetables and placed them on a platter to cool. He sprinkled them with a little sea salt and covered them with foil. He then took another piece of foil, and placed it on the grill. He the lined up the scallops on the foil, sealed them, and closed the grill's lid. Next, he focused his attention on the side burner. Tommy had placed some chicken stock and seasonings in a small All-Clad pan, and was waiting for it to boil. He lifted the lid. Satisfied with its progress, he poured in the couscous, gave it a stir and removed the pan from the heat. He re-covered the pan and placed it on the shelf attached to the grill.

"The couscous will be ready in five minutes and the scallops right after. What do you say we start with a little salad?"

"Sounds great."

Tommy opened a little Tupperware container and poured the contents onto their salad plates. It was a Tommy original: a peasant bread salad. Susan just sat, mesmerized. "This looks great. It almost looks too good to eat."

"It's not that good," Tommy joked.

"Do you want to say grace or shall I?"

"You're the guest. It's your prerogative."

"How about we both say it together?"

"Very well."

The two said a quick grace and dove in.

Susan was the first to break the silence. "So where did a tough cop like you learn to cook like this?"

"You think I'm tough?" was Tommy's reply.

"You know what I mean. I thought I'd be dropping by for some burgers, dogs and store bought potato salad. I guess I didn't think your cooking would be so refined."

"Let me tell you a little secret."

"I'm all ears."

"Cooking is how I unwind."

"I don't know, for some reason I pictured you as someone who'd go golfing or lift weights to unwind. That's what most cops do anyway."

"I do golf, but truthfully, I'm pretty inconsistent. And the gym, don't get me started. I haven't seen the inside of a gym in years. Wait, that's not entirely true. I did bust the owner of a gym last year for selling large amounts of steroids. But I guess that really doesn't count."

"So where did you learn to cook anyway?"

"Hold that thought. Let me serve our main course and then we can continue where we left off.

Tommy grabbed their dinner plates and walked over to the grill. He removed scallops from the foil and tossed them on the grill. While they finished up, he plated the couscous and the veggies. When the scallops were golden brown, he added them to the plates.

"Tommy, you won't mind if I take a doggie bag home. I don't think I can finish all this food."

"Just do the best you can."

"I'll try." She cut into one of the jumbo scallops and took a bite. "Wow, that is good…it's like butta."

"Thanks."

"Maybe I'll finish all this after all. So where did you learn how to cook?"

"Well my mom is a great cook. I've gotten some great pointers from her over the years, not to mention the many jobs I've had in the food service industry. I wasn't always a cop."

"If you do decide to leave law enforcement anytime soon, at least you have something to fall back on."

Susan and Tommy finished up their dinner and agreed to go for that walk on the beach. Susan could hardly move; she was quite full. She usually ate like a bird. Then again, when she cooked for herself her meals consisted largely of cereal and yogurt. Besides, she didn't want to insult the chef by leaving too much food on her plate.

They refilled their glasses, kicked of their shoes and walked down the steps into the cool sand. Although Tommy had limited views of the Sound, his place was right on the beach. They walked around Mr. McMansion's houses, sat down and gazed at the sky.

It was a clear night and even though the sun had set, the stars illuminated the sky above. Tommy dared Susan to go into the water. She obliged. He followed and they splashed around like a couple of kids; they even managed to avoid spilling their drinks. They both had a wonderful time.

Chapter 12

Discovered in 1614, the Thimble Islands are an archipelago of granite islands located just off the Connecticut coast. Many believe the notorious pirate Captain Kidd buried his famed treasure somewhere in the small island chain. Among them is local attorney Jerry Rivers. An amateur treasure hunter, Jerry purchased one of the smaller islands eight years ago. It was dumb luck really.

He'd represented a guilty client in a murder-for-hire case who would've spent his remaining years in prison had Jerry not come to the rescue. Jerry got him an acquittal; unfortunately, the man lacked the ability to pay his large legal bill. Instead, his client assured Jerry he could arrange a good deal on a certain piece of waterfront real estate if the debt would be forgiven. Jerry was skeptical, but decided to hear the man out. Getting something was better than nothing. After meeting with his client and the owner of the property, Jerry agreed to take the property off the gentleman's hands. The deal was great; his client must have had something on the guy, but Jerry didn't care what it was. He'd been trying to buy one of the Thimble Islands for as far back as he could remember. It was an extravagant purchase, but Jerry thought it was worth it. Even if he never located the buried treasure, the island would become his home away from home.

One of Connecticut's most sought after trial lawyers, Jerry reluctantly began his legal career some twenty-five years ago. His father was an attorney, and it was assumed that Jerry would carry on the family practice after the elder Rivers retired. After all, Jerry was the eldest son.

Although Jerry had little interest in the law, he had very few options at the time. Jerry had been a great athlete during his youth and had hoped to play professional baseball. However, he blew out his knee during his senior year in college and his dream of going onto the big leagues came crashing down. After graduating, Jerry moved home and languished, unsure where his life would lead him. He spent most of his time drinking or playing golf or both. His parents gave him a great deal of leeway at first. They knew how much baseball meant to their son. But after two long years, Jerry's lack of motivation and direction began to frustrate his parents, and they finally had enough. His father approached him one day and made him an offer. If Jerry enrolled in law school, his father would foot the bill; he would rent him an apartment, pay his tuition and any other necessary expenses. If Jerry refused, he would have to move out and go it alone. Jerry was at a crossroads; he could go to school for a few more years or work. He chose the former.

Jerry began his legal career by first taking the LSATs. He dreaded standardized tests, but needed an LSAT score to be considered at any law school. Unfortunately, he didn't do very well the first go around, so he retook them. And as luck would have it, his follow up score was lower than the first. Jerry's father was well respected in the New Haven legal community, and had many friends. He put a call into a friend at the University of Bridgeport and Jerry was ultimately accepted at their law school on a conditional basis. If his GPA fell beneath a 2.0 average, he would be kicked out. Having little choice, Jerry agreed.

Truthfully, Jerry enjoyed law school. However, he was a mediocre student at best. He spent most of his time in the local watering holes and on the public courses. He honestly didn't care about his grades; the gentleman's C was good enough for the school and it was good enough for him. Unlike most soon-to-be lawyers who'd have to go out and hit the pavement in search of a job upon graduation, Jerry's future had been secured the moment he agreed to go to law school. He took the required classes and any class that would help him prepare for the bar exam. He ended up earning his JD in three years. Upon graduating, Jerry crammed for weeks for the bar exam. It was the hardest he'd ever studied in his life. As it turned out, Jerry would pass the bar exam on his first try. His parents were elated. And for the first time since he blew out his knee, Jerry was proud of himself as well.

The man walked across the rocky beach, pulling his Zodiac Zoom 260 Aero behind him. It was only a short distance to the water and the man handled the heavy load with ease. He deposited the boat at the water's edge and walked back to where he'd left his gear. He grabbed a large black duffel bag, a small back pack and a pair of night vision goggles, and stowed them in the Zodiac. Slowly he eased the boat into the Sound. He walked beside the boat, guiding it, until the water came up to his waist. Satisfied with the water's depth, the man climbed in, retrieved a small paddle and eased the tiny craft out of the small inlet. Within minutes, the shore faded into the darkness. He placed the paddle at his feet, turned and lowered the Yamaha twenty-five horse power engine into the dark water. He hit the starter button, revved the engine, and pointed the boat away from the Branford shore. He'd arrive at his destination in about fifteen minutes.

Jerry arrived at the island at about 6:00 pm. He had a few loose ends to tie up at the office, so he couldn't pull himself away any sooner. He planned to stay on the island for an entire week this time. He just wrapped up an epic long murder trial and desperately needed some down time. The thought of a week of fishing, reading and looking for Captain Kidd's treasure really brought a smile to his face.

The sun had set and he and his partner Bruce Damon finished up a lovely dinner of lobster, corn on the cob and baked potato. Jerry picked up the dishes and brought them into the kitchen. He dumped the lobster shells and the corn cobs into the trash, and placed the dishes in the sink.

"Bruce, I'm going to take a long, hot shower. Would you mind finishing up in the kitchen? I'd do it, but I really need to go and hose myself off."

"You're not going to get any arguments from me. You smell like the ass end of rhino. If you want to get anywhere near me this weekend, you'd better clean yourself up mister."

"Is there any doubt why I love you?"

"Do you want me to answer that?"

"What's that suppose to mean?"

"I'm just giving you shit. Go clean yourself up so we can have a little dessert!"

"Feel free to join me."

"Are you out of your mind; and mess up this perfectly coiffed do? No thank you. It takes me forever to get this pretty."

"Suit yourself. I'll see you in a few."

Jerry ascended a flight of stairs and walked down the hallway to the master bedroom. His house was Victorian in style with grey clapboard siding. It had a wrap-around porch and a balcony off the master suite. Jerry opened the French doors and stepped onto the balcony. What a beautiful night he thought. He spat into the night air, took in a few deep breaths and walked back inside and into the large adjacent bathroom. He disrobed, turned on the shower and let the water run for several minutes. When the temperature was to his liking, he hopped in.

The man slowed the Zodiac's speed as he drew closer to the island, eventually turning off the motor entirely. A boat engine would hardly draw attention in the Thimble Islands, even at this time of night, but the man thought it was better to play it safe. He retrieved the paddle once again, and paddled the remaining distance to the island's shore. The island came equipped with a large dock; the owner had a cigarette boat that he used to go to and from the mainland. It was a little extravagant, but he wouldn't expect any less from the man who owned the island. The man steered the small boat towards the dock, and tied up on the far side of the larger boat. He looked around; the island was in total darkness. There were a few lights on in the house, but their glow wasn't likely to reveal his position.

The man opened his large duffel bag and removed several items: a snorkel and mask; an underwater flashlight; and two small devices containing C4 and timing mechanisms. He put on the mask and snorkel, and slipped into the water. When he resurfaced, he reached into the boat for the flashlight and the two incendiary devices. He placed the light into the water, turned it on, and descended beneath the hull of the cigarette boat. He attached the small devices to the bottom of the boat; one towards the bow and the other towards the stern. He set the timers on each and climbed back into the Zodiac. It would be five minutes before the muffled explosions went off, slowly sinking the boat into the murky water. It was unlikely his quarry would be able to make a run for the boat. However, if they somehow managed to escape the house, they would find themselves trapped on the island.

The man paddled away from the dock, navigating the Zodiac to the opposite side of the island. The boat dock was situated on the front side of the island, that is, the side of the island where the front of the house faced. The man brought the Zodiac to rest directly behind the house. He slipped on a pair of black boots, climbed out of the boat, and quickly secured it to one of the jagged rocks lining the shore. He grabbed the small backpack and the night vision goggles and made his way up the steep incline towards the house. As he reached the top, he encountered a large outbuilding about ten yards from the crest of the hill. The building housed a large propane tank and the generator that supplied the island with its electricity. It was exactly where he wanted to be.

Bruce finished clearing the table and washing the dishes and decided to have himself a cigarette. Jerry hated his smoking habit but he really needed one. He'd had a stressful week. His former in-laws had initiated a civil suit against him on Monday and he couldn't stop thinking about it. Jerry assured him that it wouldn't go anywhere, that he would get it thrown out. However, Bruce wasn't so sure.

Jerry had been Bruce's attorney for over fourteen years and his lover for almost as long. Bruce had been driving drunk and had crashed into a parked police cruiser and was in desperate need of an attorney. He'd had seen Jerry's picture on a billboard and decided to give him a call. After all, if he was on a billboard, he must be good, Bruce reasoned. His trial lasted three days, and by the end it looked like the prosecution had him dead to rights. A guilty verdict would certainly have landed him in jail. When the jury came back and delivered a not guilty verdict, Bruce could hardly believe his good fortune. He was so grateful that he offered to buy his attorney dinner at the restaurant of his choosing. It would be a several months before Jerry called in that favor.

Jerry chose Foe, a little Bistro in nearby Branford, and Bruce obliged. They had a wonderful evening. Bruce couldn't thank him enough. They talked about sports. Jerry was a Yankees fan, Bruce loved the Sox. They talked about his trial; and Jerry talked about his wife. They had been going through a rough patch. Jerry was a great listener. He wished his wife listened as well; maybe they wouldn't be having problems if she did. By the end of the night, they felt like old friends. Bruce didn't have many friends. He spent most of his time at work or with his wife. Meeting someone like Jerry gave him hope that he could make new friends. And as luck would have it, over the next year or so, the two became close friends. Bruce couldn't be happier. He was teased and picked on as a kid, so he never thought he'd have a cool friend like Jerry. But for some reason, Jerry liked him.

And Jerry seemed to know everyone. He even had Yankee season tickets. Sure Bruce hated the Yankees, but they did play the Sox a few times a year so it was worth it. Coming back from the Yankees/Sox games was when it happened. The two were driving back from the Bronx when Jerry pulled off the highway to get some gas. Bruce offered to go out and pump. When he returned to the car, Jerry surprised Bruce and kissed him. His first impulse was to punch Jerry in the face, but the more he thought about it, the more he knew Jerry was right for him. The feelings he'd been having over the past months were confirmed by the kiss. He couldn't deny his love for Jerry any longer. From that day forward, things would never be the same again. What a great life they had built for themselves. He and Jerry had come so far and now this. He thought his ex in-laws would be out of his life once their daughter died, but he was sadly mistaken.

It all started two years after Jerry and he first started seeing each other. From the beginning, they had been very discreet; neither wanted their relationship made public knowledge. After all, Jerry was a famous local attorney, and Bruce certainly didn't want the guys who worked with him at the mortgage broker's office to know his personal business. He had been extremely careful, but that all changed when his wife stumbled upon an e-mail he had written Jerry. He'd deleted all the e-mails Jerry had sent him, but forgot to erase one that had been sitting in his sent box. Bruce couldn't put that evening's events out of his mind. It was a Friday, and he had come home late, again. He told his wife he'd been working late, but he'd met Jerry. When he arrived home, she confronted him with the e-mail; he didn't know what to do. She threatened him with divorce, but the thought of his relationship with Jerry becoming public drove him into a violent rage. He grabbed his wife by the throat and started choking her. In several minutes her face turned blue, her body began to convulse. And finally, she was motionless. He panicked; he didn't know what to do. He called Jerry, but he was no where to be found. He thought about throwing her lifeless body in the pool, but reconsidered it. It was a cold day, and the last thing his wife would have been doing was swimming. He decided to call 911; he explained that when he'd arrived home, he'd found his wife's lifeless body on the floor of their living room. He suspected she'd suffered a seizure. She was breathing, but barely. The paramedics arrived almost immediately, and rushed her to the hospital. Bruce rode to the hospital in the ambulance. He was beside himself. What would happen? His relationship with Jerry would become public knowledge and in all likelihood, he'd go to jail.

The doctors were able to stabilize her, but explained that her prognosis was not very good. The "seizure" dramatically decreased the flow of blood to her brain. This oxygen deprivation caused her to suffer severe and irreversible brain damage; it was very unlikely she would ever regain consciousness. Bruce played the role of distraught husband to a T. And once again was spared time in jail.

Jerry finally called Bruce back later that night and he relayed the entire story. It was so great to hear his voice, he thought. Jerry explained that everything would be fine so long as his wife did not regain consciousness. Bruce agreed. He asked Bruce if he and his wife had prepared living wills. He responded that they had not, although he was certain that his wife would want to be kept alive. She was very religious. So taking his wife off of life support was not an option. Jerry stated that the sooner they could pull the plug, the better off the two of them would be. Bruce understood that ending his wife's life was the only way out. It had taken years of battling it out in the court system, and finally his wife was no longer a threat to himself or his lover. His wife's parents fought him tooth and nail to keep her alive, and now they had initiated a wrongful death action. Bruce didn't think he'd be as fortunate this time. Something told him his lucky streak was about to come to an end.

THE MASTER PLAN

The man entered the outbuilding and located the generator's main power switch. He removed and unzipped his backpack. He took out a Blackjack and two pairs of plastic restraints. It was likely that only one of the inhabitants would come out to check on the power, but he was ready if they both came to pay him a visit. He placed the night vision goggles on his forehead and turned the generator's power switch into the off position. Almost immediately, the house was in darkness. The man moved the goggles over his eyes and waited.

As Jerry was stepping out of the shower, the lights went out.

"What the fuck?" he yelled. "Bruce, is this some feeble attempt at being romantic? Shit. Could you have at least waited until I was done?"

Undeterred, Jerry reached for his towel on the nearby rack, but couldn't seem to locate it. He took a few more steps, and slipped on the wet floor.

"This is just not my day," he uttered, nursing his right arm.

He climbed onto all fours, and felt around for the vanity. Locating it, he opened the second drawer and removed a flashlight. It wasn't the first time he'd lost power. He turned it on and moved the beam around the small room, eventually locating his towel. He placed the flashlight on the sink and quickly dried himself off. From the back of the door, he removed a silk kimono. It was a little hot for a robe, but he didn't feel like wandering around outside in the nude. He cinched the belt around his waist and called to Bruce again.

"Bruce, what happened? Bruce?"

He picked up the flashlight and walked into the hallway. Not hearing anything, he headed down the stairs and into the kitchen. He looked around, but couldn't seem to find Bruce. He walked to the front of the house and noticed a candle burning on the porch. Bruce was sitting in a nearby chair smoking a cigarette. Jerry opened the door.

"Bruce, I was calling you. Were the hell were you?"

"I was out here having a smoke."

"I thought you were trying to be romantic by turning out the lights."

"Guess again. If I was being romantic, I'd dim the lights, not turn them all off you idiot."

"What's eating you?"

"I don't know, this lawsuit is really scaring me," he sighed.

"I thought I told you not to worry about it; that I'd handle it and…"

"That's easy for you to say. You're not the one who killed his wife."

"What are you talking about? You didn't mean to kill her. You made a mistake. It happens to all of us."

"I didn't mean to hurt her, this much is true. But I purposely pulled the plug, didn't I?"

He took Bruce by the hand. "Listen, we'll get through this. When have I let you down before?"

"I know, but I'm having a bad feeling about this one. Sure it won't land me in jail, but it will certainly open my life up to a great deal of scrutiny."

"Would you do something for me?"

"Name it."

"Relax. Let's enjoy this weekend. I'm on vacation all this week. In between fishing, reading and who knows what, I will work on your case."

"You promise?"

"I promise. But first, I've got to go and fix the power. Damn generator; what a piece of shit. Go pick out some music and a nice bottle of wine and I'll meet you inside."

"OK."

"And one more thing, brush your teeth. You know how much I hate it when you have smoker's breath."

"Anything for you."

Jerry grabbed a pair of flip-flops from the porch and descended the nearby steps onto the grass. He walked around to the back of the house and headed towards the building that housed the generator. This was the fourth time this season that he had to come and check on a problem with it. What a pain in the ass. He'd had enough. He was going to sue the generator company until it hurt. Sure, he didn't mind forgoing phone service or cable or internet while on the island, but he could only take small doses of life without electricity. The generator company would pay.

He reached the front off the corrugated steel structure and he pulled open the rusty door. It almost fell of the hinges. He moved the flashlight around, looking the generator over from top to bottom. He approached the massive machine and noticed something odd; the power was off. Either Bruce was full of shit or someone else was on the island. At that moment a severe blow struck Jerry's head, the flashlight fell out of his hand and he went crashing onto the ground. He never saw the man, but he certainly felt the effects of the Blackjack. The man quickly secured Jerry's hands and feet and dragged his body behind a pile of old lawn furniture. One down, one to go, he thought.

Chapter 13

After Bruce finished brushing his teeth, he splashed a little cold water on his face. What a week. Maybe Jerry was right. The lawsuit was much ado about nothing. He had Jerry and Jerry was the best. In all the time that he had known Jerry, Jerry had always come through for him. Why should this time be any different?

He picked up the scented candle and ambled down the hall to the cellar door, the planks of the pine floor creaking beneath his bare feet. He opened the door and proceeded down the rickety steps, holding the banister to keep his balance. When he reached the dirt floor below the bottom step, he took a right and lifted the candle above his head, gazing at the wide expanse of wine. There were hundreds of bottles to choose from. Jerry was the wine expert, not him. "Hmmmm, what goes with a man sandwich?" He chuckled to himself.

He grabbed a bottle of champagne, but returned it to its shelf. Maybe after this whole legal mess was behind him they could celebrate with a little champagne, he thought, but not tonight. He then picked up a nice pinot noir. It looked nice anyway. Isn't that the wine they drank in the movie *Sideways*, he uttered to himself? Jerry and he just loved that movie. Maybe one day they could take a trip to wine country, rent a convertible, and stay in some cute little

B&Bs. Wouldn't that be lovely? He thought.

Happy with his choice, Bruce headed back upstairs and into the living room. He sprawled out on the couch, resting his head on a velvet throw pillow. He just loved velvet. What was keeping Jerry, he thought? He leaned over, placed the wine on the coffee table and remembered that Jerry wanted him to pick out some music. Jerry had an awful taste in music, so Bruce made sure to always bring some of his CDs whenever he came out to the island. Jerry was so well versed in the ways of the world, but his musical taste bordered on the ridiculous. For some reason Jerry just loved show tunes. If Bruce had his way, there would not be a single show tune played the entire weekend. Bruce was gay, but he wasn't about to hop on the show tune band wagon. He could never understand why his gay brethren fancied show tunes. Like the Bermuda Triangle and Stonehenge, it was a mystery to him. He opened his black carrying case and flipped through a dozen discs before finding the one he'd been looking for. Ah, there it is: Peter Cetera's Greatest Hits. Now we're talking. He just loved Peter Cetera. Not only was he a musical genius, but he was gorgeous as well. He looked at the song titles. Yes, The Glory of Love would be perfect. After all, Jerry was the man who continued to fight for his honor.

Fifteen minutes had passed, and the power still hadn't come on. What the hell is taking so damn long, he said to himself? He was getting restless. He thought about having another cigarette, but decided against. Instead, he'd go and investigate what was keeping Jerry. Maybe he could help. He walked to the back door, pushed open the screen door and stepped out onto the porch. "Jerry, how are you making out? I picked out some wine and music, but I need some electricity if we're going to have a listen. Hello? Did someone forget to pay their gas bill? Jerry?"

Jerry did not respond. "Do I have to come out there and bitch slap you to get you moving?" he joked. "Jerry, what gives, my handsome stallion?" Frustrated with Jerry's lack of response, he made his way down the stairs and across the back yard in the direction of the utility shed. He walked around the steel building, but Jerry was no where to be found. Next, he tried the door closest to the house. Its rusty hinges creaked open. He gazed inside. "Jerry?" Shit, I should have brought the candle, he thought. He loved the smell of cinnamon, and it would have made it a lot easier to see, he thought. He walked over to the giant propane tank and rapped on it three times with the knuckles of his right hand. Sounds full to me, he thought. He then turned his attention to the generator. He edged closer to get a better look, and heard a noise that sounded like footsteps on gravel. "Jerry, is that you?" As he turned to look behind him, a person dressed all in black appeared. But before he could say a word, the Blackjack came crashing down on his temple; a searing pain echoed through his head. As his legs buckled and he collapsed to the ground, all he saw was darkness.

The man retrieved the remaining plastic restraints, and placed them on Bruce's hands and feet, just as he had done with the lawyer. He lifted Bruce's limp body over his shoulder and began the trek to the house. He deposited Bruce face down on the living room sofa and headed back outside to grab Jerry. Upon arriving in the utility building, he removed his night vision goggles, and placed them into his backpack. He turned the main power switch back on and walked behind the pile of old furniture to retrieve the lawyer. To his amazement, he was gone. He quickly exited the rear door of the building, looking around. The lawyer was no where to be found.

"Shit," he uttered under his breath. He ran back through the door, gravel crunching under his feet. He killed the power to the generator and retrieved the night vision goggles and a nine millimeter pistol with a sound suppressor from his pack. He zipped up the pack and quickly exited the rear door of the building. He surveyed the immediate perimeter. Where could the lawyer be? He made a sweep of the area surrounding the structure - nothing. He headed to the edge of the steep hill where he'd left the Zodiac. Perhaps the lawyer made a run for the water. The man peered down the embankment hoping his instincts were correct. To the right of the Zodiac was the lawyer laying face down among the rocks. Jerry had managed to undo the restraints on his feet, but his hands were still bound. In a calm and even voice the man addressed his prey: "Counselor, you better not be dead, as I am not through with you yet. Although by the time I am done with you, you will welcome death just as you'd welcome an old friend."

The granite was uneven and course, but the man was an expert climber. With gun in hand, he quickly descended the treacherous hill and reached the lawyer in under a minute. The attorney lay motionless, but the man knew that could change in an instant. He underestimated him once, and he'd make certain it would not happen again.

The man took the butt of the gun and slammed against the lawyer's skull. He was out cold this time. Next, he removed his trusty diver's knife from its sheath on his right leg. He had acquired the knife a lifetime ago and had used it to kill twenty-four times. He could still picture the faces of each of his victims. Will you be kill number twenty-five, Mr. Rivers? His gaze rested on the glowing steel of the sharp blade and he whispered: "Counselor, you could have made this easy on yourself. Instead, you chose to put up a fight. Truth be told, I admire your fighting spirit. The world is full of cowards. If given the choice between fighting a coward or a man with fortitude, I'd choose the latter every time. After all, where is the satisfaction in beating a man who is not even your equal? In any case, if it is a fight you want, I can oblige." The man leaned over and drew the knife across the Achilles tendon of the lawyer's right leg, severing the bridge between the calf muscle and the heel. A small trickle of blood exited the wound and dripped onto to his foot. When he had finished with the right leg, he repeated the same procedure with the left. Jerry would not run away from him again.

He re-sheathed the knife and replaced the pistol in the outside pocket of his backpack. He secured the pack to his back, and leaned over and lifted up the lawyer. Luckily, the lawyer was in better physical shape than Doctor Green. He couldn't imagine lugging the overweight doctor up such a steep incline. He carried the lawyer to the house and brought him to rest on the floor of the living room, adjacent to the couch. He then checked on his lover. He was still unconscious and very secure.

In the dining area of the lawyer's island home sat a charcoal Farmhouse table with matching Bowback chairs. There were three on either side and one at each head of the table. The man grabbed the end chairs and carried them into the living room one by one. He moved the coffee table and its contents to the side and placed the two chairs facing away from one another in the center of the room. He lifted up the lawyer, and placed him in the chair closest to the dining area. He then lifted the other man and placed him in the second chair. He removed his backpack and pulled out a roll of duct tape, two dozen polypropylene straps with steel cam-action buckles, a canister of piano wire, a pair of cutters, a set of pliers and a small metal clamp. He used the straps to secure the men to their respective chairs and the duct tape to cover their eyes and mouths. Next, he took the piano wire, fashioned a figure eight and placed a loop around each man's neck, securing the wire in the center with the tiny clamp. He then used the pliers to tighten the clamp. If either man moved his head too much in any direction, he would choke himself and his lover in the process.

Satisfied that the lawyer and his lover were secure, the man retraced his steps and proceeded to the utility shed. He turned the main power back on and knelt down in the white gravel next to his black duffel bag. He opened the bag and examined its contents. He removed an incendiary device, much like the ones he'd placed on the hull of the cigarette boat. Although it was almost identical in construction, it was larger in size and contained a detonator that could be triggered remotely. He placed the device under the propane tank, zipped up the bag and headed back to the house. He'd take care of arming it on his way out. Right now he had a few other things to attend to.

Tommy and Susan finished frolicking in the water and headed back up to the house. Ever the quintessential gentleman, Tommy opened the slider and stood back to allow Susan to enter first. She shook the sand off her feet as best she could and crossed the narrow opening into the living room. In her best British accent, Susan voiced her thanks:

"Why thank you kind sir."

Tommy bowed in her direction. "You're welcome m'lady. It is my pleasure serving you."

Susan smiled. "Tommy, you continue to surprise me, and that's no easy task."

"What can I say, I am full of surprises."

Tommy headed to the hall closet to get some towels and another bottle of wine. When they were done toweling off, the pair settled onto the couch. Susan was the first to speak.

"I can't even begin to tell you how much fun I've had tonight. It's a welcome change."

"I have had a nice time as well."

"It's just that lately I've been so wrapped up in my work, I have taken little time to stop and just enjoy myself. Don't get me wrong, I love being a cop, but I've let the rest of my life slip by while I've focused on my work. It's kind of sad."

"I know exactly where you are coming from. Why do you think I took such a long vacation? I needed to clear my head. Only a cop can really understand what another cop is going through. It's this constant tug. On the one hand you love the work and can't think of anything but the job. At the same time, that same job can squeeze the life out of you."

"It's a tricky balance for sure."

"So what made you decide to become a cop anyway?"

"That's a long story."

"I have all night. Please do tell."

"You asked for it!"

"I am a glutton for punishment."

"I guess it's not so long after all."

"OK."

"Well for me it boils down to just one word: *CHIP's.*"

"Did you say, *CHIP'S?*"

"Yes."

Tommy laughed. "You mean the TV Show *CHIP'S?*"

"That's the one. When I was a kid, I loved that show. Ponch and John were my heroes. I guess I wanted to be just like them."

"You've got to be kidding." Tommy stuck his hands out and

pretended to ride an invisible motorcycle. He made motorcycle noises like a little kid.

"Why? Is that funny to you?"

"Well no, no, maybe, I don't know. I guess the thought of you riding around on a motorcycle seems a little far fetched. I thought you were kidding."

"I am."

"Very funny."

"I actually come from a long line of cops. My dad is a cop. He's the police chief in Stonington. My brothers Patrick and Brian are cops and my Grandfather was a cop as well. We're a cop family."

"I think I like the *CHIPS* story better."

"Ha ha. I guess growing up around cops makes you appreciate all that they do, all the sacrifices they make. Cop families are a different breed. I guess what it boils down to is that I was born to be a cop. Besides, I think it's cool to have a job where you can carry a gun!"

Tommy laughed. "I agree."

"So when it came time to pick a college, the University of New Haven was the obvious choice; great criminal justice program."

"The best."

"I got my Bachelor's degree in three years and stuck around and earned a Master's in Forensic Science a year later. Then it was off to the academy."

"How did you end up with the State Police?"

"As it turned out, they were hiring."

"That certainly helps."

"Not to mention the great reputation they have. I really think I made the wise choice. I learned a lot, and I was able to put my training to good use. Plus, you've got to love those cool hats we get to wear."

"Yes, hats are an important part of the job," Tommy joked.

"So how did you end up as a cop?"

"I guess it all started when I was a kid. I remember one Christmas getting a badge and a toy gun from Santa."

"Please tell me you don't still believe in Santa Claus."

"Excuse me, are you insinuating that there is no Santa Claus?"

"Yes I am."

"You're so mean. I'll bet you beat suspects as well."

"Only if they deserve it; please continue."

"Thank you. So I get this badge and gun and I end up spending most of my free time playing cops and robbers with my friends. Now I know what you're thinking, all kids say they want to grow up to be a cop or a fireman or an astronaut. Well, this kid never changed his mind. Being a cop was the right fit for me then and it's the right fit for me now. It's simple really; the cops are the good guys. When you're a kid, that's really all you know. As an adult, I approach being a cop much the same way. I am there to protect those who can't protect themselves, and to deal with those persons who'd do harm to those who can't protect themselves. It's the classic struggle of good versus evil, and I choose to be on the side of good."

"So you're the man on the white horse?"

"The white GTO anyway."

"I think I like the *CHIP'S* story better as well."

"Very funny."

"So where did you go to school?"

"What is this, twenty questions?"

"Maybe more."

"You're quite persistent."

"Persistence comes in handy when you're a cop."

Tommy gave in. "I went to UCONN and majored in…"

"Drinking and chasing unsuspecting coeds?"

He laughed, "Not officially, but yes, there was some of that. On the books I majored in economics and foreign languages."

"You don't seem like the economics type."

"I get that a lot."

"I'll bet."

"After graduation, I joined the Marine Corps."

"Yeah, I hear they are really courting economists in the Corps these days."

"You'd be surprised. Anyway, after I finished OCS and the Basic School, I left Quantico and headed out to The Defense Language Institute in Monterey. I really loved California. It was great living on the coast, but, my time in the Corps would be short lived. I was driving up the Pacific Coast highway from Point Sur back to Monterey, when I was hit head on by a drunk driver. As it turned out, the guy was an illegal alien with no license, no insurance and no money. The crash shattered both of my legs, broke five ribs, collapsed a lung, and to top it off, the air bag broke my nose. The doctors said I would never walk again. For the longest time, I thought they were right. Anyway, after receiving a medical discharge, I moved back to Connecticut and spent all of my time rehabilitating my legs. And in two years, I was back to ninety percent." As he was finishing this sentence, Tommy turned his attention to the bottle of wine on the table. He opened the new bottle and filled his glass. He was having such a good time he didn't want the night to end. He hoped Susan felt the same way.

"Susan, can I offer you a little more wine?"

"Why yes you can. Thank you."

"You're welcome. And when I was back in shape, I went to the academy. I knew I always wanted to be a cop; it just happened a little sooner than I imagined. I really wanted to serve our country as a Marine, but it just wasn't in the cards. So what brought you to New Haven anyway?"

Susan nervously shifted her body like a shy school girl. "Honestly?"

"No, I was hoping you'd lie to me," he joked.

"I wanted to work with the best. I wanted to work with you."

"Work with me?" Tommy could hardly believe his ears. The expression on his face revealed his surprise.

"Does that surprise you?"

"A little, I guess."

"I remembered a murder case you solved, the banker who killed his wife."

"You mean the Teddy Kerry case. Yeah, that was an interesting one."

"Everyone thought it was the gardener, but not you."

"The gardener was too obvious a choice-- in *Clue* he might have been your man, but not in real life. Yes, he had a record; yes he'd spent time in prison, but he'd never committed a violent crime in his life. And when I questioned him, for some reason, I knew he was telling the truth."

"It would have been easy to roll over and put him away for that crime, and no one would have second guessed you."

"I would have."

"That's what makes you different. You don't want the easy collar, you want the right collar."

"That's true. Man that was a tough case. I knew that scumbag did it, but the powers-that-be didn't want to hear it. Not the mayor, not the chief, no one. Mr. Kerry is a fine upstanding citizen, blah,

blah blah. I thank God for Tony, he didn't back down one inch."

"That's because he's a cop, not a politician."

"I know I joke about Tony quite a bit, but I have the utmost respect for him. He's a great man and a great cop."

"So I hear."

"It's funny that you mention the Kerry case. I'd say it's the one I am most proud off. I just can't stand guys like Teddy Kerry. They think their money can buy them whatever they want and they think they can get away with anything. There's this sense of entitlement. And when they don't get what they want, look out. But in the end the law, the law is the great equalizer."

"It is."

"It's the same thing with the asshole who owns the houses in front of mine."

"You mean the jerk that blocks your view?"

"One and the same; he has offered to buy my place for five times what it's worth, just so he can put up some giant shit box that he'll probably visit once a month."

"You want to go and ring his doorbell and run away?"

"What, are you in the third grade?"

"I'll have you know that I rang doorbells up until the ninth grade."

As she spoke those words, Tommy' doorbell rang.

"Man, that's spooky."

"What do you mean," she replied.

"The doorbell."

"I told you I stopped ringing doorbells long ago."

"No, my doorbell just rang."

"That's a relief; I thought I was starting to hear bells in my head from all this wine."

"Excuse me while I get the door. With my luck, it's probably that asshole next door complaining about something. Maybe I'll shoot him. That would certainly shut him up."

"I'll pretend I didn't hear that."

"Thanks. Sometimes I let that temper of mine get the better of me."

Tommy walked past the kitchen into the foyer. He glanced through the peephole and saw a young woman. At least it wasn't his neighbor. She was eighteen, maybe twenty with blond hair and hazel eyes. She was wearing a pair of cut off jeans and a blue Polo shirt. He pulled open the door.

"Can I help you?"

"I was wondering if Susan could come out to play."

"Excuse me?"

"Isn't Susan Kendall here? This is where she told me to meet her."

Susan walked down the hallway and met Tommy and the girl in the foyer.

"Maybe I can shed some light on this mystery woman. This is my niece, Lyla."

"Hi Lyla; nice to meet you."

"And you as well, Mr. O'Leary."

"Tommy, please. My dad is Mr. O'Leary."

She smiled at Susan. "Susan said you'd hate being called 'Mr. O'Leary' and she was right."

"Your aunt is a funny lady."

Susan interrupted. "Tommy, since my ride is here, I think it's time for me to go."

"Your ride?"

"Yes, my ride. Tony said you liked to throw them back, so I

figured I might need a designated driver. Lyla's it."

"You're right. It is getting late, and we have a bad guy to catch. What do say I meet you at the clinic at 9:00?"

"How about 8:30?"

"I like 9:00 better."

"OK you win. See you at 9:00."

"Goodnight Susan; nice meeting you Lyla. Drive safe."

"Will do, Mr. O'Leary," she joked.

"Thanks again for a wonderful evening Tommy. I won't soon forget it."

"Me too. Bye bye."

Susan and Lyla departed through the front door and Tommy waved as they walked towards the driveway. He closed the door and walked back into the living room and sprawled out on the couch. What a night, he reflected. Tommy hadn't had that enjoyable of evening in a long time. Maybe ending his vacation a little prematurely wasn't such a bad thing after all. Susan Kendall was amazing. He couldn't wait to get to know her some more. He closed his eyes with that thought still lingering in his mind. He fell asleep five minutes later.

Chapter 14

The man entered the living room and placed the black duffel bag on the oriental carpet and unzipped it. Inside were four wireless video cameras, a battery pack as well as a cordless drill. In addition, the bag contained a folding antenna and a transmitter to relay the camera signals back to a receiver he'd set up on the mainland. He took the antenna and the drill and headed up the staircase to the second floor of the house. He walked down the hallway towards the master suite, but stopped just before the entrance. Above his head hung a white string; he pulled the string and down came a set of retractable stairs. He rapidly ascended the stairs. At the top of the landing he pulled a second string; this string illuminated the surrounding area, revealing a hatch leading to the roof. He removed the hatch and slid the square cover to the side and onto the open roof above. He pulled himself through the hole and found himself standing on a widow's walk. The light from below penetrated the night air. The man looked around; even under the darkened sky, the view was spectacular. Using the drill, he quickly mounted the antenna, grabbed the attached cord and brought it with him down the foldaway stairs. At the bottom he turned and continued down the hallway and the staircase back to the first floor. Next, he took the cameras and mounted them in the four corners of the room. He attached the wire from the antenna to the transmitter, checked the power and the video feed. Everything was set. Perfect.

When he finished installing the cameras, the man removed the black diver's hood from his head, exposing his face to the outside world. He wanted to make sure the lawyer knew who he was. The lawyer had made quite a few enemies over the years and the man planned this for too long to forgo that satisfaction of having his victim realize how he'd come to such a pass. The man drew his attention to the lawyer. He and his lover were conscious and making noise. However, the sounds were inaudible thanks to the duct tape. He was certain the lawyer was in pain. Perhaps he was screaming because of his injuries. The man did not care. The lawyer was finally getting what he deserved.

He walked over and removed the tape from the lawyer's eyes. His eyes said it all; he was terrified. Before the lawyer could make a sound in response to this revelation, the man approached the second chair and restored the second man's eyesight as well. He began to slowly circle the men. "Good evening gentleman." He smirked. "Please don't get up on my account." He walked the room confidently and with purpose. "Seriously, if either of you moves too far in any direction, that wire around your neck you will strangle you as well as the fellow on the other end." He continued. "Mr. Damon, I'm sure you are wondering why all this is happening to you. It's a fair question. I would be wondering as well. It started long ago. You see, Mr. Rivers did a very bad thing. I know what you're thinking; Mr. Rivers has done many bad things in his lifetime. However, not all of Mr. Rivers' misdeeds have touched my life, save one in particular."

"Mr. Rivers committed this bad deed while he was still a young lawyer trying to make his mark on the world. Let's face it, Mr.

Rivers knew he would never be the lawyer his father was. His father was a saint in the legal community. He's the type of lawyer that every first year law student should aspire to be. You might be surprised to know that I was an acquaintance of Mr. Rivers' father. He was a good man, unlike his son. In any case, Mr. Rivers worked for his father, but pursued other legal matters on the side. He did some pro bono work for some local miscreants. Now that might sound admirable, but he wasn't doing it out of the kindness of his heart. He took these clients in order to use them and blackmail their acquaintances in furtherance of his legal career. He was quite successful at it, by the way. I'll go into more detail about that momentarily. At the same time he was doing his 'charity work,' he did some work for The United States Civil Liberties Association. He prepared briefs and other legal documents for the good folks over at the USCLA and argued before state and federal courts on their behalf. One of those briefs put you in these chairs tonight. As it happened, a bill came up in the Connecticut legislature that would have required the parents of minors seeking abortions to be notified of their child's pending surgery. It was a sensible law, it was an important law and there was a great deal of support for it in the legislature and the community at large. After all, a child must have permission from her parents to get an aspirin at school or to pierce her ears or to get one of those dreadful tattoos on her body, but that same girl can go and get an abortion, no questions asked. Common sense would say that notifying one's parents when a child is about to undergo major surgery is a good thing. Unfortunately, reasonable minds do not always prevail."

"Despite fierce opposition from the Majority leader W. Arthur Townsend and his cronies the measure passed by a slim margin. After all, it was an election year. Our elected officials didn't want the good church going folks here in the Nutmeg State to think that they'd let a child get an abortion without their parent's knowledge. It was unthinkable. Most saved their seats and they planned other ways to undermine the pro-life movement in the future behind closed doors. In any case, the matter did not rest there. Undeterred by the vote, the Majority leader and his minions did the next best thing: they contacted their buddies at the USCLA. Now their buddies had been following this issue very closely, they are the keepers of 'a woman's right to choose' as we know. It's kind of ironic though. They claim to support the rights of women, but half of the lives terminated by abortion are female. Hence, by supporting abortion, they end up killing the people whom they espouse to protect. It would be funny if it wasn't so sad. Sorry about the little detour. The logic of the left or lack thereof I should say, never ceases to amaze me. Anyway, the USCLA were counting on the Townsend's ability to derail this thing, so they hadn't made the necessary preparations to appeal this matter in state court should the vote not go their way. In walks Mr. Rivers. He stepped to the plate and working in concert with the Majority leader and his staff, crafted a brief in opposition to the law. With his help, they filed a lawsuit the day after the governor signed the bill into law. I know what you're thinking; Mr. River's legal track record was untested at best, pathetic at worst. He was a horrible student, right? This is true, but when he really wanted something, Jerry here busted his hump to get it. It was around this time that he finally rediscovered the competitive edge that made him a great athlete. But I digress. Where was I? Oh yes, the lawsuit doesn't end there. Not by a long shot. After they filed suit and made their oral arguments, the lower court eventually ruled against them. They were down, but not out. As you'd expect, there were appeals. And as luck would have it for the pro-life movement, the USCLA and their fellow travelers lost at the intermediate appellate level as well. They were coming to the end of the road and they knew it. If they lost the battle at the State Supreme Court, they had pretty much lost the war. There was always the hope of appealing to the U.S. Supreme Court. However, the chances that the justices would grant Cert., that is allowing the case to come before them, were slim at best. Not to be outdone, Mr. Rivers had a plan. It seems that one of his pro bono clients, a prostitute by the name of Mandy Dupree, had a 'relationship' with one of the more conservative members of the State Supreme Court. Up to this point it looked like the court would be split right down the middle, or if anything, the court was more likely to lean towards upholding the lower court rulings rather than going against them. Of course, that was before Mr. Rivers played the ace up his sleeve. Through an intermediary, he contacted the justice in question. As you can imagine, the judge was flabbergasted. After all, he was a respected member of the legal community, not to mention a dedicated family man. Word of his relationship with Mandy would have destroyed the life he'd worked so hard to build. As it turned out, it took very little convincing on the intermediary's part for the justice to come around. When the court handed down their ruling several months later, it came down five to three in favor of striking down the law. The USCLA were ecstatic and Mr. Rivers became a hero of the progressive left."

At this point the man paused and stood directly in front of the lawyer looking him dead in the eyes. He then continued. "Now you are probably wondering what this has to do with me." His tone changed. Before, he was cool and composed; now, his anger was apparent. "Had this law been in place a young girl would still be alive today. But because of you, Mr. Rivers, and your ilk, she died after having visited an abortion clinic without her parent's knowledge. Maybe this doesn't trouble you, but it certainly troubles me. After all, that girl was my daughter!"

The lawyer became agitated and did his best to move in his chair, but he was restrained by the piano wire noose, and his attempts were futile at best. He wasn't going anywhere and he knew it. He reflected on what he'd just heard and it finally occurred to him that he'd taken one too many shortcuts in his career. He knew it all along, but he never thought it would come to this. Maybe he'd lose his law license some day. Maybe he'd be sued, but not this. This couldn't be happening. The man walked and faced the second prisoner. He had a word or two for him as well.

"Mr. Damon, let me assure you, you are not without blame; I know your story as well. You are just as bad as Mr. Rivers over here. It's like the Terri Schiavo case all over again." As he said this, he slapped the lawyer across the face, sending his head forward, and as a result, the piano wire dug into Mr. Damon's narrow neck, pulling his head back. "Mr. Damon, you were a married man, and you cheated on your wife. You broke the scared bond of trust married couples assume when they swear their love before God. It's irrelevant who you cheated with. However, you couldn't have picked a more despicable person in Mr. Rivers. But it does not end there. I know how you attacked your wife and how you claimed it was some sort of seizure. You're lucky the authorities didn't pursue the matter any further. You might have spent the rest of your days behind bars if they had done so. I'm not sure if Mr. Rivers told you, but he had a hand in preventing your indictment in this matter as well. It seems Mr. Rivers had some useful information on the would-be prosecutor in your case. He couldn't have you indicted. After all, he's the one who convinced you to pull the plug on your wife in the first place. If you did, she would not longer be a concern to you or him. And when she died, he was just as culpable because he was an accessory to murder after the fact. Mr. Rivers knew that he couldn't advise you to take further illegal action, but he didn't care. He needed to protect himself, and maybe you in the process. Needless to say, you will both receive an adequate punishment if I have anything to say about it."

Jerry was shocked. He couldn't imagine how this man knew all this about them, but he did. His future and Bruce's looked very bleak. He could only imagine what he was capable of. He knew the man's reputation. Who didn't? He was a tough bastard who never gave up and always fought for what he believed in. Jerry was certain that this would not end peacefully. The man had already severed Jerry's Achilles tendons; he wasn't ready for his idea of an adequate punishment.

The man was drained. He hated reliving the sequence of events that brought him to this tiny island this summer night. He wished things had been different, but he couldn't change the past. Instead, he could only do his best to ensure a future where these two men could bring no more harm to the world or its inhabitants. Having said his piece, it was time for him to go. The man picked up his black bag, slung it and the backpack over his shoulder. He quickly closed all of the windows in the house and he turned the heat all the way up. He then exited through the back door without saying a word. Of all of the deaths the man planned, he was certain this would be the worst, but it was fitting and just. Mr. Damon ordered the assisted living facility to end his wife's life by depriving her of hydration and food. He would end their lives in a similar fashion.

It was a horrible way to go, but these two guilty men deserved the same horrible end that Bruce subjected his wife too.

He walked back through the utility shed and made a quick stop. He armed the bomb, and exited the back door. If the men were not dead by the end of the week, he'd blow the island. There was enough C4 and propane in the tank to take out the house and a good portion of the island as well. The man descended the rocky incline and boarded the Zodiac for his trip back to the mainland. He made a quick pass by the boat dock to confirm the cigarette boat sank. It had. He knew Mr. Rivers and Mr. Damon would not be making it off this island alive, and for that he was pleased. He increased the power on the engine, and made his way back to the shore. He needed to get a good night's sleep, for he had one more person to deal with and he needed to be at one hundred percent when he did.

Chapter 15

Clinton 7:38

The bright morning sun beaming in through the slider woke Tommy from his slumber. I knew I should have drawn the drapes, he thought. He woke up in the middle of the night, but didn't have the motivation to drag his drunk ass into the bedroom. The couch was comfortable enough, so why move? He lifted up his tired head and cringed as his temples began to throb. Maybe we had a little too much wine, he reflected. He rolled off the couch and slowly made his way to the bathroom. After relieving himself, he thoroughly brushed his teeth. Much better, he thought. When he woke up, his mouth tasted like something had crawled in there and died. He walked back to the kitchen and put on a pot of coffee. Despite the slight hangover, he was in good spirits. He'd had a wonderful time with Susan and it looked like they had a few avenues of inquiry in the murder of Doctor Death. He poured a big cup, tossed in a few ice cubes, and drank it on the spot. He then gobbled down a couple of blueberry Pop Tarts and headed to the bathroom for a half hour shower. He loved taking long hot showers; it relaxed him and for some reason he did some of his best thinking in the shower. By the time he had toweled off, the caffeine was beginning to take effect and he was starting to feel human again. He dressed a little more conservatively than yesterday, khaki shorts and a button down, and he was out the door.

He took his usual route to the highway, but made a quick stop at the *Shell Mini Mart* to gas up and grab the morning papers. He wasn't a big fan of *the Register* or *the Courant*. Like most papers these days, *the Courant* and *the Register* were far too partisan for his liking, but he made it a point to read any and all articles about his current cases. *The Register* had a nice picture of the outside of the clinic on their cover with the headline *Respected Doctor Brutally Slain*. Respected by whom was the question. *The Courant* had a piece, but it was small by comparison. He threw the papers on the back seat and hopped on the highway in the direction of Fair Haven. Hopefully the knuckleheads working construction at the Frontage Road exit had the morning off, but he doubted it.

Susan was waiting out front when Tommy pulled up to the New Haven Reproductive Clinic. She gave him a wave as he passed by in search of a place to park. She looked beautiful, he thought. He nearly hit a parked car because he couldn't take his eyes off her. Note to self: keep your freakin' eyes on the road. He climbed out of the car and walked in the direction of the entrance. Susan was talking to a young woman he had never seen before. He didn't want to interrupt, so he slowed his pace. After a few moments, the two said their goodbyes and Tommy took that as his cue to pick things up and finish his trek to the front door.

"Who was that?" Tommy asked.

"A scared girl."

"A scared girl?"

"Apparently she hadn't heard about doctor Green's demise. She had an appointment with him this morning."

"What did you tell her?"

"I told her the truth; that he was brutally killed inside and then I referred her to a place called Birthright. She actually seemed quite relieved."

"I can imagine."

"So how's my dinner companion feeling this morning?"

"Quite well, thanks. And you?"

"I've never felt better, well, that's if you don't count my terrible hangover."

"I know what you mean."

"I talked to a locksmith I know, and he said he'd be able to meet us here in an hour at the earliest. Unfortunately, he's a busy man."

"Aren't we all? How about we try and get that safe open ourselves."

"I'm game, but I must admit, I'm not much of a safecracker."

"Neither am I, but I figure we should at least give it a try."

"Lead the way; just try not to destroy any evidence."

"You're no fun."

Tommy removed a knife from his pocket and used it to slice through the Police tape that sealed the door. He then produced a key and used it to unlock the deadbolt and the lock within the door handle.

"Where do you get that," Susan inquired?

"Ms. Carpenter gave it to me. She figured she wouldn't be needing it anymore."

"She's probably right."

"I told her if her boss is somehow raised from the dead, I'd be sure to give it back to her."

"Very funny."

"I thought so and so did she."

Tommy pushed open the door, and felt around until he found a light switch; there were four. He turned them all into the on position and made his way in the direction of the walk-in refrigerator. Susan closed and locked the door behind them and followed Tommy's lead. Tommy had noticed the walk-in yesterday, but didn't place much significance to it at the time. Unless the killer was hiding in there, it didn't seem like it played much of a part in the saga. He reached out and put his hand on the steel handle; it was cool to the touch. He gave it a pull and cold air came rushing out. It was both refreshing and eerie at the same time. He stepped into the small room and looked around. There were shelves in front of him and on both sides, lined with dozens of plastic storage containers. He could only imagine what was inside. His attention was drawn to the left and he noticed the safe among the final resting place of so many innocent lives. The techs were right, someone tried to get in. Maybe he'd have better luck than the killer.

"Susan, would you excuse me. I'll be right back."

"Sure. Don't be long. This is the last place I want to be standing all by myself."

"What are you, some kind of 'fraidy cat?"

"Something like that."

"Don't worry, I'll just be a minute."

Tommy walked down the hall and into Operating Room Number One. He opened a few drawers and found what he was looking for. He walked back down the hall and rejoined Susan.

"If you had to use the restroom, you could have waited until we got back to the station," she joked.

Tommy's face turned red. "If you must know, I was up to something else, thank you."

Tommy produced the item he'd retrieved from the operating room: a stethoscope.

"Tommy, I'm all for an old fashion game of doctor, but I'm trying to solve a murder here," she joked. "It would have been a little more appropriate if you broke it out last night."

"I thought it might lighten the mood."

After wiping the eartips down with an antibacterial wipe, Tommy placed them into his ears and he positioned the diaphragm onto the door of the safe. He slowly turned the dial until all the tumblers had clicked. He turned the handle and pulled the safe door open as an amazed Susan looked on.

"Tommy, that was incredible," she remarked with genuine surprise.

"If you think that's great, wait until you see me pull a rabbit out of my ass."

"Don't you mean hat?"

"Anyone can pull a rabbit out of a hat."

"You are disgusting."

Tommy removed the eartips and looked into the safe.

"Well, what do we have here?"

He removed the items one by one and handed them to Susan. There were the usual things one might find in a safe: legal documents, some jewelry, a ledger of some sort and more cash than Tommy had made during his entire life.

Susan was the first to speak up. "Are we sure this guy wasn't up to something a little more underhanded?"

"You mean more underhanded than abortions."

"Good point."

"Don't fool yourself Susan. The abortion business is a profitable racket. They might say it's all about 'a woman's right to choose,' but they fail to mention that this so-called right lines their pockets with piles of money. Doctor Green's little stash here is proof enough of that. And I'm sure if we looked at the Clinic's financials, we'd see that doctor Green was making out quite well."

"I guess I never looked at it that way."

"It's a business, pure and simple. Sure there are ideologues within the industry, but the simple fact is that these people are in it to make money. They are not doing it out of the kindness of their hearts."

"Do you think one of Doctor Green's competitors could be our killer?"

"It's possible, but I don't know. The last thing one of his fellow abortionists wants to do is to put their industry in a bad light. As it is, most Americans are against abortion. If they were going to kill old Edgar, I'm sure they'd have chosen a different method. Unless they are a bunch of morons, but even then, I'd find that hard to believe."

Tommy and Susan placed the safe's contents into several large evidence bags; he closed the door to the safe, but left it unlocked.

"I guess you can call your locksmith friend and tell him we won't be needing his services today."

"I was thinking the same thing. By the way, you are going to have to teach me to crack a safe sometime. It sure can come in handy."

"I wish I knew how. I just copied the guys on TV."

"Please."

"I swear. It seemed easy for them, so I thought why not give it a try?"

Susan shook her head in disbelief. She the pulled out her phone and dialed the number for her locksmith friend. As she was doing that, Tommy wandered back to the operating room to return the stethoscope to its proper place. He'd have to thank his uncle when he got a chance. His uncle had been a locksmith for thirty-eight years before he retired. Tommy worked for him over two summers during high school. He's the one who taught him how to open a safe. At the time, Tommy wasn't sure if he'd ever have use for that particular skill, but it certainly proved useful today. He removed his cell phone from his pocket and placed a call to the Medical Examiner's Office.

A friendly man answered after the first ring: "Medical Examiner's Office."

"Michael Patel, please."

"Who may I ask is calling?"

"Detective O'Leary."

"Please hold detective, I'll see if he's available."

"Thanks."

Dr. Patel came on the line in several seconds; his accent reflected his years of study in the UK. "Tommy, I was just about to give you a call."

"I've heard that one before. I left you a message last night. I thought for sure I'd hear from you first thing this morning."

"I'm sorry, I'm a busy man; my work's been piling up!"

"For a medical examiner, you're pretty funny."

"You're a little snippy this morning; long night?" he sarcastically replied.

"You know how those luaus can be."

"Luau? I heard you had a date with your new partner."

Tommy sheepishly replied: "I wouldn't call it a date. It was more of a working dinner."

"Did you make her your famous scallops?"

"Yeah, so?"

"Than it was a date, at least it was a date from your perspective; God only knows what was going through her head. You always make those scallops whenever you want to impress a lady. After all, you've never made them for Maria and me."

"I never made them for you because I thought Indian's weren't allowed to eat shellfish."

"Hindu's don't eat shellfish by the way. We are Christian, so we eat whatever we want, except for meat on Fridays during Lent."

"You're right. I knew it was a Hindu thing. And yes, I only make scallops for the ladies, but I promise to make them for you the next time I have you guys over, unless of course Susan is there as well. In that case I can't serve her the same food two times in a row."

"Fair enough."

"And for your information, Susan expressed that she had a wonderful time, thank you."

"You don't have to be so defensive, Romeo."

"Just because you are blissfully married doesn't mean you have license to pick on us unfortunate single people."

"Sure it does."

"OK, that's enough abuse for one day. Did you find out anything that might help me catch our killer or do I have to call in that psychic again?"

"I've got a little something, but I wouldn't take the psychic off your speed dial just yet."

"Alright, cough it up."

"First of all, our victim was drugged. I found a puncture mark on the right side of his neck, and he had traces of Sodium thiopentone in his system."

"At least we know how our killer knocked him out. But doesn't Sodium thiopentone wear off pretty fast?"

"Yes, but regardless of its duration, the killer seemed to have more than enough time to take care of Doctor Green. Of course it didn't help that Dr. Green was legally drunk at the time he was killed as well. I'm sure the booze didn't make those reflexes any faster."

"That's for sure. It also confirms that our victim was probably awake when he was killed."

"Unfortunately for him, that was most likely the case. Although after he received that blow to the head, he was probably unconscious in a matter of seconds. The worst part for him must have been the anticipation, I would guess."

"I'd have to agree."

"Also, I was able to ascertain the time of death after an internal examination of Dr. Green. Based on the stomach contents, it looks like our victim took his last breath at 10:00 pm, give or take a few minutes."

"That verifies your initial assessment."

"It does. On the bright side, at least our victim had a nice dinner before he was killed; nothing like being killed on an empty stomach," he replied sarcastically.

"What do you mean?"

"If I knew I was going to be killed, I'd stuff my face. Think about it, you don't have to worry about those empty calories anymore, so why not treat yourself?"

"No, what do you mean by he had a nice dinner?"

"I mean Dr. Green ate some kind of stew and bread a short while before he died. His stomach was still full; he didn't have time to digest it. At least he didn't die hungry."

"There weren't any leftovers or take-out containers found at the scene."

"So he must have eaten somewhere close by..."

"...And our killer was able to intercept him and drug him, but that would be asking a lot. Then again, our killer certainly doesn't disappoint."

"Say, where can you get some stew around here? I'd say that very few places would be serving stew in the middle of the summer, unless they specialize in it."

"I know just the place," was Tommy's response, realization coalescing in his mind.

"Where?"

"Liam McGuire's. I should have thought of it before. Listen Michael, I have to get going. Thanks for the help. I really appreciate it."

"No problem; any time. Just so you know, I will be eagerly awaiting my invitation for that scallop dinner."

"Tell Maria I said hello.

"Will do."

Tommy walked over to talk to Susan. She was sitting in the waiting area reading a magazine.

"And people say that women like to gab. You seem to spend more time on the phone than my niece Lyla. What's the story, morning glory?"

"If you must know, I was checking on our lunch reservations."

"I didn't know we had any."

"We don't, but I'll explain that on the way."

Chapter 16

Tommy and Susan exited the clinic and quickly headed back to the station. Tommy headed inside to drop off the items they removed from Doctor Green's safe with the property clerk, save the ledger, while Susan hunted around for a parking spot. By the time Tommy had finished and walked back outside, Susan was leaning on the GTO waiting for his arrival.

"I can see why you park on the sidewalk. Parking really sucks around here."

"I told you. They purposely left that little tidbit out of the brochure."

"I'm still considering that truth in advertising suit, and this just adds to the case."

"It most certainly does. I'd be glad to be called as a witness. I am quite good on the stand."

"I just might take you up on that."

"Speaking of taking, how about I take you out for a nice lunch?"

"Do I have a choice?"

"As it turns out, you do not."

"In that case, I'm all yours."

Toby Scott had been with *the New Haven Register* for most of his life. He'd started out as a paperboy when he was twelve; he delivered the *Journal Courier* in the morning before school, and *the Register* in afternoon. He loved newspapers. His friends who delivered papers looked at it as a way to earn a few bucks, for him, it was much more. After he'd finish his route, he'd read the papers cover to cover, time permitting. After all, there was no internet, so the newspaper was a young man's ticket to the outside world. Sure, he read magazines and watched the news on TV, but there was something about thumbing through the pages of a newspaper and getting your hands all dirty, that made it special. It was the only time his parents didn't get on his case for getting dirty. They were just so pleased that he took an interest in reading. After high school, Toby studied journalism at Northwestern before heading back to Connecticut in search of a job. He worked as a stringer for several local papers before being hired full-time by *the Register* three years later. In the beginning he was given bottom-of-the barrel stories to cover, but as the quality of his work improved, so too did his assignments. And now, after years of hard work, he was one of the youngest news editors in the business.

It had been a slow news week, at least until Doctor Green got himself killed. Now Toby didn't wish bad things upon people. Far from it, but in his business, sensationalism sells. And up until the time they wheeled the fat doctor out of his clinic on the gurney, there hadn't been a sensational story to report for a long while. Sure he could report about the war in Iraq, but even there things seemed to be settling down. He did his best to make the paper's loyal readers think things were going terribly in Iraq, but even now they were starting to question the paper's sincerity in that matter. It was a tough spot to be in. But a murdered abortion doctor, talk about a story. He was so excited that he personally went out to the clinic to get the scoop. No junior reporter was going to take this little slice of glory away from him.

As Toby reveled in his good fortune, the kid with the mail cart happened by his office. He deposited Toby's mail on his desk, picked up the little pile of outgoing mail and headed to the next stop on his route. Toby quickly sorted through the pieces of mail: junk, junk, bill, junk. When he came to the manila envelope, he paused. What do we have here? He asked himself. He tore open the parcel and removed the one page of paper that was holed up inside. He read it to himself:

By now the bound body of Doctor Green has been discovered on his table of death. Let it be a lesson to all of you who continually defy the will of God; there will be consequences to your actions. As you sow, so shall you reap. Doctor Green ended the lives of countless children in that chamber of death. I ended his life in a similar fashion, sending him to the bowels of hell. So I tell you again, repent now or you will face a fate far worse than Doctor Green's.

Toby's first reaction was to think that this was some kind of hoax. If he'd had a nickel for every whack-job who'd confessed to a crime, or wanted their manifesto published, he could have retired years ago. But something about the piece struck him as odd. How did this guy know Doctor Green was bound to a table? The cops didn't release that; they only mentioned that he'd been stabbed and bludgeoned to death. Ok, you could guess that he might have been bound, but it would be difficult unless you knew someone on the force.

He turned the page over. He hadn't noticed it before; there were words scrawled on that side as well: *I've admired your work for years, so you were the logical person to send this to. Publish this and*

I might overlook your past transgressions, in particular, that tryst you had three years ago with that underage girl in DC. I'm sure your wife would find that a little disturbing. A chill went up Toby's spine. He'd never told anyone about that. It had happened when he was on assignment. He was in the mood for a little action, so he headed to the part of town where the 'working' girls gathered. As it turned out, the pickings were slim. He almost drove away until he spotted her. She was a beauty. He thought she looked young, but he was pretty confident she wouldn't be calling the cops. He pulled over and named a price. She agreed, and off they went for a ride. He'd left town the same day and thought no one would be the wiser. He knew the girl couldn't identify him. He'd made sure to wear a disguise, he'd didn't even mention his name, plus she wasn't really looking at his face anyway. Shit, if this guy was capable of knowing the smallest of details of his life, he was certainly capable of killing an abortion doctor. He'd publish the piece in tomorrow's paper and hope this man didn't come looking for him.

Tommy took the scenic route to Liam's so he'd have plenty of time to explain to Susan what they were up to. "Doctor Green's burned-out car was discovered up the street from the Liam McGuire's. In addition, during the autopsy, Dr. Patel removed some sort of stew from the victim's stomach. And based on the condition of the stew, it was apparent that Doctor Green had just eaten. So we put two and two together and…"

Susan was incredulous. "…So you're not buying me lunch?"

"Very funny."

"I'm serious."

"Well, I…"

"Got ya!"

"Oh, I'll buy you lunch. Just don't judge the food by the look of the place."

"I never do. If I did, I wouldn't have eaten the food at your house last night."

"You really know how to hurt a guy."

"Don't worry; I actually went to Liam McGuire's a few times during my college days. You gotta love a dive. Who needs the fake ambiance you get in those chain style bars? If you ask me, it's the dive bars that really have the character."

"Detective Kendall, I couldn't agree with you more."

Tommy pulled the GTO into the dirt parking lot adjacent to bar. He surveyed the area. It was the first time he'd come here so early in the day. The glow of the morning sun illuminated the usually dreary exterior. It almost looked welcoming. Tommy closed the driver's side door and waited for Susan to make her way around the car. The movement of her feet sent a cloud of dust into the humid morning air. Tommy covered his mouth with a fisted right hand and feigned a coughing fit. "Could you try and keep some of that sand on the ground? Jeez."

"Sorry, but there's not much a girl can do when you make her cross the Sahara on the way to lunch."

"I didn't want to park the GTO in a place where it might get dinged. It would bring tears to my handsome brown eyes if that were to happen."

"Men and their cars; what's so special about a car anyway?"

"It's not cars, it's this car. It's a classic."

"Whatever. So are we going in or what?"

"After you mademoiselle."

"Very classy. So was French one of the many languages you

studied in college and Monterey?"

"As a matter of fact, it was. I took Spanish in high school and became fluent very quickly. My teacher told me I had an aptitude for languages. Go figure? During college years, I worked on French, Italian and continued with Spanish. And when I got to Monterey, I worked on Arabic and Farsi."

"Tommy, I never pegged you as being so worldly."

"What can I say? I am a regular Renaissance Man. I even play the lute."

"You don't say?"

Susan approached the door and Tommy leaned in and extended his hand to open the door.

"Thank you. I guess chivalry isn't dead after all."

"It's not dead, but I'd say it's got one foot in the grave. I do my best to keep both feet from fallin' in."

"You are a good man, Tommy O'Leary."

"That's what they tell me."

Tommy had to laugh. He hadn't been here in a while, but the place looked exactly the same. Susan spoke: "It's funny, I haven't been here in years, and yet it still looks the same."

"What are you, some kind of mind reader? I was thinking the same thing."

"Great minds think alike."

The two sat down at the antique mahogany bar. It seemed out of place in the otherwise run down establishment. Nick was unloading a rack of pint glasses into the small freezer behind the bar when Tommy placed their order. Shit, Nick had been here forever and he hadn't aged a bit, Tommy thought. "Nick, can I have two pints of *Guinness* please."

Nick smiled in Susan's direction. "And for the lady?"

"She'll have the same," Susan replied.

"Four pints coming up."

Susan leaned in and whispered into Tommy's ear: "Do you think I should tell him I only wanted one?"

"I think he knows."

"I'd hate to have it go to waste."

"Don't worry, it won't."

"That's a relief. My Irish grandfather would be rolling over in his grave."

"I know what you mean. I figured you were a *Guinness* drinker."

"How'd you figure that?"

"I'm a detective, don't forget."

"No, really?"

"I noticed that *Guinness* calendar hanging in your cube."

"I guess you have an eye for things besides wine."

"I sure do try."

Nick placed the frosty glasses of stout on the bar. There was a pile of cocktail napkins nearby, but he paid them no attention. "Would you like to order some food?"

"That's a silly question," Tommy replied.

"Why's that?"

"I guess I'd assume that most people who come in here in the middle of the day are looking for something to eat."

Nick laughed. "You'd be surprised."

"How about a bowl of stew for me."

Nick looked towards Susan. "Ma'am?"

Behind the bar was a blackboard with the day's specials scrawled on it. Susan gave it a quick once over and made her decision. "I'll have the corned beef sandwich. But could I have rice instead of fries?"

"Try again."

"Onion rings?"

"You're getting closer, sort of."

"Mashed potatoes?"

"That we have. Coming right up."

"Thank you."

"You're welcome."

"You didn't want to try the stew? It was the final meal of our victim, after all."

"Nah, but I'll have bite of yours."

"Good luck."

Nick returned with two paper placemats, some napkins and the necessary utensils. The placemats had a picture of Ireland on them. As he was laying them out Tommy spoke up. "Are you familiar with a Doctor Edgar Green?"

"I never thought you'd ask."

"You knew we were cops?"

"I've been doing this a while. I can pick out a man's occupation from a mile away."

"Really? What tipped you off about me?"

"I guess the gun bugling out from the back of your pants did it. You were either a cop or here to rob me. Since you ordered some food, I figured cop was a good guess. Plus, I remember when you were a beat cop in these parts. You broke up a number of fights on St. Paddy's Day a number of years ago."

"Nick, I didn't think you remembered me. Tommy, Tommy O'Leary's the name." The two shook hands.

"It's good to see you Tommy. You haven't paid us a visit in a while."

"I live farther east these days, so I spend less of my free time here in town."

"I don't blame you. The traffic sucks. When I'm not working, I stay as far away as possible. Anyway, yeah I knew Doctor Green, and yeah, he was in here the other night. He was in here every night."

"Did anything seem out of the ordinary with him?"

"Out of the ordinary? I guess you'd never met Edgar while he was among the living. He wasn't what one would call ordinary on any day. He was a weird guy, and he pretty much kept to himself."

"Did you see him talking with anybody last night?"

"Not really. He had some words with some kid in the can, but nothing came of it. I was getting some ice and I heard him and the kid exchange pleasantries, if you know what I mean. Dr. Green left soon after and the kid was here until close. I don't think he went and killed him if that's any help."

"Was there anyone in here who seemed out of place?"

"Tommy, we get all kinds in here. It's hard to say who looks out of place and who doesn't. It was a pretty small crowd that night, so it would be easy enough to spot a new face. It looked to me like everyone had been here before."

"Did Doctor Green have any problems with any other patrons on any other nights?"

"Nah. He didn't say enough to get people pissed off at him. He came in, had his usual, *Dewar's*, straight up. That particular night he had three. He ate some stew. That was his favorite. And he was out of here within an hour. That was his usual routine. He'd come in after work, have a bite and a few drinks and then he'd head home. You could set your clock to it."

Tommy let those last few words sink in: you could set your clock to it.

"Thanks Nick."

"I'm sorry I couldn't be more helpful. Most people didn't like the doctor, but for some reason, he was nice to me. I certainly didn't like what he did for a living, but nobody should be killed in such a horrific way."

"Nick, you were plenty helpful. In this business, it's the little things that help you solve a case. Thanks."

"You're welcome. I'll go and see how your food is coming."

"Thanks."

"Tommy, I'm sorry I wasn't more proactive there. But you seemed to be handling things quite well yourself." She took a big sip of her *Guinness*, the foam leaving a creamy mustache on her upper lip. "Besides, it's hard to come between a lady and her pint of *Guinness*."

"So true."

Susan grabbed a cocktail napkin from the nearby pile and wiped her mouth. "You know, I am no advertising guru, but I think the *Guinness* people should do adds like the milk people. You know the ones I am talking about?"

"Oh yeah."

"Let's face it, *Guinness* leaves a far better mustache than milk. Got *Guinness*? That would be perfect."

"Don't quit your day job."

"Some partner you are. I though we were suppose to support each other."

"I'd be glad to support you in areas where you show aptitude."

"But advertising isn't one of them?"

"Something like that," he joked. "I'll tell you, the good doctor made the killer's job pretty easy. Nick said something that really struck a chord with me: you could set your clock to it. The killer knew Dr. Green's routine and was probably waiting for him outside.

He knew the doctor would only be in here for an hour, so it was a matter of waiting for him to exit the building."

"And when you add the fact that the doctor was probably feeling the effects of those drinks…"

"…We have a recipe for murder. And that's the reason the car was left behind. The man subdued the doctor in his car or on his way to the car and dragged him into his own vehicle, presumably that van, and off they went for a little late night surgery."

"What van?"

"The one I was trying to commandeer for you. It was found within a mile of the clinic. Who ever left it there set it ablaze and fled the scene, just like they did with the doctor's BMW."

"Now that we've got the how, we just have to figure out the who and the why."

"The who and the why. Is that all? Yeah, those are million dollar questions for sure. Maybe one of the items we grabbed from the safe will shed some light on the who and why. I checked everything with the property clerk, but kept that ledger. Dr. Green must have placed some value to it in order to keep it in his safe."

"Maybe it's his diary."

"That would be great. I'd love to know if he was passing notes to someone in study hall."

"I meant a personal journal. Maybe he put his deepest thoughts and reflections in there and didn't want the outside world to see."

"I guess that's as good an explanation as any. I left it on the backseat of the car. Hopefully nobody bagged it."

"Are you crazy?"

"It's actually in the trunk under all my dirty laundry. I'm pretty certain no person would risk going through my dirty boxers to retrieve a book of any kind."

"It's safe to say that I will likewise not be riffling through your trunk any time soon."

Nick brought out their order. First, he placed the corned beef in front of Susan and he followed it up by giving Tommy his stew. "Is there anything else I can get you guys?"

"We're fine. Thanks Nick," Tommy replied.

'Maybe he's fine, but I could use a little mustard if you wouldn't mind."

"Coming right up."

"Thanks. Oh, and a refill would be great." She looked at Tommy's beer. It was nearly full. She turned to face him. "But I think Sally over here is all set."

Nick smiled. "Don't worry, I'm sure he'll catch up."

"Don't bet on it Nick."

"Hardy har har. One of us has to drive."

"I'm aware of that, but two Guinness's aren't likely to impair your judgment. Well, not like three *Dewar's* anyway."

"Just eat your sandwich."

"As a matter of fact, I think I will."

Chapter 17

Tommy and Susan headed back to the station, but not before making a quick stop at *Dunkin' Donuts*. Susan ordered a hazelnut with two shots of espresso, and Tommy got a large regular, black and a glazed cruller. He finished the cruller on the way. The pints of Guinness and the hearty lunches made the pair a little sleepy, so they figured some caffeine would do them good. The ledger they retrieved from the safe was extensive in size, so it might take hours to peruse. But with any luck, it would shed some light on their killer. Tommy walked back to his cube to grab a legal pad while Susan made a quick dash to the ladies room.

After retrieving the pad, Tommy walked down the rows of cubes in the direction of a small conference room. The cubes he and Susan occupied were too tight for this task. They needed some room to sprawl out. Plus, he could always take a snooze if the need arose. Unlike his cube, the conference room had a door, and the door was closed. He knocked and got no response. He turned the handle and peered inside. It was empty. Great. He took all the items he was carrying and placed them on the table. He then took a sip of his coffee and let out a big sigh. If the ledger didn't pan out, he was out of ideas. The brief conversation with Nick helped, but not as much as he would have liked. "Who killed you, Edgar Green?"

he muttered under his breath. He shook his head from side to side. What the hell am I missing?

"Hello, is anybody in there?" Tommy picked his head up and looked in the direction of the door. It was Susan. "Oh, there you are. I'm sorry, I'm still getting used to the layout of this place."

"I understand. It can be a little confusing at first. But don't worry, you'll get the hang of it in no time."

"I sure hope so. It looks bad if a detective can't find her way around her own station." Susan grabbed the chair next to Tommy, pulled it out and sat down. "So, are we ready to get down to business?"

"I was just waiting for you."

She slid the ledger in front of her so as to get a better look at it. The faux leather cover had faded over time. The red spine was coming apart, and was threatening to separate the cover from the rest of the book. Susan cracked it open and glanced at the first page. "Here we go."

Her eyes made their way down the page; the book contained names and dates, patients presumably. There were little notations next to some of the names. Some of the notes contained additional names. It meant nothing to Susan.

"Do you think this is a list of his patients?"

"I guess, but why keep it in the safe? Presumably he has the names computerized like every other physician on the planet. So why would he write them out by hand and store them in the safe along with his other valuables? If someone wanted to check out his list of clients, they could hack into his computer or simply steal it. Do you mind if I take a look?"

"Sure."

Susan slid the book to her right so Tommy could see it equally well. There were hundreds of pages and thousands of entries. It would take quite a while to sift through the entire book if they went line by line. The dates went back twenty-five years; the most recent entry was from five days ago. Tommy took a special interest in the names with notations next to them. It didn't take long before he'd found one he recognized. He put his index finger next to the entry and drew Susan's attention to it. "Do you know who that is?"

"It says August Gardner."

"Do you know who she is?"

"She's an actress, isn't she?"

"Yeah, and she goes to Yale. She just finished her first year and is getting ready for year number two."

"How do you know so much about August Gardner? Don't tell me you read those gossip magazines."

"Please. I watch *E*, thank you. Just kidding; no, we were notified that she'd be starting school last year. Like most of Hollywood's 'A List,' she's had her fair share of stalkers. And since I lived in California for a short while, they figured I was the closest thing to an expert in stalkers on the department. Yeah, lucky me. Anyway, the movie industry big wigs weren't crazy about her going to college in the first place. She's been in some high grossing movies over the last few years. But she was determined to go. So we got a call from her agent asking us to do all we could to keep her safe."

"I just loved that romantic comedy she starred in with the dog. You think she came in to have an abortion?"

"Well, I don't think she dropped in for a pap smear."

"You think she's our killer?"

"Hardly; have you seen her? She's a waif. She'd get knocked over by a strong breeze. No, I don't think it was her. Could she have hired someone? Maybe, but I don't peg her as the type. Even in Hollywood murder is still a no-no. On the other hand, if it came out that she'd had an abortion she'd be hailed as a crusader for women's rights. You know how the Hollywood crowd is. Abortion is a sacrament of sorts in their eyes."

"It's sad, but true."

"She probably didn't kill him, but there's a good chance the person who did is among these names or associated with one of these names. I say we start with the names that have notations next to them from the last year or so. If nothing comes of that, we can go back a year at a time. Sound good?"

"Works for me."

Tommy and Susan diligently read through the ledger for a solid four hours. By the time they'd finished, they were exhausted. They ended up going all the way back to the initial entry from twenty-five years ago, and were more than surprised with the results. The ledger entries containing notations were people of influence or the person who accompanied a patient to the clinic or someone related to them. It was a who's who of Connecticut society and beyond. It was something to behold.

"OK, I don't even know where to begin. It's fair to say that quite a few of the people on our list would be damaged in some way if the knowledge of their trip to the clinic came out. With that said, is there anyone who would kill to keep that a secret? Let's not forget, abortion is taboo. However, at this time, it is a legal one. Although many of the people on our list would be embarrassed if their abortion came out, there are quite of few on our list who have been vocal supporters of so-called woman's rights in the past. "

"Well, let's look at the list. Who do we think has the most to lose should their little secret come out?"

Their list contained thirty-eight high profile names, and fifty or so semi-high profile people. The rest with notations had died, were well known abortion advocates or just didn't ring any bells with the two detectives. Any one of them or none of them could be the culprit. Tommy ran his finger down the list, but none seemed to jump out. "I think I've been looking at these names for too long."

"You're telling me."

There was a knock at the door. Susan answered. "Come in."

It was Tony. "Hey, how are you two kids getting on? Have you caught my killer yet? That damn mayor won't stop calling me. He's a real pain in the ass."

"Tony, you really have it tough. But as luck would have it, Susan just solved the case."

"I what?"

"It was the mayor's wife's lover."

"What?"

Just kidding. We're making progress. You can tell him that."

"Making progress is code for I don't have a freakin' clue."

"Yeah, but he doesn't know that."

"He will soon enough."

"Look Tony, Susan and I have been grinding hard on this. You know as well as anyone how tough it is to get an investigation rolling with the little bit of evidence our killer left behind. What we do know is this: Lester Bell is not our killer."

"I would hope not. That wouldn't say much for our brethren in corrections."

"Very funny. How about this, we are also pretty sure no one associated with Lester committed this crime. He's been out of the loop far too long to have had a hand in this. Next, we think it's unlikely it's some pro-life lunatic. It just doesn't fit. Sure there's the drama of being on the table much the same way as woman who's about to have an abortion. However, I think our killer is more sophisticated than that. He planned this down to the last detail. He knew Doctor Green's schedule. He knew that he'd go to Liam McGuire's for dinner and drinks. He did that every night. And Edgar only spent an hour there. So our killer waited for him to come out, he intercepted him, drugged him, and dragged him back to the clinic where he had his way with him."

"He raped him too?"

"Sorry, just a figure of speech."

"Very funny."

"I wasn't trying to be funny."

"I know, but somehow, someway, you always seem to make a joke."

"It's a gift."

"Yeah, the gift that just keeps on giving."

"As I was saying, I think we have a good profile of our killer."

"That's all well and good, but we need someone to pin it on. Do you have anyone in mind?"

Susan produced the list they'd compiled. She handed it to Tony. "These are some of the names we put together from Doctor Green's ledger. As you can see, there are many people who would be rather pissed off if their names were exposed."

"Shit. This isn't good. When I asked for a killer, I was kind of hoping it wouldn't be a well known someone. This will put the mayor in a bad place. As it turns out, our victim and our killer might be his buddies."

Tommy chimed in. "Yeah, the irony certainly is not lost on me."

"I'm sure it isn't. Just keep digging and let me know."

"Will do."

Tony made a hasty exit and Tommy turned to Susan. "What do you say we take a little break and get a bite to eat? I'm so hungry I could eat one of Tony's wife's dinners."

"Is she that bad a cook?"

"Bad doesn't even begin to describe it. It's funny, if Tony invites you over for dinner and his wife is the one cooking, you know you did something to piss him off. But if he invites you over and he mans the kitchen, you know you are still in his good graces."

"He actually invites you over when he's mad at you?"

"Maybe mad is too strong a word. Let me give you an example: one night I was sitting on my couch watching TV and it was getting kind of late."

"And that bothered him," she sarcastically replied?

"You like interrupting stories, don't you?"

"Just bad ones." She smiled. "Please finish your story; I can't wait for the big climax."

"Anyway, you know during late night TV you are inundated with those infomercials?"

"Sure."

"Well I decided to send Tony some of those promotional videos care of the station. I sent him a workout machine video, an adjustable bed video, a hearing aid video. You name it. But I also sent him one of those hair restoration videos."

"I'm not only the CEO, I'm also a client," Susan proclaimed.

"That's the one. Well, the packages start rolling in, and he can't quite understand why they're coming to him. Oddly enough, he decided to buy the workout machine; go figure. So a few weeks pass and he gets a phone call from the hair restoration place. Apparently it's their policy to follow up with the people who request their literature. On this particular day, as luck would have it, I was sitting in his office. So the woman politely asks him how he liked the video; whether he had any questions. Tony thought this was part of the joke, and he'd had enough of the shenanigans. He couldn't quite figure out who'd done this to him and it was driving him crazy. So he replies 'I do have one question, does your product restore pubic hair?' As you can imagine, the woman was speechless. It was at that point Tony realized that despite the fact that he didn't order the video, this woman was legit. I've never seen someone's face go so white. He couldn't apologize enough. He ended up buying some of their product after all. Truthfully it did his balding head some good. Anyway, I fell out of the chair I was laughing so hard, and he finally figured out who was responsible for his large increase in parcels. Needless to say, I was invited for dinner a short time later and he wife treated me to the worst meal of my life."

"What was your point again?"

"Let's eat."

"That's all you had to say."

"Where too?"

"You like sushi?"

"Who doesn't?"

"A lot of people, actually. Although for the life of me, I don't understand the aversion."

"I hear you. Would it kill some people to move out of their comfort zones ever once in a while?"

"I agree."

"As luck would have it, I'm not one of those people with an aversion to sushi."

"Well then, I've got just the place."

The man had used the early part of the day to rest. Although he was in peak physical shape, the last few days had taken their toll on him physically and emotionally. It had been a long while since he'd taken another person's life, let alone four. Sure, the two men on the island were probably still alive, but they would soon be drawing their last breaths as well.

He finished applying the prosthetic nose and the fake beard and looked at himself in the mirror – Perfect. His own mother, God rest her soul, wouldn't even recognize him. He put away the make-up kit and proceeded to get dressed. He had gathered the rattiest clothes he could find; they would certainly do the trick. New Haven was going through a renaissance as of late. However they didn't let the pan handlers in on the news. He would head down and wait for his fifth and final victim. And with any luck, he'd make a few bucks in the meantime. He had always wondered how much a panhandler could earn on a given day. He had his own theory, and now he was finally going to put it to the test. Why not kill two birds, he thought? He decided to take the motorcycle one last time. After all, parking was problematic in the city. And he always found a spot with his bike. He donned the nylon suit over his ratty clothes and gently put his helmet on over his facial disguise. The last thing he needed was to have his fake nose fall off before the big finale. Of all his victims, he had the most reservations about killing his fifth and final one. It's not that he felt remorse about it. On the contrary, he hated this man with a passion. No, he had other reasons to be cautious. Yes, it was possible to kill a two-bit lawyer and draw virtually no attention. Although they wouldn't utter it aloud, most people could care less. However, if you were to kill a U.S. senator, the crime was less likely to go unnoticed.

Chapter 18

Senator W. Arthur Townsend spent the early part of the day engaged in one of his favorite pastimes, golf. He had been playing most of his life. And although he'd never mastered the game, he was quite fond of it just the same. Senator Townsend was the quintessential WASP. His ancestors made passage on the Mayflower or so he said. Unbeknownst to his constituents and the public at large, this was a fabrication. Townsend's great grandfather had arrived on the shores of the U.S., but not on the Mayflower. No, he came stowed away on a merchant ship bound for Boston in the latter part of the eighteenth century. The captain was a very accommodating man so long as the price was right; he cared little of the man's past. In truth, Townsend's grandfather was a master thief who'd fled England to stay ahead of Scotland Yard. With him, he brought a small fortune in jewels, cash and gold, as well as a number of rare paintings. It was only one of the many secrets Townsend kept hidden from the outside world.

In many ways he had followed in his grandfather's footsteps; he too was a thief. But instead of stealing art or jewels in the dead of night, he stole every last cent he could from the American taxpayer and used this money for his favorite causes and pet projects. Earmarks, as they are known, were his revenue generator of preference. In reality, these earmarks were nothing more than bribes. And Arthur did everything in his power to steer as many of these earmarks to his home state and other states where he could rely on the constituents for support. Sure the out-of-staters couldn't vote, but that didn't matter. They aided him in other ways, for those who received these earmarks responded in- kind. They in turn donated to Arthur's favorite cause, among them, the Townsend Foundation. In reality The Townsend Foundation was a shell charity constructed by Townsend to bankroll his private slush fund. He had tucked so much cash away in his years in office that he would never have to worry about money again. That was quite a feat considering he'd only been a U.S. Senator for sixteen years. And this didn't even take into account the many "contributions" he'd received during his time in office. When all was said and done, he would be a far richer man than his grandfather ever dreamed.

Arthur examined his extensive wardrobe. He wanted to look his best for this evening's affair. The first Saturday of the month he met his Yale Law School cronies at *The Union League* for an evening of eating, drinking and womanizing. Sure, he was married. But what his wife didn't know wouldn't hurt her. And even if she did find out, Arthur didn't give a shit. He had an iron clad pre-nup, and his wife was well aware of this fact. Besides, she knew what a player he was when they'd married. If she thought he was going to become a one woman man just because he said 'I do,' she was fooling herself. He provided her with a damn fine life; better than she would have had otherwise. When he'd met her, she was waiting tables. Now, she was wife to one of the most powerful men the state and the country had ever known. He knew she wouldn't trade this life for her old one. Arthur had learned early on that he came first. This was true in his career and his sexual conquests, as he remarked to anyone who cared to pay attention. As much as he enjoyed life within the Beltway, he looked forward to his evenings at the Union League with eager anticipation.

He slicked back his grey hair with some pomade and rubbed his face with a little bronzer. He'd gotten some sun today, but why not add a little more color? He thought. He had to admit, he looked great. Who could tell that during his spring vacation he'd had a face lift? Next, he put a little wax on his mustache to round things out. He then put on a pair of white briefs and a matching V-neck under shirt. Over that he wore a pink oxford shirt and a pair of white trousers. He had only a few short weeks before Labor Day, and he was determined to wear his favorite white pants a few more times. He looked at himself in the mirror yet another time. "How did you get so damn good looking?" he laughed. "Oh, what a nice piece of ass you'll get tonight."

The man eased the bike onto Interstate 95 and followed it over the Q Bridge, making his exit onto Route 34 towards downtown New Haven. He caught the Police Station out of the corner of his eye. Yes, you will have another murder on your hands this evening, gentlemen. Maybe the people of America will finally open their eyes and realize what kind of men and women are running their country.

The sun finished its descent as the man made his way through the ever crowded city streets. He knew exactly where to park. He owned a great deal of real estate around the city. Two of the buildings were located adjacent to one another. The alley that lay in between would be the perfect spot. There was just enough space to accommodate his bike. The buildings housed offices for lawyers, doctors and accountants, and were sure to be empty at this time of day. And even if they weren't, the man cared little. No one would recognize him. In addition, his parking spot had another advantage as well; it was a short distance from a building owned by Connecticut's junior Senator. It was a little known secret that Senator Townsend kept a little love nest in the city. His principle residence was located in Greenwich. However, he'd purchased this building by way of a dummy company several years ago, to be used for his monthly trysts. It had come in quite handy. For the longest time he kept a suite of rooms at a local hotel for his stable of high priced whores. However, he much preferred the secrecy and discretion the building allowed.

Over the years the man had looked deeply into the Senator's past. He probably could have blackmailed him or even turned him into the authorities, but ending his time on earth seemed the best idea of all.

The man hated very few people; the Senator just happened to be on the list. Not only had the Senator's actions harmed him personally, he was the kind of man who would sell out his country for a dollar and not give it a second thought. It made the man sick. Just as he had spent his life protecting the nation, Senator Townsend had spent his life undermining it. The senator had been instrumental in drafting countless pieces of legislation with the goal of undermining the United States and her sovereignty. He was a whore for the U.N. and wanted a one world government where the U.S. would finally be put in its place. There was talk that the Senator would enter the next Presidential race. The thought of Townsend running the country sent chills up the man's spine.

Although the Senator chaired the Military Appropriations Committee, he did everything in his power to destroy those who gave their lives to protect America. He belittled them, spat on them and persecuted them. He even burned a flag as a young man to protest the fallacious atrocities in South East Asia. While the man was fighting and bleeding half way across the world, this piece of human waste was getting high and pissing on the land of his birth.

Unlike the Senator, the man had volunteered to serve his county during the Vietnam War. He considered it his honor and his duty. The man believed that The United States of America was a true gift from God. And with any gift comes responsibility. The man's ancestors all served God and country. He too would follow in their footsteps; he too would defend liberty, he would preserve God's gift. The Senator on the other hand avoided the war as many rich and gutless men did at the time; he paid a psychologist ten thousand dollars to declare him mentally imbalanced and unable to serve. In a way, this made the man laugh. He knew the truth; he knew the Senator truly was mentally deficient. Sure the Senator was one of the most powerful men in the county, but the mere fact that one attains power doesn't mean one possesses a balanced mind. After all, what man spends all his waking hours doing everything in his power to destroy his county? What kind of man would side with the enemies of America in a time of war? What kind of man would not give America the benefit of the doubt? What kind of man would help foster a society marked by godlessness and hedonism? An insane man of course. The man didn't know what caused this mental illness; maybe it was the drugs, maybe it was some sort of genetic defect, maybe it was the primal lust for power. Whatever the case may be, he'd do his part to bring this Senator's crazy train to a screeching halt.

He down shifted the bike into second gear and crossed the center line, pulling into the narrow alley between the two brick buildings.

There were a few lights on in the building to the left, but nothing to worry about, he thought. He dismounted the bike and rolled it behind a small dumpster. A black pipe ran up the side of the building to his right. He pushed the bike until it was only a few inches away. He removed a lock and chain from one of his saddlebags and secured the bike to the pipe. He didn't think anyone would steal it, but one never knew in this day and age. In the land of entitlements created by the likes of the good Senator, who knew what some people thought they were entitled to? He carefully removed his helmet and riding clothes and stuffed them into his saddlebags. He then examined his face in the small mirror that rested on the left hand side of the handlebars. His disguise remained intact. He reached into his pocket and removed his hat and placed it on his head. He slumped over the way a man who has been beaten down by life does, and made his way down the tree-lined sidewalk. He had some time to kill, so he reached into a nearby trash can and pulled out a discarded coffee cup. He then walked two more blocks and found a place to rest and wait. The Senator wouldn't be along for bit. Until then, he'd just occupy his time by pan handling. As soon as he placed the cup on the ground, a man tossed in twenty six cents. He growled out a thank you and continued to hold his head down. However, he never took his eyes off the surrounding landscape. To do so would put him in peril.

The Senator's drive to New Haven was uneventful. He preferred to take his helicopter to New Haven, but he was having some problems with his favorite mode of transportation and the morons to whom he paid large sums of money could not figure out what the hell was wrong with it. He couldn't stand dealing with these peons. After all, they were beneath him. Why couldn't they just do their jobs and go home to their pitiful little lives at the end of the day? What riff raff. They told him it wouldn't be ready for at least a week. Who did they think he was some ordinary schmuck?

So he decided to drive himself. He was a man of the people, right? Well that's how he was perceived anyway. And in his world, perception was reality. Truthfully, he hated his constituents and held them in utter contempt. They were sheep who would do anything he said. How pathetic. Maybe it would do him good to take a little drive, he thought. Those tree hugging, Prius driving, hemp wearing supporters of his would probably shit themselves if they knew he flew the short distance from Greenwich to New Haven on a regular basis. He relied on them heavily for votes and money. He would do what he had to in order to keep up appearances.

He pulled onto the Merritt Parkway and began the short journey to the Elm City. He liked the Merritt. Of all of Connecticut's major roads, it was the most scenic. And besides, he just didn't have the stomach to drive on Interstate 95. What a mess that highway was. Sure, he'd made a great deal of money over the years steering highway projects to certain friends and donors. However, it didn't mean that he enjoyed being inconvenienced on these same roads. He was an impatient man by nature. He adjusted the air and hit play on the CD player. Seconds later, Vivaldi echoed through the car's interior. He didn't really like the music, but he was told by the people in his circles that it was something he should like. He just grinned and bared it. Despite having to drive himself, he was in good spirits. His companion for the evening would be an attractive whore named Monique. She'd been with him for a while. He didn't think that was her real name. But it didn't matter. Her name could have been Bertha for all he cared. She was a good lay; that's all that mattered. She was to meet him at the Union League, and he was awaiting her arrival with deranged anticipation.

Chapter 19

Located in the Historic Sherman Building, *The Union League Café* is not only one of the Elm City's top restaurants, it's also a proud landmark. Just steps away from Yale University and the City Green, the site once housed the home of Roger Sherman. In addition to being New Haven's first mayor, Sherman has the distinction of being the only American whose name appears on the Declaration of Independence, the Articles of Confederation and the Constitution. Some one hundred years after Sherman's time, a local industrialist by the name of Gaius Fenn Warnier constructed the brownstone that rests on the site today. Up until the forties, the Union League operated as a private club. To some, like W. Arthur Townsend, it still functions as a club of sorts.

Townsend pulled his late model Mercedes up in front of the restaurant and impatiently waited for the valet. "What the fuck is taking so long," he muttered to himself. He pulled down the sun visor and lifted the tiny panel revealing a mirror. As he did this, a small light came to life. He gazed at his reflection and gave his porcelain veneers a once over. Great, nothing in my teeth, he thought. As he pushed the visor back into the up position, he heard a rap on the driver's side window. Finally, he thought; about fucking time. Townsend opened his door and stepped out and onto the sidewalk.

He was greeted by a young Middle Eastern man no older than twenty. The man was wearing a red jacket and a pair of black trousers. The plastic name tag pinned to his breast revealed his name – Amir. The young valet flashed the Senator a big smile. His teeth were gleaming white; his face a dark brown with only a small hint of facial hair around his chin and upper lip.

"Hello, sir, can I be of assistance?"

"I don't want any assistance; I just want you to take care of my car."

"Well, you have come to the right place. Amir is all about taking care of cars."

"I'm sure. Make sure it doesn't move from this spot."

Amir coyly stuck his hand out; his gaze rested on the open palm.

"I can't promise that, sir. We have very many cars on a Saturday night."

"Don't you know who I am?"

"You are a valued customer, sir, that's for sure."

He handed Amir the keys.

"You listen to me. I am a U.S. Senator. You fuck up my car and I'll send you back to the third world toilet that produced your sorry ass. If I see so much as a speck of dirt on this car when I come out, you'll be parking camels back in that shit hole you came from. Got that Amir?"

"Oh sir, I'll be very careful, don't you worry."

The Senator closed the car door behind him and walked up the steps towards the building's entrance. When he was out of earshot, Amir shook his head. "What an asshole."

The senator gazed around the bar area in search of his dinner companions, but to no avail. I must be the first one here, he thought to himself. He rudely pushed his way past several waiting patrons and flagged down the bartender. "Give me a Grey Goose martini and make it quick."

"Coming right up sir," the man replied.

"And try and keep the ice to a minimum, alright?"

"Whatever you say sir."

A spot opened up at the bar a few seats down, and the Senator wasted little time snatching it up. A few of the people who'd been standing there for a while gave him a dirty look. He swiveled around on the leather chair like a kid on a carnival ride and rested his arms on the mahogany bar. The bartender delivered his drink and placed it on a white cocktail napkin.

"Will that be all, sir?"

"Yes. How much do I owe you?"

"With tax it comes to $9.88."

He opened his wallet and removed a ten dollar bill and placed it on the bar. "Keep the change."

The bartender walked over to the register and rang it up. He placed the ten dollar bill in the drawer, and removed a dime and two pennies and threw them in the tip jar to the right of the register. He'd met some cheap bastards in his time, but none were cheaper than Senator Townsend. He couldn't believe that he actually voted for this asshole. Well, he wouldn't cast a vote for this parsimonious miser ever again. The bartender dreaded the Senator's monthly visits to the Union League. On the bright side, the Senator only spent a short time in the bar area, if at all. It was the wait staff that really endured his wrath.

The Senator took a big swig from his martini and gazed around the room. He felt like he owned the world. Did the people around him know they were in the presence of greatness? Probably not; the peons scattered around this room probably wouldn't know greatness if it came up and bit them on the nose. He consumed the remainder of his drink and shouted to the bartender for another.

Tommy and Susan returned to the station after a light dinner. And although dinner brought out a few funny stories, the two were no closer to catching their killer. Tommy was profoundly frustrated, for he had an uncanny knack for piecing together the disparate particulars of most crimes. This crime was different; the answer wasn't as clear as that big nose on Tony's face. What were they missing? They had even stopped by a nearby church to light a few candles and say a prayer with the hope of receiving some Divine inspiration, but to no avail. Tommy's pondering was interrupted by his desk phone. The loud ring startled him.

"O'Leary here."

"Tommy, it's Atkins at the front desk. There's some guy here from the *Register* who wants to talk to someone about the Green murder. What should I do with him?"

"What, does he want a quote or something?"

"Nah, he says he received something in the mail that may or may not be from the killer."

"Did he say what it was?"

"His dirty underwear! I don't know, I didn't think to ask."

"You're some kind of cop, Atkins."

"That's what they tell me."

"Just tell him to wait there and I'll be right out."

"Will do. Oh, and Tommy, that new partner of yours sure is a hottie. You thinking about layin' into that thing?"

Despite the vulgarity of the remark Tommy grinned. "Atkins, it's no wonder you're forty-eight and still living with your mother."

"She's a great cook and my laundry's always done. What more could a man ask for?"

Tommy pondered that a moment and sarcastically replied, "I stand corrected. Maybe things aren't so bad at the Atkins house after all."

He walked the short distance to Susan's cube and tapped her on the shoulder. She flinched, and Tommy felt goose bumps go up his arm.

"Hey, some guy from the *Register* is here." Susan continued to type away on her keyboard. "What, did you let you subscription lapse or something?"

"First, I only buy that rag when it contains articles about my current or past cases."

"So you like to see your name in print, is that it?"

Disregarding the flirtatious dig, he continued. "Second, it could be an important lead."

"Did some paperboy see our killer? Do they still have paperboys any more?"

"Not to my knowledge, Miss Wisenhiemer."

"That a paper boy saw the killer or that there don't seem to be any paper boys anymore."

"Neither."

"I'll tell you, I miss the paperboy. They were so Rockwellian, don't you think?"

"Apparently he's heard about you and wants to do a story on New Haven's newest detective. Reporters are funny that way."

Susan's demeanor changed, her face seemed to light up. "They want to write a story about me?"

"No, but you were giving me shit, so I figured one good turn deserves another."

"Thanks, Mr. nice guy."

"The guy believes the killer sent him something."

"Maybe we should talk to him then."

"That's why I came to get you."

"No duh," Susan sarcastically replied.

Tommy and Susan walked through several sets of doors before they found themselves in the station's lobby. There was one man seated on the faded orange vinyl chairs that lined the far wall. He was kind of scrawny with disheveled blond hair. Tommy thought he'd seen him before, but couldn't be certain where. This must be the guy, they thought.

Tommy was the first to speak. "Can I help you?"

"Are you working on the Green case?"

"Yes sir we are."

"My name's Toby, Toby Scott." The man extended his hand and Tommy took it, reluctantly.

"Toby Scott. Yes, you've written some great pieces on me. I had hoped that I'd get a chance to meet you face to face some day."

"I'm sorry, what was your name again?"

"I didn't give my name although I was getting to it. I'm Detective Thomas O'Leary, and this is Detective Susan Kendall."

Toby started to get a little anxious. He recognized the name immediately. He'd written a number of stories about the detective, the majority of which weren't too flattering. He had to retract most of them. Shit, he thought.

"Well detectives, the reason I'm here is because of this."

He reached into the pocket of his powder blue windbreaker and pulled out an envelope. He had wrapped it in a plastic bag so as not to mess up any fingerprints, although he was certain the killer hadn't left any, but you never knew.

"Here," he said, offering it timorously. "I got this from the killer or someone who claims to be the killer."

Susan took the small package from his hand. "What makes you think this is authentic? You guys must get plenty of people claiming they've done this and that, just like us."

"Typically I'd agree with you, but something tells me there's more to it than that. Read it and see what you think."

"Fair enough."

"Listen, while you look it over, I am going to grab a smoke."

"Sure thing," replied Susan." Toby started to walk towards the doors, but Tommy stopped him. "Oh Toby," Tommy called out, feigning compassion.

"Yes, Detective O'Leary?"

"Cigarettes are killers, maybe you should rethink that habit."

"You're all heart detective. If you must know, I haven't had a cigarette in ten years."

"Why the change?"

"Read the letter and maybe you'll understand."

Toby stepped though the double doors and walked out into the humid August night. He'd gone over it in his head hundreds of times and this seemed like his best course of action. Sure, the killer knew that he'd picked up a hooker. That wasn't good, but maybe, just maybe if they caught this sonofabitch, he could sleep at night. He riffled through his jackets pockets and found the Parliament's and a book of matches. He drew the match across the back of the back and watched as the flame came to life. He lit the small tube of tobacco and God knows what else and inhaled deeply. What have I gotten myself into?

Tommy followed Susan to a small room that contained supplies. They each put on a pair of latex gloves and prepared to open the letter.

"You and Toby seemed to hit it off out there Susan. You still hoping he'll write a story about you?"

"Me, what about you? You were practically kissing his ass."

"It's called sarcasm. I thought an educated gal like you would know the difference."

"I guess your sarcasm is a wee bit too subtle for me."

"I'll try and give some kind of sign next time. I certainly wouldn't want you to miss out on a fine bit of humor."

"That's very kind of you. Maybe you could wink a few times; that would certainly get my attention."

"I'll make a mental note."

"So what's your beef with this guy?"

"Toby? He's a weasel of the lowest order."

"What newspaper person isn't?"

"Good point, but he goes beyond that. He has a real hard on for cops."

"He wants to get in your pants?"

"What did you say?"

"I said, he wants to get in your pants."

"What are you talking about?"

"You said he has a hard on for cops. I take that to mean that he is sexually aroused by men in blue, and let's face it, you fit the bill."

"No, I meant he doesn't like cops."

"I know. I was just wondering what your reaction would be to Toby wanting a little something from you."

"That's a disgusting thought."

"I try."

"And you succeed."

Tommy opened the bag and slid out its contents. "What do we have here," he mused.

"The last time I checked, they called that white stuff paper."

"It's no wonder they made you a detective."

"And they other thing is an envelope."

"Lucky guess. You're two for two today."

"What does our white paper say?"

"I was getting to that; you want to be the one who reads it aloud, be my guest."

"Why don't we just read it to ourselves, and then discuss?"

"What is this, some kind of focus group?"

"Something like that."

"Anyway, it sounds good. For one, I don't have to hear myself butcher the printed word out loud and I get to have a break from hearing you and your ongoing commentary."

"Tommy, you know you just love working with me and you especially love my musings. Be honest, you haven't had this much fun on the job in years."

"That's certainly a fair statement. Why don't we read the letter now and we can exchange pleasantries later?"

"I've already finished reading it."

"You're quick."

"I bet you say that to all the girls."

"No, just the ones who read fast. If you don't mind, I am going to take my time."

"No problem, I've got all night."

"Ha ha."

Tommy looked over the first page of the letter, and although

Susan had already finished reading it, she gave it a second look. When they had both covered the entire page, Tommy turned the letter over and read the paragraph that was addressed to good old Toby. Tommy read the few lines several times before raising his eyes from the page. Susan was the first to open her mouth. "What do you think, oh great one?"

"We can assume our letter writer is OCD free."

"Profiling is all well and good, but I'm not sure how someone's OCD or lack thereof helps us."

"It doesn't or at least I don't think it does. But after meeting with Dr. Patel, I am reminded that I could use a little work in that department. Our killer doesn't appear to suffer from the same affliction. In any case, someone with OCD would in likelihood match his stationary with his envelope, but I digress."

"What?"

"Sorry for the tangent." Tommy smiled. "Seriously, I can see why Toby brought us this letter. If what the writer of the letter was saying is true, Toby is probably scared shitless. What kind of person knows your every move?"

"God?"

"Very funny."

"It's true."

"I know, but I don't think God strapped Dr. Green to the table and had his jollies with him."

"Good point."

"No, whoever wrote this letter is as professional as they come. There's no way some pro-life extremist had the resources to follow a man as insignificant as Toby Scott. Our killer is good, maybe too good."

"Tommy, there's no such thing as the perfect crime. Every

criminal makes mistakes, thankfully. Otherwise we'd be out of a job. We just have to find that one mistake Dr. Green's killer made, and when we do, we've got him."

Tommy smiled. "You make it sound so easy."

"I'm not sure easy would be the right word. But we do know that this guy, whoever he is, is probably not out to grind some political ax. My guess is that this letter to Toby is a smokescreen. This guy is as serious as a heart attack. On the plus side we haven't had any other bodies turn up in the last few days, so maybe Dr. Green was a one shot deal."

"We should only be so lucky."

Chapter 20

The Senator was sipping his third martini of the evening when he felt a soft tap on his shoulder. He turned his head to see the hostess standing beside him. She was wearing a white silk blouse and black slacks. Her auburn hair fell just above her shoulders. She forced a smile for the restaurant's most despised patron.

"Good evening Senator, your party has arrived. They are being escorted to your usual table as we speak. They asked me to see if you were waiting in the bar."

"Where else would I be?" He barked.

"Perhaps they thought you might have stepped out or were running late."

"I'm never late sweet ass. Tell them I'll be there in a minute."

"As you wish, Senator."

Not bad, he thought. He stared at her ass as she walked away. Maybe he'd ask her if she wanted to have a little threesome this evening. She'd been checking him out, all women did, he thought. Luckily, his dinner companion was not opposed to having another woman in on the fun. It wouldn't be the first time and certainly not the last. Yes, it was going to be another memorable evening.

He finished the remainder of his drink and tossed his glass on the bar, spilling the remnants all over the man to his left. The man looked at him with disdain. The Senator didn't care. The man was a nobody and he, he was a somebody. Townsend stepped away from the bar and walked the short distance to the private dining area where his friends had gathered. Like the bar area, its walls were lined with dark wood and stylish accents.

It was the usual cast of characters. There was Judge Nelson Pickford, a distinguished jurist of the Connecticut Appellate Court. He was a thin man with a narrow face to match. Above his lip sat a mustache that a pubescent boy could put to shame. To Pickford's right was John Christopher, Dean of a local law school. Although roughly the same age as the other men at the table, he looked ten years their junior. He had a full head of blond hair parted to one side. His angular nose and blue eyes were the focal point of his boyish face. Unlike his friends, he took very good care of himself. He hadn't had a drink or cigarette in twenty years; his only vice was young women. Rounding out the table was Townsend's closest friend and confidant: Dennis Edwards. The Senator and Dennis went way back. They had been roommates at Princeton and both applied and were accepted to Yale Law. Neither man liked the practice of law. However, they knew that a Yale Law education would open countless doors. For Townsend, it paved the way for his political career. For Edwards, it ushered him into the world of investment banking.

The three men stood and greeted their long time friend and Connecticut's most liberal elected official. They embraced, shook hands and exchanged pleasantries.

"Where are the women?" asked Townsend as he took one of the table's empty seats.

"You know women," exclaimed Pickford.

"You bet your ass I do," replied Townsend. The men all laughed.

"It sure is good to see you sons of bitches."

Edwards ordered several bottles of Burgundy and an assortment of appetizers from the waiter while the men sat discussing old times and the current political climate. It would be another forty minutes and four bottles of wine before the women arrived.

The man had pretty good luck as a panhandler. He'd taken in over $25.00 and he'd only been at it for a little over an hour. Oh the liberal guilt, he mused derisively. If they only knew how much these unfortunates were taking in and what they were spending it on, they might think better of forking over their hard-earned money. So far so good, he thought.

In addition to filling his coffee cup with cold hard cash, many passersby had laid eyes on his disheveled face. And this was exactly what he wanted. When the authorities questioned people in the surrounding area, they'd say they saw a homeless man begging for change. The police and FBI would be tearing the city apart looking for homeless men and thanks to the city's lax policy in this regard, there would be no shortage of suspects. By then the man would have disposed of his motorcycle and anything that could trace him to the crime. He regretted having to give up the motorcycle, but it was the cost of remaining ahead of the authorities.

The man looked around and slowly climbed to his feet. He wanted anyone watching to think he was drunk or disabled or both. He dusted himself off, hung his head low and walked in the direction of the Senator's love nest. It would all be over in a short while, he thought. Even if he was apprehended after the fact, which was unlikely, he didn't care. He'd have accomplished what he set out to do; he'd have fulfilled his master plan. As it was, his time on earth was fast coming to an end. His doctor gave him no more than a year to live. And that was six months ago. It was on that day he started planning this, his final mission. If the authorities were smart enough to put the pieces together, the puzzle would point to him, but it was an intricate puzzle only very few people could decipher. They could put him in jail, but he really didn't care. A short stint in jail would pale in comparison to the pain he had endured throughout his life.

By the time they had finished dinner and dessert, the Senator was so drunk he could hardly stand. If his arrogance was not apparent while sober, it was quite evident when he'd had too much to drink. He excused himself from the table with an inaudible grunt and stumbled to the restroom. He positioned himself in front of the urinal. However, his vision was so blurry that he all but missed. When he finished relieving himself, he hastily left the bathroom and a puddle of urine in his wake.

Despite his intoxication, he was ready to take Monique home and have his way with her. He liked spending time with his buddies, but he liked getting laid more. He pulled out his wallet and feigned paying the bill. He knew one of the others would politely stop him. It was a little game they played. He had repaid them many times over in the past and they knew it. Besides, he was picking up the tab for the whores. He always paid for the whores. He grabbed his date by the hand and forcefully pulled her from the chair. She was taken aback, but had come to expect such things from Townsend. For the amount of money he paid her, she would take just about anything.

The two exited the dinning room and made their way towards the front door. While in route, the Senator made a quick stop at the hostess station. By this time, things had slowed down a bit, however the hostess was speaking with someone on a phone that hung on the wall adjacent to the podium that served as the station. When she had replaced the phone in its cradle, he leaned in and put his hand on her backside. The two exchanged words and the Senator slowly retreated and rejoined his date. To his dismay, the hostess was unable to join them due to a prior commitment. That's what he told Monique anyway. In reality the hostess told him if he ever touched her again, she would shoot his dick off with the *9mm* Glock she carried in her backpack. Senator W. Arthur Townsend was speechless.

The Senator led the way out the front door and down the steps. He tripped as he stepped down on to the sidewalk, but miraculously regained his balance. "Didn't I tell you that I always land on my two feet?" The woman nodded her head. How long is this going to take? She thought.

Arthur scanned the street in front of the building, but did not see his beloved car. "I told that camel fucker to leave my car where it was. He'll be sorry he fucked with me."

"Arthur, it's alright. I'm sure it's near by," she replied.

"No it's not alright, damn it."

As he was uttering those words, two young Yale coeds happened by. They looked in his direction.

"Is that Senator Townsend?"

"Yeah, it's him," the other replied. "Oh my God!"

The pair moved closer in the hopes of meeting the honorable Senator Townsend. The first one interrupted the Senator and Monique.

"Senator Townsend, I hate to bother you, but I just want to say what an honor it is to meet you. You have done so much to help the environmental movement. We can't thank you enough."

Next, it was the second girl's turn. "Yes, she's right. You sure do put those right wing fanatics in their place. How can they even begin think that global warming is not man made? Can you say flat-earthers? Gosh."

Despite his intoxication, the Senator decided to engage them. He could actually be charming when it suited his needs. Truth be told, he didn't think man had a thing to do with global warming, but he wasn't going to tell them that. "Why thank you girls." He put his arms around them. "You are the reason that I got into politics in the first place. For too long I stood by and watched as others destroyed our beloved planet. There were times that it almost brought me to tears. I swore that if ever I had the chance, I would become an advocate for the environment. After all, we are the party of the voiceless, and who or what in this day and age is more voiceless than our beloved environment? I hear the cries of our environment loudly and clearly and I will not stand idly by letting those screams go unanswered."

The two girls were practically gushing. The first one spoke again.

"Sir, you'll always have my vote."

"Mine too."

"Thank you for your kindness," was his reply. He handed them each his business card. "If ever I can help either one of you, please feel free to give me a call."

"Bye."

"Thanks, sir."

The girls walked away.

"You certainly have a way with young girls, Arthur. I thought you were going to ask them to join us. Even for you three would be something of an accomplishment."

"Those girls? Please. Those tree huggers are good for one thing and one thing only: votes. Our system of higher learning is churning out political zombies by the thousands and do you know who they are voting for? People like me. No, I'd just as soon fuck women like you."

"Arthur, you certainly make a girl feel wanted."

He was starting to get a little emotional, something that was very out of character for him. "You know what I mean. You see right through me. Those girls attend one of the greatest universities in the world and yet they cannot even think for themselves. Sure they will probably succeed financially, but they will always be the clay that we liberal politicians mold for our own purposes. Don't let my little speech fool you. I don't give a shit about global warming. On the contrary, I use the global warming issue to gain votes and to make money. Who do you think convinced our former VP to start his carbon credit business? Me, that's who. That guy is so clueless it's almost sad. But you know what's more sad? The fact that people buy into this nonsense. Shit," he spat out vehemently.

"For once Arthur, we are in agreement."

Amir, appeared from out of nowhere. He walked around the corner to have a smoke and on the way back noticed the unlikely couple waiting by the valet stand. "Good evening, do you have your ticket?"

"What ticket?"

"Oh sir, it is you. I remember you. The ticket I gave you when you arrived. Of course, you didn't have that pretty lady with you when you arrived."

"I don't need a ticket. Do you know who I am?"

Shit, not this again, he thought. "You are the gentleman with the Mercedes." Before Townsend could complain, he said "I'll be right back." He grabbed a pair of keys from the valet box and quickly headed up the street. In the meantime Arthur sat down on a nearby bench. It was covered with bird shit, but he was oblivious. Within seconds, he had toppled over and had passed out. When Amir returned he was behind the wheel of the Senator's car. He pulled it into the valet zone and exited. "What happened to him?" he asked as he handed the keys to Monique. "He had a little too much fun."

"I think you'd better drive."

"I think you're right." She smiled and handed him a $50.00. "My guess is that he didn't tip you on the way in."

"Good guess."

"Help me drag him into the car and we'll call it even."

"Works for me."

They lifted him off the bench and carried him to the car, one on either side. Rather than carrying him around to the front seat, they opted to stick him in the back. They shoved him in and quickly closed the door before his body had a chance to fall out onto the curb.

The woman leaned in and gave Amir a kiss. "Sorry about his bullshit. He can be a real jerk sometimes."

"Are you his wife?"

"Nah, I just get paid to sleep with him."

"And I thought my job was bad."

Chapter 21

The man entered the Senator's love nest via the rear door. He didn't even have to pick the lock as the Senator had a key hidden beneath a small flower pot. The Senator was notorious for losing things and his keys were no exception. Many, including the man, thought he had also lost his mind as well, but that was a discussion for another time. Despite his disdain for the Senator, the man gave him credit for his choice of buildings. It was a lovely brownstone constructed in the late 1800's and the Senator spared no expense in restoring and decorating it.

The man closed the door behind him and removed a small pen light from his pocket. He turned the light on and cautiously moved from room to room. The bottom floor contained the kitchen and a small living area. He quickly covered the distance from the backdoor to the staircase, taking the steps two at a time. He noticed a light on the next floor, but paid no attention. The Senator had several of his lamps on timers. The Senator was a huge proponent of giving breaks to criminals. However these breaks did not extend to allowing them to pay visits to his unlit, empty house. The man likewise passed the third floor landing and proceeded to the top floor. The top floor housed the Senator's master suite. There was a king sized bed as well as a hot tub that held up to eight people. In addition, there was a walk-in closet containing some spare clothes as well as dozens of adult movie titles. The man opened the door, and stepped inside the roomy closet. He looked around for something to sit on and found an old foot stool. He pulled the stool out from under the closet organizer and sat down and waited. It wouldn't be long now.

The Senator's date did her best to navigate through the city streets. By now she should have been used to driving Arthur's car around New Haven. After all, every time they went out, she ended up driving the drunken politician home. But deep down, she was still a country girl and riding through the city streets still caused her some anxiety. Where did she go wrong? She thought. Her life was a lot different than those days growing up in the country. Despite her misgivings about her chosen profession, she laughed to herself. That valet thought she had a pretty bad job. Maybe so, but luckily for her, she hadn't had sex with the Senator in months. He was always so drunk that he usually passed out on their so-called dates. And even when he was semiconscious, he had trouble performing. It was like taking money from a baby.

She turned down the one way street that ran behind the Senator's brownstone. The Senator had a small car port located directly behind the building. She pulled into the small enclosure and shifted the car into park.

"Time to get up sleepyhead. We're home."

The Senator let out a series of moans and groans from the backseat.

"That's what I thought."

She climbed out of the driver's side door and stepped onto the cobblestone pavers that lined the ground. She had half a mind to leave him there. Maybe next time, she thought. She opened the rear door and Arthur fell out of the door and landed on his face.

"That had to hurt," she said.

"What the fuck," was his response.

"Here we go again." She lifted him up by placing her hands under his arms. With her help, he managed to get to his feet.

"Ok Arthur, we'll just take this nice and slow."

"Yeah, ok." She did her best to hold him up and they made their way to the back door.

The man heard the car pull in and he slowly eased the door open and walked over to ornate floor to ceiling window. He looked down and shook his head. "Arthur, drunk again. And I thought this was going to be fun."

He continued to watch as the woman attempted to carry him to the door. The man considered his location. It didn't seem plausible that the woman would be able to get him to the top floor. Arthur was in decent shape, but that girl would have quite the difficult time helping him up to his room. The man quickly descended the staircase and slipped into a coat closet on the second floor.

The woman leaned Arthur against the wall and fumbled with the keys. After two attempts, she gave up and decided to look under the flower pot for the key. That's odd, she thought. No key. She put the pot back in place and tried a few more keys. Finally the key turned and the door opened with a click. "Come on Arthur, just a few more steps."

The pair stepped up and entered the brownstone. She quickly made a right hand turn and deposited Arthur on a nearby loveseat.

"I know it's not comfortable, but I can't carry you to your bed."

"Can you get me a drink?"

"Coming up." She walked down the hallway to the nearby kitchen. "Yeah, I'll give you a drink." She opened the *Sub Zero* refrigerator and removed a bottle of *Pelligrino*. She poured some of the sparkling water into a tumbler and topped it off with a few ice cubes.

She walked back and handed him the glass. "Here, drink this."

"What is it?"

"Just drink it." He took a big sip and leaned back on the loveseat.

"Thanks for a wonderful night," he said.

"You're welcome. Listen, I'm going up to bed. If you can make it, I'll be there waiting."

"I'll be up in a little while," he said. "I just need to rest a little."

She smiled and climbed the stairs. Sometimes he wasn't a total jerk, she thought. As she reached the second floor landing she heard a noise, but before she could figure out what it was, she was hit with the Blackjack. The man quickly bound her hands and feet with duct tape and stuffed her in the closet he'd used as a hiding place, shutting the door behind him.

"Judgment day has arrived, Arthur."

Tommy leafed through the stack of newspapers on his desk. Although he wouldn't admit it to Susan, or anyone else for that matter, he did like seeing his name in print. He read a couple of articles about the case. Neither mentioned his name. Oh well, we are pretty early in the investigation, he thought; maybe tomorrow. He thumbed through the paper and when he came to the local section, he started to read. The headline on the top of the page caught his eye.

Woman Dies in Drowning Accident

Middlesex Academy Mourns The Loss Of Its Beloved Head Mistress

> Westbrook- Margaret Baldwin's lifeless body was found yesterday by a local fisherman at the bottom of Messershmidt Pond. Witnesses state that Ms. Baldwin was seen kayaking in the area prior to the incident. An outdoor enthusiast, Ms. Baldwin spent most mornings kayaking around the majestic pond. The State Police have ruled it an accidental drowning pending an autopsy. A student favorite, Ms. Baldwin won her way into the hearts and minds of students as a teacher at the prestigious school and in recent years took over as the schools Head Mistress. An ardent supporter of the United States Civil Liberties Association, Ms. Baldwin was to be honored by the civil rights organization on the very evening of her death. In lieu of flowers, donations can be made in Ms. Baldwin's name to the USCLA. A memorial service is planned for Tuesday.

Tommy put the paper down. When it rains, it pours he thought. Ms. Baldwin. Wow, he hadn't thought about that name in forever. Tommy just sat there in a daze.

"What's on your mind, Tommy?" It was Susan. She had walked up behind him, but he was so distracted that he didn't even notice her.

"What?"

"You were just staring into space, almost trancelike."

"I'm sorry, it's this case, plus I found out that someone I

once knew just passed away."

"Oh Tommy, I'm so sorry. Was it an old friend?"

"Of sorts."

"What is that supposed to mean?"

"Can you keep a secret?"

"I'd like to think so."

"It was the woman with whom I…"

"I what?"

"…I lost my virginity."

"Oh, I see."

"Anyway, I was thumbing through the paper and it looks like she drowned."

"Tommy, that's awful."

"So she was an old girlfriend?"

"No, she was actually a teacher of mine."

"Here's to you Mrs. Robinson," sang Susan in her best Simon and Garfunkel voice.

"Very funny. No, she had just started at the Academy, so she had to be twenty-two, twenty-three at the most."

"That's not the Catholic school you went to I hope?"

"No, I spent my high school years at a secular school."

"You know that's a crime?"

"Going to s secular school?"

"No, sleeping with a student."

"That's what they tell me."

"Sorry, it's just the cop in me. I do that sometimes. Please continue."

"It was weird. She was very liberal, dare I say a Marxist. Well she did her best to educate me in the plight of the working masses, that sort of thing while using her womanly charms to seduce me."

"Sounds like someone who truly cared about her students. Not!"

"You're telling me. Well, I saw right through her propaganda, but if she wanted to have her way with me, I figured, why not? All of my friends had lost their virginity long before me. It was late in my senior year, and I was what you might call a late bloomer, so when the chance came, I jumped on it."

"Literally..."

"And figuratively, yes."

"Did you have a crush on her?"

"No, far from it. She was pretty, but not attractive if you know what I mean."

"You lost me."

"To look at Ms. Baldwin, you'd have to say that she was good looking, but there was something about her that made that beauty hard to see."

"She was beautiful on the outside, but not so beautiful on the inside?"

"That's about right."

"Regardless of her personality, I am really sorry, Tommy. It's tough to lose someone, especially when that someone helped you get your jollies for the first time."

Tommy smiled.

"Susan, you're a great listener. The funny thing about Ms. Baldwin was that she was a champion swimmer. I guess I never thought swimming would be the way she went."

"Maybe she bumped her head or something. It's a little hard to swim when you are unconscious."

"You think? Yeah, I guess. They are having a memorial service for her in a few days. Maybe I'll go. It might help to exorcise some of those demons."

"It couldn't hurt. And if you want someone to go with, I'd be happy to escort you."

"That's very nice of you, thanks."

"Plus I get to see the high school that helped shape that twisted mind of yours."

"An added bonus, yes."

"Well listen, I am going to head home. It's been a long day. Rest up Tommy. Something tells me it will be a busy day tomorrow."

"Do you know something I don't know?"

"No, it's just that the criminals don't ever seem to take a vacation."

"You got that right. Good night, Susan."

"Good night, Tommy."

Chapter 22

Arthur sipped his sparkling water. Maybe Monique was right, he thought. The last thing he needed was another drink. A little hydration never hurt anyone. He held the cold glass against his aching head, the condensation dripping down his face. "Shit that hurt," he said to himself reflecting on his fall out of the car.

"Arthur," the voice said. "I always told you that your drinking was going to get you into trouble, but you never did listen to me."

The voice was definitely male, so it couldn't be his lady friend. "Who the fuck is that?"

The room was dark, and Arthur's eyes had not yet adjusted, not to mention his eyesight was rather blurry due to his night of heavy drinking.

The man stepped into the small room. In his hand he held a pistol with a cylinder attached to the end of the barrel, a silencer.

"I think you know exactly who it is."

The man took a seat in an oversized chair directly across from Arthur. Little by little Arthur's eyes began to adjust. At first he could make out the image, but the edges seemed a little fuzzy. Finally, he was able to see the disheveled man in front of him. Although he didn't recognize the man's face, the voice somehow seemed familiar.

"Who the fuck are you?" he slowly slurred.

"Arthur, can we dispense with the vulgarity for once? I'm so tired of it. How you became a U.S. Senator with that mouth is beyond me. You really are an embarrassment."

"Wait, I know that voice," he said angrily. "You! What the fuck are you doing here? How did you know where to find me?"

"Arthur, I am a resourceful man when I want to be. You should know that by now."

"Get the fuck out of here."

"I'm not staying long, believe me. On the contrary, the less time I have to spend with you, the better."

"Don't give me that shit."

"Arthur, please, can't we have a civilized conversation for once?"

"Get the fuck out of here before I call the cops."

Finally, the man had had enough. "Don't worry Arthur, once I put a few holes in you, I'll be on my way."

Arthur struggled to get up, but was unable to balance himself and fell back down onto the loveseat.

"What are you talking about? What's with the gun?"

"Arthur, if you must know, I am here to kill you."

"Excuse me?"

"Yes, for your crimes against America as well as for a crime you wittingly perpetrated against me some years ago."

"I've never broken a fucking law in my life you piece of shit."

"Is that so? For some reason Arthur, I have a little trouble taking you, of all people, at your word."

"Go ahead, judge me you self-righteous asshole."

"Arthur, this is not about me looking down my nose at you. This is about revenge."

"Revenge?"

"Yes, and who knows, maybe we can get a conservative person to take your Senate seat," the man chuckled.

"Wait…"

But it was too late. The man raised the gun and put two shots into Arthur's tanned forehead. Although he knew they were coming, Arthur's look revealed his surprise. Arthur's lifeless body came crashing down on the glass topped coffee table sitting between the two men, shattering the top and splintering the wood that held it in place. The man rolled him over with his foot and looked at him one last time. "Good riddance," he uttered as he put the remaining bullets into Arthur's groin.

A crime of passion, that's what they'll say, he thought. Arthur had slept with so many women that he had certainly pissed off a husband or two in his day. No doubt he had received a threat or two as well. It was not uncommon for men in his position to be threatened. It was however a rare occasion when one acted on such a threat.

The man slowly backtracked away from W. Arthur Townsend's dead body. If the man thought ending Arthur's life would make him feel better, he was mistaken. Taking human life never brought joy. On the contrary, it wrought only pain, he reflected. But in the end it wasn't about making him feel better. No, it was about righting a wrong. He knew this wouldn't bring his daughter back, but maybe some father somewhere wouldn't have to feel the same pain that he had. In that the man could take solace.

He closed the rear door and replaced the key under the small flower pot. It was a short distance to his motorcycle, but he decided to take the long round about route. It was a pleasant evening, he thought, and after finishing his business with Arthur, he had nowhere in particular to be. He unlocked his bike and in a few minutes was riding out of the city. As he came closer to the Quinnipiac River, he slowed the bike down. Just ahead there was a small park abutting the river. It was deserted at this time of night. He removed his disguise, including his outer clothes, and tossed them into the water along with his gun. What remained was a tank top, a pair of athletic shorts and white socks. Next, he removed a pair of running sneakers from his saddlebag and quickly put them on. When he was dressed and ready to go, he pushed the motorcycle into the murky water and began running out of the park. It was about five miles to his home, but the man was not worried. He had run twelve marathons in his day. Compared to those races, this run would be a walk in the park. No pun intended, he thought.

As he jogged, he thought about Arthur. Where did that man go wrong? He was such a smart man, and at one time, a decent man, or so he was told. But somewhere, somehow along the way something changed; he changed. As best as the man could figure, Arthur changed after he'd gone to college. After that, he had never been the same. He went in as an America loving everyman, and left as a Marxist intent on destroying the America the Founding Father's intended. If only the man had a little more time, perhaps he'd put some of those radical college professors in their places as well. Were it not for them, maybe Arthur would have gone on to be a man that helped the less fortunate rather than exploit them. In any case, it was too late for anybody to help Arthur.

The man pushed himself and in several minutes he had left the New Haven city limits. What a busy few days, he thought. If he didn't hear anything by the morning, he would make an anonymous call to the police notifying them of the whereabouts of the state's junior Senator.

When Senator Townsend's date awoke, she was quite confused. What the hell had happened? The last thing she remembered was depositing Arthur on the couch. Then she headed up stairs, heard a strange noise and after that she couldn't remember a thing. Her hands and feet were bound, that much she could decipher. In addition, there was something covering her mouth. She fumbled around and bumped into a small metal box. I must be in the downstairs closet, she thought, and that must be the little toolbox that Arthur left for small jobs around the house. Although her hands were tied, she was able to move her fingers. She felt around and quickly found the latch that opened the lid. When she got it open she felt around and in no time located the item she'd been looking for: a box cutter. She pulled the box cutter out of its place and began working on the tape that bound her feet. When she'd gotten her feet free, she kicked the door open and pushed herself into the living room, hoping to God that whoever did this had already left. Next, she cut the tape off of her hands and removed the tape from her mouth. "Thank God," she said as she took in a deep breath.

"Arthur, Arthur. Are you there," she cried.

"Arthur?"

She wasn't sure how long she'd been out. Was it a matter of minutes or hours that had lapsed? Was Arthur still here? Maybe Arthur had already left. She retraced her steps and when she arrived in the small living area off the kitchen she screamed in horror. "Arthur!"

There was so much blood she could hardly believe it. What happened? She thought frantically.

On the kitchen wall hung a telephone. She ran into the kitchen nearly slipping on the Italian tile floor, grabbing hold of the phone with both hands as she went. Her hands were shaking, but she managed to dial 9-1-1.

"911, what's your emergency?"

"Somebody just murdered my ah, boyfriend."

"Please remain calm. What's your name ma'am?"

"Monique. Oh, I can't believe he's dead; oh God." By now, she was hysterical.

"Monique, where are you? In order for us to help you, we have to have your location." She gave the dispatcher the address.

"Hang tight Monique, the police will be there right away."

"Thank you."

"Would you like me to stay on the phone with you?"

"Please."

"Are you physically alright?"

"Yes, I'm just a little shaken up."

"Well, you're doing great, just hang in there."

"Thank you."

"Don't mention it dear. That's what we're here for."

"How much longer will it be?"

"Just a few minutes, don't you worry."

She began crying.

"It's OK dear, just let it out."

In the distance she could hear the sirens. She thanked the woman again and hung up the phone. She ran upstairs and waited on the front steps for the police to arrive. When she saw the flashing lights, she knew everything was going to be alright.

"Thank God you're here," she shouted at the approaching officers, tears streaming down her face.

Tommy was just about to leave when his phone rang. "O'Leary."

"Tommy, just got a call from dispatch." It was Tony. "It seems we've got ourselves another murder."

"Great, and we are doing so well on Dr. Green's murder as it is."

"Look Tommy, if it was any other time of the year, I'd assigned someone else. However, there are bunch of folks on vacation, so you're the guy."

"I thought you said cops don't go on vacation."

"I lied."

"Tony, one of these days I am going to beat the shit out of you."

"Are you finished?"

"Finished with what?"

"Venting."

"I guess. Just give me the address, before I change my mind." Tony did.

"Nice neighborhood."

"What can I say, only the best crime scenes for you."

"You're all heart and full of crap. Should I call Susan, or will you?"

"How about you give her a call. I was getting ready to head out."

"It must be nice."

"It must be nice what?"

"It must be nice being you, Tony."

"It has its good days and its bad days."

"Give the mayor my best."

"Very funny. Give me a call on my cell once you've had time to assess the crime scene."

"You bet your ass I will, although don't be surprised if I wait a few hours. Maybe I'll wake up that sorry of ass of yours when you're in the land of slumber."

"You'd do that after all I've done for you?"

"Forgive me if all you've done for me slipped my mind."

"What about your new partner? It knew you two would hit it off."

"If this has all been your idea of the 'Dating Game,' don't expect an invite to the wedding."

"So you do like her?"

"Cupid, what do you say we continue this conversation another time; I have some bad guys to find."

"Good night Romeo."

Tommy hung up and headed to his car. He'd wait and see what the crime scene had to offer before he bothered his new partner. If it was open and shut, he'd let her rest. If there was more to it, well, he'd just have to wake her up.

Chapter 23

Tommy wound his way through the city streets until he came upon the crime scene. He kept the windows rolled down the whole way. Luckily there was a nice breeze blowing off the harbor. He found a place to park and made his way up the front steps of the brownstone. Tommy knew the neighborhood quite well. The notorious banker Teddy Kerry had lived just around the corner. He'd killed his wife and Tommy put him away for life. With any luck, he'd find and put away the perpetrator of this crime as well. Tommy looked around the interior of the brownstone. Nice digs, he thought. The usual cast of characters were mulling about. Except for some shredded duct tape on the floor, there seemed to be nothing out of the ordinary.

There was a young woman sitting at a large dining room table. Her eyes were swollen and red. She'd been crying. To her right was Officer Gloria Jenkins, holding her hand and doing her best to console the girl. Tommy would talk to her once he'd seen the body. He flagged down one of the evidence techs and she pointed him in the direction of the body. "It's downstairs Tommy," she replied. Tommy looked in on the body. In the gore department it was a toss up between this man and the good doctor. Doesn't anyone poison their victims anymore? He wondered. He looked around, but there was no sign of Dr. Patel. He'd wait until he arrived before spending any more time with the body. After all, time spent with a mutilated body was sure to ruin your day, he pondered. Tommy made his way back upstairs, exhaustion apparent in his gait. It never gets any easier, he mused.

The woman seemed a little more composed than when he'd arrived. As she sipped what appeared to be a cup of coffee, Tommy approached her.

"Excuse me, miss."

Tommy made eye contact with Gloria as if to say "is she the one who made the call?" Gloria's expression revealed this to be the case.

The girl took another sip and finally looked up from the fine china wedged between her tiny little hands. They were so small that they almost looked like the hands of a child.

Gloria spoke. "Monique, this is Detective O'Leary. He'll want to ask you some questions. Do you think you're up for it?"

"Yeah, yes, I guess."

"Great. Tommy, if you need anything let me know."

"Thanks Gloria." Gloria got up from the table and walked out of the room.

"Monique, I know this must be difficult, but I'm wondering if you can tell me what happened. Do you think you can do that for me?"

"I'll try."

"Ok, great. Let's start from the beginning."

"Well, Arthur and I had some dinner with friends tonight."

"Where at?"

"The Union League."

"Nice."

"Yeah, I guess. Anyway, Arthur had a little too much to drink, so I drove him back."

"Do you live here with him?"

"Sort of."

"Sort of?"

"Well…"

"Let's not worry about that right now. Please continue."

"Well I managed to get Arthur in the door and to the little living area off the kitchen."

Tommy thought back to his recent visit to the room in question. "Yep, I know where you mean."

"I got Arthur something to drink, non-alcoholic, and I told him I was going to bed. It wasn't the first time he'd gotten this drunk. I told him that if he could manage the steps that I'd be waiting for him."

"So what happened next?"

"After we said our goodnights, I headed upstairs, although when I got to this floor, I heard something or someone. After that it's a total blank until I woke up. Gloria said it looks like someone hit me over the head with some blunt object."

She rubbed her head. "It sure feels that way." She continued.

"Anyway, I woke up and I was in that closet over there." She pointed to a nearby door that stood ajar.

"And whoever did this wrapped tape around my hands and feet."

"How did you get out?"

As luck would have it, we keep a small tool box in that closet, just in case. I managed to get it open and cut the tape."

Tommy smiled. "Nice job."

She really needed some encouragement. The compliment

seemed to melt away some of the tension in her voice. "Thanks. It was hard for me to figure out how long I had been in the closet. It was all a blur. My first thought was to look for Arthur."

"Your boyfriend?"

She hesitated. "Yeah."

"OK."

Not wanting to lie she added, "I'm sorry detective, I'm more like a mistress..."

Tommy felt embarrassed, but tried not to let it show. "I see."

"A paid mistress."

Tommy knew exactly what she meant, although he wasn't about to get on her case about it. That was between her and her maker. He needed her to trust him.

"You were saying," he interjected.

"I figured the best place to look for him would be where I last saw him. The rest is history as they say."

He took her by the hands and looked her in the eyes. "Monique, you've been really brave. Believe me I know how hard this can be. We'll find the person who did this. That's what we do."

"Please do. I've never been this scared in my whole life."

"You don't have to be scared anymore."

"I'll try."

"You said your boyfriend's name was Arthur?"

"Yes."

"Arthur Townsend." Tommy's heart quickly skipped a beat.

"Excuse me, could you repeat that?"

"His name is W. Arthur Townsend, Oh I'm sorry, Senator W. Arthur Townsend."

"Holy shit," was all Tommy could think to say.

~

Tommy was totally flustered, and it showed. He waved his hands and flagged down Gloria. "Gloria, please sit with her. I've got to call Tony."

"Tommy, what's wrong? You don't seem yourself. You're usually the king of cool."

"This king just had the shock of his life."

"Would you mind letting me in on it?"

"Our victim…"

"Yeah."

"It's Senator Townsend."

"Wow, that's big," was her reply.

"I know. Listen, I've got to call Tony and the FBI will certainly be joining the party. Whatever you do, don't breathe a word about this to anybody outside of this building."

"Who would I tell?"

"I can think of lots of people." He smiled, half heartedly. "Just kidding."

"Very funny."

"Please gather everybody together while I call Tony."

"I'm glad I'm not you right now."

"Believe me, if I could be anybody else right now, well except for Senator Townsend, I'd jump at the chance."

Tommy walked outside into the night air while Gloria pulled the half dozen or so people together.

Tony's phone rang five times before he picked up.

"Tommy, this had better be good. When I told you to call me, I was only being nice."

"Tony, believe me, I had hoped it was a little domestic squabble gone awry, but we have got bigger problems my friend."

"OK, spill the beans, what's the big deal?"

"Our victim…"

"Our victim is…who?"

"W. Arthur Townsend."

There was dead silence on the other end of the line. If Tommy didn't know better, he would have thought their connection had been broken.

"Tony, say something."

"Kid, I'm at a loss for words. Man, this can't be good."

"Look on the bright side."

"There's a bright side to all this?"

"Yeah, there's a pretty good chance that the higher-ups will forget all about Dr. Green."

"Thank heaven for small favors."

"Small favors indeed."

The man made it back to his house in just under forty minutes. Not bad, he thought. He walked to the fridge and pulled out a bottle of Poland Spring Water, removed the cap and finished it in one big gulp. Not satisfied, he grabbed another and walked over to a small desk. On top of the desk sat a laptop. He opened the top and booted it up. When the laptop came to life, he entered a series of passwords and on his screen appeared the living/dining area of the island home of the lawyer and his boyfriend. His eyes focused on the two men slumped over in their chairs. If they weren't already dead, they were well on their way, he thought.

As the man stood up, he felt a sharp pain in his head, and after that, nothing. When the man awoke several minutes later, he was soaked with his own urine and his head was throbbing. The brain tumor, he surmised. His doctor stated that he might experience intense pain or seizures. Up until now he'd been lucky. The man didn't fear death. On the contrary he often welcomed it. What he did fear was dying painfully. He picked up the *Poland Spring* bottle. There was a little bit left. He walked through his bedroom into the master bath. He fumbled through the drawers of the vanity and found what he was looking for: a bottle of *Alleve*. He popped two in his mouth and washed them down with the water. Hopefully that will help, he thought. He did have more powerful medications, but he would only turn to those as a last resort. For now he wanted to keep his wits about him. He threw his dirty clothes into the hamper and jumped into the tub for a cold shower. As the cold water hit him in the face, his headache began to dissipate. When he'd finished in the bathroom, he had a quick bite and turned in for the night.

Tommy called Susan's cell phone and left a message. Where are you Susan? Undeterred, he called information and obtained her home number. She picked up on the second ring.

"What city please?"

"What, Susan, is that you?"

"Sorry, Tommy. Just a little phone humor, that's all."

"Please tell me you're not in bed."

"No, but I was going to go to bed after my long soak in the tub."

"You're in the tub?"

"Why, does that make you feel a little uncomfortable?"

"No, it makes me realize I haven't bathed in a while, but don't rub it in."

"Sorry, just messing with you. You were saying?"

"We've got ourselves another murder victim. I wasn't going to call you, but it turned out to be a little more complicated than I originally thought."

"How so?"

"It's the victim."

"And..."

"If you thought Dr. Green's murder was big, wait until I tell you who tonight's victim is."

Tommy relayed the name of the victim.

"Holy shit," was her reply.

"My sentiments exactly."

Chapter 24

Senator John Maitland stood on his expansive deck gazing out at Long Island Sound. The sun shown brightly on his face; he sat transfixed by the beauty unfolding before his eyes. He had stood in this same spot for years, yet never tired of the view. In his hand he held a tall glass of orange juice. He took a sip and pondered the phone call. It came at 5:30 AM and it woke him from a dead sleep. It was his chief of staff, James Wiener. It seems Arthur Townsend had been murdered last night. The details were sketchy at best, but it appeared he was in the company of a woman who was not his wife. Arthur Townsend's extramarital affairs were no secret to beltway insiders and it was for that, and countless other reasons, that Senator Maitland despised the junior Senator from his home state. Unfortunately, protocol dictated that he put those feelings aside, at least for a time, while the authorities had time to sort the matter out.

The Senator dreaded the days ahead. He could picture the media frenzy just on the horizon. In death, W. Arthur Townsend would be lionized, glorified despite the circumstances he found himself in at the time he met his maker. The mainstream media would do everything in their power to paint this man as a saint. Ok, maybe saint was too a strong word. The Senator was quite sure that most of the media types he had encountered wouldn't know a house of worship if it came crashing down on their warped little heads. Regardless, they would rehabilitate him in death, a near impossible feat were he still among the living. All his past deeds, all those transgressions, of which there were many, would be cast aside and a new image of W. Arthur Townsend would emerge. The Senator hoped the new media would do everything in their power to keep the true image of W. Arthur Townsend alive. The Senator finished off his orange juice and walked back into the house. He had to make a phone call of his own.

Tommy had gotten zero sleep over the last twenty-four hours, and it was starting to show. There were dark circles under his eyes and the stubble on his face seemed to get thicker by the minute. He told Susan to wait until morning before coming in. There was no use in having both of them sleep deprived. Besides, the FBI was all over this case now, and despite the fact that murder was a state charge, he was quite certain that the feds were by no means going to let him see this through.

Susan came walking in with a surprising spring in her step. She carried two coffees.

"Tommy, good to see you; sleep well I trust?"

"If you call the ten minutes I rested my head on the desk here sleeping well, then yes, I slept well."

"Sorry, I'm sure it was a rough night."

"Calling last night a rough night would be the understatement of the decade."

"That bad?"

"Yes. I got to play nursemaid to several FBI agents who had

never seen a body, let alone one that's been shot up."

"So this case is out of our hands?"

"Essentially. Sure, we'll go through the motions, but it seems our little band of misfits isn't good enough to find our killer."

"At least that takes some of the heat off of us."

"You'd think so. However, my guess is that we'll get roped into doing our usual legwork, without the benefit of the collar, and if this case goes south, which is entirely plausible, guess who'll be the ones getting the blame?"

"Us?"

"Yep. So my advice is do as little as possible and watch your back."

"Come on Tommy, I think I know you better than that. You can't let things go this easily. You want to catch this killer. That's what we do."

"It sure is, but outside of us and Tony, we are just helping out our federal friends."

Tommy's phone rang. He immediately recognized the number. "Would you hold on for a second? I really need to take this."

"Take your time."

"Thanks." He hit the talk button. "Detective O'Leary."

"Tommy, why so formal?"

"Hello, sir. Just habit I guess."

"Tommy, I'm sure you know why I am calling."

"Yes sir, I've been expecting your call."

"Listen, I hate to do this on the phone. What do you say we play a round of golf and have a little chat? I could meet you at Pine Orchard at 12:00."

"Sir, that sounds great, but make it Clinton at 12:30. I still owe you a round of golf after our last outing."

"Yes, I don't know what happened. You were kicking my butt until we got to the back nine."

"You win some, you lose some. I've been hitting the range, so you'd better watch out."

"Clinton it is. I've always liked that course."

"Thanks, sir. I'll see you then."

"See you at 12:30."

Tommy pressed the end button. Susan looked at him, curiosity evident in her eyes.

"Who was that, your dad or something?"

"Or something."

"Come on Tommy, do tell."

"It was Senator John Maitland."

"Calling you?"

"Yes."

"Tommy, you sure do keep interesting company. A dead Senator last night and a live one today. The next thing you'll tell me is that you are having lunch with the governor."

"Is that today?"

"What?"

"Kidding. It's not like that."

"Just how is it?"

"I drive for him and do security when his regular guy is off or unavailable."

"How did you land that job?"

"He trusts me."

"How did he come to earn that trust?"

"I saved his son's life."

"How come I never heard about this?"

"Because it happened when we were fourteen. You see, his son is my best friend. I've known the Senator since I was a kid, although back when I first met him, he was still Admiral Maitland."

"That's right, he was a decorated war hero before he ran for office."

"Yeah, anyway we were riding our Jet Skis out in the sound behind a big fishing boat. The wake it threw up was enormous and we were jumping the waves when Daniel somehow lost control. To make a long story short, the Jet Ski hit him in the head and knocked him out. I managed to scoop him onto my Jet Ski and after what seemed like hours, we made it back to shore. He had a concussion, but other than that, he was fine."

"That's amazing."

"So the Senator and I have been close ever since."

"I can see why. Where's Daniel now?"

"Iraq. He's a major in the Marine Corps stationed in the Al Anbar Province."

"Just like his dad?"

"Well his dad is a Navy man. Believe me, that was a huge bone of contention in the Maitland house. Daniel did go to the Academy, so his father wasn't totally pissed off."

"I guess almost drowning as a kid would turn anyone off from the navy if you ask me."

"That's true; I never looked at it that way. Anyway, he had hoped that his son would follow in his footsteps. And he has, in a manner of speaking."

"Both military men?"

"Both elite fighting men. The Senator was a Seal, the Navy's elite; Daniel heads up a Force Recon team."

"Well, that's not so bad. It could have been worse. He could have joined the Army."

"Very funny."

"I am well aware of the rivalry between our armed forces."

"Well, I have a round of golf with the Senator at 12:30."

"It must be nice."

"You're more than welcome to join us."

"No thanks, I'll let you guys bond. It's too damn hot out there today to be doing anything outside."

"It's never too hot to play golf."

"That's what all my guy friends keep telling me."

Chapter 25

Tommy's golf outing couldn't have come at a better time. He was stressed and needed something to help him unwind. More often than not, golfing brought the worst out in him, but today he didn't care how poorly he played; he just needed to get away from work for a little while. Sure he and the Senator would talk about the case, but talking about the case on a fairway was a heck of a lot better than talking about it in his cramped little cube.

Tommy left the station almost immediately. It was 8:30, but he wanted to go home and catch some z's before hitting the links. Also, he couldn't seem to remember the last time he'd had a shower. Bathing was certain to do him some good. On the way home he hit the *McDonald's* on the highway and got an egg sandwich and a hash brown to go. He washed it down with some coffee. By the time he had finished his food, he was heading down the exit ramp en route to his house. As he pulled into his driveway, he noticed his pain-in-the-ass neighbor approaching his car. Now is not the time, he thought. As he exited the GTO, the dumb bastard opened his mouth. All Tommy could see was a mouth full of porcelain veneers. And if that wasn't bad enough, the guy had no hair, but chose to have one of those goofy ponytails anyway. What an asshole. Didn't he know he looked like an idiot? Apparently not.

"Hello neighbor. Have you given any more thought to my offer?"

Tommy was exhausted. Was this guy for real? Tommy did his best to hold his temper, but it was no use. The lack of sleep and the burden of the two cases made him snap. "Listen you little yuppie weasel, maybe you can buy everyone else, but you are never, ever going to buy me. I don't give a shit what you offer me. You will never own this house as long as there is breath in my lungs."

The man was taken aback. "But…"

"No buts. Get out of my face before I grab you by that ponytail and throw your sorry ass into Long Island Sound."

"But my offer is very generous."

"What part of 'get out of here' didn't you understand? Listen, I am in a terrible mood. I have two cases that could make or break my career; I can't remember the last time I slept or bathed, and all I want is to lie down on my bed. But instead, I am standing here arguing with a spoiled pain in the ass who never worked a hard day in his life."

With that Tommy walked to his front door. As he gazed back, he saw a look of surprise on his neighbor's face.

"And one more thing, you're bald, asshole. Get rid of the ponytail before I cut it off while you're asleep."

The man was shocked. He was not accustomed to people talking to him that way. How could this be? He always got his way. Why should this time be any different?

"That was kind of rude," he uttered out loud for anyone to hear. No one did. He'd tell his friends at his morning Yoga class. They'd surely understand, he thought.

Tommy went straight to his bedroom and dove head-first onto his bed. He reached up and turned the AC on high. The last thing he wanted was to wake up all sweaty. He was fast asleep in a matter of minutes.

Tommy logged only two and half hours sleep, but it did him a world of good. He parked his car and walked over to the bag room to get his clubs. He usually walked the course, but on a blistering hot day, getting a cart was a sensible idea. He loaded the clubs onto the cart and drove the short distance to the driving range. He hit a bucket of balls while he waited for the Senator. He had a few good shots, but nothing worth writing home about. As he was picking up the empty bucket, he saw Senator Maitland pulling into the parking lot. You couldn't miss him. He drove an old T-Bird convertible. He could have afforded a much more expensive vehicle, but chose to drive this car more often than not. Tommy remembered when he and Daniel were kids Daniel's dad would always be outside washing and waxing it up. He loved that car. Daniel told him that his father had totally redone the car all by himself. Apparently it was quite a mess when he bought it, but now it was a work of art. Tommy really admired that about the Senator. The Senator came from a wealthy family, but unlike that toad who wanted to buy his cottage, the Senator never took it for granted, and always, always worked his ass off. Tommy wished he was a little more like the Senator.

The Senator found a spot and Tommy climbed back in the cart and headed across the parking lot to meet him. He was pulling the clubs out of the trunk as Tommy approached.

"Tommy, it is good to see you."

"It's good to see you too, sir."

"What's with the cart? Are you going soft on me all of the sudden?"

"Very funny, sir. I figured it's pretty damn hot, and who knows, maybe with the cart we can squeeze in eighteen."

"I like the way you think. These days it seems harder and harder to squeeze in eighteen. It's certainly not like the summer of your twenty- first year."

"You still remember that?"

"How could I forget? You guys spent more time on the golf course than you did anywhere else."

He was right. What a great summer, he thought. When he was twenty-one, he, Daniel and a bunch of their buddies got junior memberships to the club. And unlike the senior members, the vetting processing was non-existent. It was the best $650.00 he'd ever spent. What a steal. And what a great time they had; golfing, eating and drinking, without a care in the world. And when they were not golfing, they were hanging out at the cottage. It was great; he and Daniel lived at the cottage all summer. Tommy often longed for those simpler times.

"What do you say we go off the back nine first? I noticed a few cartloads of people near the first tee when I picked up the cart."

"Works for me."

The Senator secured his bag to the rear of cart and jumped in beside Tommy.

"Tommy, we need to talk about Arthur Townsend."

"Yes we do."

The two men hit their drives down the tenth fairway, and when they got back into the cart, the Senator was the first to speak.

"Tommy, you know that Senator Townsend and I were, how should I say this, rivals at best, enemies at worst? With that said, I want to make sure that everything is done to catch his killer."

"I couldn't agree with you more."

"I figured that since you are by far the best investigator the department has, that this one would be thrown your way."

"Good guess, although I'm not sure Tony would be quite as flattering, and the FBI certainly have their own ideas."

The Senator laughed. "In any case, I'll do everything in my power to help you out."

"I know you will sir, I know you will."

The men had a good round of golf. Unfortunately, they were only able to get nine holes in, as the sky opened up once they rounded the eighteenth tee. In any case Tommy didn't care. He'd played pretty well today as did the Senator. It was the first time in a long time that Tommy scored better than the Senator. And after talking to the Senator, Tommy was somewhat relieved. The Senator wasn't interested in pressuring Tommy about the case. On the contrary, he just asked that Tommy keep him apprised of any developments. Tommy agreed to do just that. He hoped he wouldn't let the Senator down. Truth be told, he thought Arthur Townsend was a weasel. But that weasel got killed in his city. He'd work his ass off to find the killer, but he wasn't about to make any promises. As it was, he was still hitting dead ends left and right on the Green murder. Who knows, maybe Susan would have some updates by the time he got back to the station.

Tommy offered to buy the Senator dinner at the clubhouse, but he politely declined.

"Thanks, Tommy. Maybe another time. I have a few things to attend to. Don't worry, it's not the company, I assure you."

"Sir, if I didn't know better, I'd say you were ashamed to eat with me due to your poor performance out there today."

"Very funny. You did beat me, but two strokes doesn't make for an ass kicking."

"I know, but it is nice to win once in a while."

"Don't fool yourself, Tommy. Losing always sucks."

The two embraced. "Take care of yourself, son."

"It's been a pleasure as always."

"The pleasure is mine Tommy, the pleasure is mine."

The Senator climbed into his convertible. He'd had the presence of mind to put the top up before they started to play, so he didn't have to ride home in a wet car. Tommy headed into the clubhouse to get a bite to eat and have a quick shower. After throwing back a turkey club and two Diet Cokes, Tommy was driving south on 95 back to New Haven. When he looked at his phone, he noticed he'd missed five calls.

Great, he thought. Who's looking for me now? As it turned out, it was just Susan checking in. She wondered how the men's outing had gone. Tommy wasn't sure. He had hoped the Senator could've have shed some light on the person or kind of person who bumped off Arthur. Unfortunately for W. Arthur Townsend, he was hated by a great many people.

The man logged in to his computer once again to check on the lawyer and his partner. They were both slumped over as before. He was quite sure they were dead. Unfortunately for the pair, the weather had been so hot that dehydration and death came more quickly than even the man had predicted. Ever the pragmatist, the man started to cover his tracks. He clicked on a clock shaped icon on the lower part of his computer desktop. When the program opened, he was asked to enter a password. He typed in a number of keystrokes and a digital time clock appeared on the screen. Next, he entered a frequency code. When he finished that, he set the timer for one minute and closed the lid of the laptop. He grabbed himself a beer from the fridge and walked out onto his deck. As he gazed out across the water, he saw the light of the explosion before the sound registered in his ears. "Goodbye gentlemen," Senator John Maitland uttered as he took a sip of his beer. "Goodbye indeed."

Chapter 26

The explosion was seen and heard from miles away. It lit up the summer sky like a Fourth of July fireworks display. Folks from as far as Long Island watched as the flames consumed the once beautiful island. In no time police, fire, rescue, and Coastguard boats were converging on what was left of Jerry's paradise. The locals were in a frenzy. They had never seen such a spectacle before. News crews in their small boats fought for the best shots while police did their best to keep onlookers in their pleasure crafts from getting too close to the island.

Tommy heard about the explosion on the police radio, but thought little of it. After all, the Thimble's were outside of his jurisdiction. Susan paid him a visit as he was thumbing through Dr. Green's journal for a third time.

"Tommy, just heard back from the lab on the Toby Scott's letter. It was just as we suspected; no prints."

"Great, yet another dead end."

"Any luck on your end?"

"I wish." Tommy was so frustrated that he threw the book onto his desk.

"I don't know," he uttered as he rubbed his temples.

He instinctively gazed at the page that lay open on his desk.

There were only a few highlighted entries. The one at the top of the page listed the name of the patient only as Madelyn M., brought in by Peggy Baldwin. To the right of Peggy's Baldwin's name was written the word friend. The date of the visit was August 5, 1988.

"For some reason this date stick's out in my mind."

"What date?"

"August 5, 1988 or was it August 6th? Although for the life of me I can't remember what it is. I was in high school at that time, although school would have been out for the summer."

"Tommy, I'm sorry, I wish we had more to go on," Susan offered plaintively.

Tommy waved his hand in Susan's direction. "Wait, just give me minute." Tommy sat and thought about that summer some more.

"It was like any other summer. The only thing that sticks out was the tragedy that befell the Maitland's."

"What kind of tragedy?"

"Daniel's little sister died."

"Oh my God. How awful."

"Tell me about it. Maddie was like the little sister I never had."

"What happened?"

"She had some kind of infection. All I know is it took her very fast."

"When was that?"

"I know it was in August. We were getting ready to go back to school. That much I remember. She was actually living on campus at the time. Middlesex Academy had summer school classes. Unlike most schools, their summer sessions were about getting ahead, not getting caught up. I remember that summer Miss. Bald..." Tommy paused. It couldn't be, he thought.

"Tommy, what's wrong?"

Tommy starting pulling apart the items on top of his desk. Where was it, he thought? "Shit."

"Tommy, talk to me."

Next, Tommy started digging through the recycling box beneath his desk. It didn't take him long to find what he was looking for. It was a copy of one of the newspapers from the previous day. He nearly tore the paper apart trying to find the right page.

"Can I help you find anything?"

Finally Tommy replied as he opened the paper to the article about the Head Mistress of his alma mater. He quickly passed the headlines and started reading the body of the article.

…Margaret Baldwin's lifeless body was found yesterday by a local fisherman at the bottom of Messhershmidt's Pond…

Tommy turned his attention back to Susan. "Susan, what are some of the nicknames for the name Margaret?"

"Marge, Margie, Margo. Why?"

"What about Peggy?"

"Yeah, now that you mention it, some Margaret's do go by Peggy, although for the life of me, I could never figure out how one got Peggy out of Margaret. Why do you ask?"

"Read this." Tommy handed her the journal as well as the article.

When Susan was though, she looked up. "So Madelyn is Daniel's sister Maddie…"

"As best as I can figure."

"And Margaret aka Peggy is the one who brought her to Dr. Green's office?"

"It would appear so."

"I thought you said she died from an infection."

"She did, although they were always hush hush about its

cause."

"That's understandable under the circumstances. If she some-how contracted this infection at Dr. Green's, her parent's would be certain to protect her memory from this."

"Poor Maddie, she must have been so scared. I remember how upset her boyfriend was, although there is no mention of his name in Dr. Green's journal."

"I guess we can assume only she and Miss Baldwin went to Dr. Green's that day."

"This is too much for me to handle."

"Then who killed Dr. Green, the boyfriend?"

"I hate to say it, but I think my golf partner from earlier today had some hand in this."

"Tommy, I don't know what to say."

"I think I do."

"You've got to tell Tony. This is huge."

"It's bigger than huge. My bet is that Margaret Baldwin's death was no accident either."

"It is too big of a coincidence for sure."

"Not to mention Arthur Townsend. His death might be tied to this, although I have yet to see a direct connection other than the fact that Senator's Maitland and Townsend were colleagues."

"I think colleague is too strong a word; I've seen them go at it on the Senate floor many times on *CSPAN*. It wasn't pretty."

"Maybe he killed Townsend because he figured he had nothing to lose. After all, what's the difference if you kill two people or three people? Chances are you are going away for the rest of your life. Although with the bleeding hearts on the parole board we have in this state, the Senator might be out in a few years."

"Tell me about it. Listen, Tommy, we've got to bring him in. I know he's your friend, and God knows I voted for him countless times myself, but if we don't do something, and soon, he might kill again."

"Who?"

"I don't know, but you said it yourself, if he's killed already he doesn't have much to lose."

"Would that be so bad?"

"What do you mean?"

"Would killing more people like Edgar Green or Arthur Townsend be so bad?"

"Tommy, you're starting to scare me."

"Don't worry, you're in good company; I'm starting to scare myself as well. What I mean is, I understand how he feels."

"The Senator?"

"Yes. I certainly don't know what it's like to lose a child, but I remember how sad I was when she died. I still think about her. Like I said, she was the kid sister I never had. She used to tag along with Daniel and me. Daniel used to tease me and say that she had a crush on me. I was there to look after her when she started school at Middlesex Academy. Daniel and I were juniors and she was a freshman. She didn't want to have her big brother keeping an eye on her, so I was always there when she needed anything. When she died, it was the one time I was unable to help her. After all, I was able to save her brother once, but I couldn't do anything to save her."

"Tommy, don't blame yourself."

"I don't. I blame Dr. Green and Miss Baldwin, and who knows, maybe Arthur Townsend. In any case, I will talk to the Senator, but I have to do this on my own. I hope you understand."

"Tommy, let me back you up."

"You don't understand. I don't need back up. Senator Maitland is the most honorable man I know. He wouldn't do anything to tarnish that image."

"You don't think killing two, maybe three people is a quick way to tarnish one's image?"

"Point taken."

"How about you wait in the car while I go in and talk to him?"

"I'll do whatever you think it best."

"At this point, I'm not really sure what best is."

Tommy and Susan rode in silence the entire way to the home of Senator Maitland. Tommy was so distracted that he let Susan drive the GTO yet again. Tommy had made this drive many times before, but never under these circumstances. What would he say? Would Senator Maitland put up a fight? These questions and others swirled around in his head like the billowing clouds of smoke engulfing the nearby Thimble Islands. He really needed a drink. He hoped Senator Maitland was pouring.

Chapter 27

Susan drove slowly down Selden Avenue, one of the roads that lined the Branford coast. When they got to the house in question, Tommy indicated so to Susan. She pulled up in front of the house, but decided not to pull in to the circular drive. There was a walkway from the street to the front door, so she parked the car adjacent to it. Tommy unbuckled his seatbelt and took a deep breath.

"Here goes nothing," he said.

"Just remember, if things don't go down as you expected, I'm right here, OK?"

"Thanks, although for the life of me, I don't really know what to expect. Will he deny it? Will he say 'yes Tommy, you got me?' I just don't know."

"Well, you won't know unless and until you knock on that door."

Tommy opened his door and closed it behind him with two hands. He squatted down so that his head was at Susan's eye level.

"Susan, if I haven't said it before, you're a great partner."

"Thanks, Tommy. That's means a lot. Now, go get him."

Tommy shook his head. "There's no time like the present."

He turned on a heel, and walked confidently up the walkway. Truth be told, he was scared shitless, but perception was everything.

If the suspect thought you were nervous, well, anything could happen, even if that suspect was a sitting U.S. Senator and your best friend's father. Tommy rang the bell. Despite having a staff that took care of the house, the Senator answered the door personally.

"Tommy, long time no see."

"I know sir. Can I come in?"

"Certainly." The Senator's gaze rested on the unknown woman in the GTO.

"Tommy, why don't you invite your partner in as well. I'm sure she's also wondering why I killed Dr. Green."

Tommy was startled by this admission, but didn't let on.

"Yes sir, I believe she is."

"I'll pour us some drinks and you go get Susan, that's her name, right?"

"Yes it is sir."

"Is white wine OK? I have a nice Pinot Grigio that's been chilling a while. Will that do?"

"That would be just fine, sir."

"Very well."

Tommy walked back to the car and motioned Susan to join him.

"Is everything OK Tommy?"

"So far so good."

"You up for a drink?"

"As a matter of fact, I am."

Tommy held the front door as Susan walked into the large foyer. Senator Maitland appeared with two glasses of wine almost instantly. He handed one to each officer and headed back into the kitchen to retrieve one for himself.

He pointed them in the direction of the great room. The room extended two thirds of the way across the back of the house. Its floor to ceiling windows gave a breathtaking view of the Sound.

"Will this do, or would you prefer to sit outside?"

"This is fine sir, thanks."

"Tommy, you don't have to beat around the bush. We all know why you're here."

"Sir, I think I do, but not everything seems to fit for me."

"Let me explain and then you and Susan can do what you came to do. Fair enough?"

"Yes sir."

The Senator began his heartfelt monologue.

"It all started almost twenty years ago to the day. Mrs. Maitland and I were sitting in this very room. It was maybe 4:00 pm. Daniel had been home for the summer, but Maddie wanted to attend the summer session to get ahead. It was so like Maddie. Anyway, it was 4:00 and Maddie came home and she looked awful. She was very pale and she complained of abdominal pain. When we asked her why she didn't go to the school's infirmary, she burst into tears. Of course we were concerned. Like all kids, she'd been sick before, but she had never been this upset, not even when she was a young child. After a few minutes she told us what had happened. She and her boyfriend Brian had had sex one time. They were both virgins and their passions got the better of them. Afterwards they both decided it wasn't the time for them to be sexually active. They cared for each other and didn't want to ruin what they had by turning it into something physical. That was June. Well a month passed, and Maddie missed her period. In addition, she had been experiencing what she later found out was morning sickness. I guess she panicked and she turned to first person that she thought she could trust."

"Miss Baldwin."

"Yes, Miss Baldwin. She'd been taking one of Miss Baldwin's summer classes at the time and she was one of four people in the class. During that time, the two got along quite well. As Maddie put it, they formed quite a bond or so she thought. Well, Miss Baldwin said she would bring her to see a doctor friend of hers. Maddie thought she was going to have a pregnancy test. As it turns out, Miss Baldwin brought her to Dr. Green's office. She did receive a pregnancy test and she found out that she was six weeks pregnant. Maddie was a smart girl; she knew what Dr. Green did. Miss Baldwin tried to convince her to abort the child, but she told Miss Baldwin emphatically that she did not want an abortion. After about a half hour of trying to convince her, Maddie told her she wanted to leave. The two left Maddie alone for a few minutes and went into another room to talk. When they returned, Doctor Green handed Maddie two bottles of pills. One was a bottle of prenatal vitamins. He stated that if she wanted to keep the baby, it was important that she take these in order to ensure a healthy child. The other bottle he explained would help with her morning sickness. He pointed her in the direction of a nearby water cooler and she took the pills. Miss Baldwin brought her back to school and Maddie went straight to her room and to bed. She woke the next morning with severe abdominal pain. She did go to the infirmary, but they told her it was probably something she ate. She tried to take it easy for the better part of the day, but the pain became unbearable. It was at this point that she drove herself home."

Tommy and Susan were riveted. The Senator took a big sip of his wine and settled back into telling them the rest of the story.

"We immediately drove Maddie to the hospital. As we got closer, the pain seemed to increase. We brought her to the ER and explained what had happened. They took her on gurney to examine and treat her, and that was the last time we saw her alive."

Tears began to well in Susan's eyes.

"When the doctor came back out to tell us she had died, we were beside ourselves. We couldn't believe this was happening. The days that followed were the worst of our lives. We were all totally numb. We didn't know how we were going to move forward. Were it not for our faith, I don't know how we would have made it through that period."

At this point the Senator was crying as well. He wiped the tears from his face and took a deep breath.

"As it turns out, the second set of pills was *RU-486.*"

"The abortion pill?" Susan replied."

"Yes. Maddie unwittingly took this pill and in the process she contracted a bacterium called Clostridium Sordelli. It was this bacterium that took her life."

It was at this point that the Senator broke down. Susan instinctively put her arms around him and held him.

"It's OK sir, let it out."

After several minutes had passed, the Senator composed himself enough to continue the story.

"As you can imagine, and as Tommy knows, our family was never the same again."

"What about bringing charges against them? *RU-486* wasn't approved for use in the U.S. until recently," Susan asked.

"Believe me, I wanted to do everything in my power to get back at the people who did this, but my wife, a trial of any sort would have killed her. I promised her that I wouldn't do anything if it was going to cause her undue harm. If she ever had to get on the stand to talk about bringing our dying child to the hospital, it would have destroyed her. In the mean time, I gathered everything I could on

Miss Baldwin and Dr. Green. I hired investigators, you name it. I reasoned that some day maybe Wendy would come around."

"But she didn't."

"No. I'm not sure if Tommy told you, but I lost her two and a half years ago."

"I'm so sorry."

"Thank you, it's still hard to think about life without her. Anyway, after she died I thought about doing something, but the statute of limitations had long since run out on the criminal charges or for bringing a civil suit for that matter. And six months ago, I went to the doctor. I'd been having some terrible headaches. He referred me to specialist. After a CT Scan, it was discovered that I have an inoperable tumor."

It was Tommy's turn to speak. "Sir, I am so sorry."

"Don't be, Tommy. This old man has had a good life. Despite losing Maddie and Wendy, I have been quite blessed. Daniel still amazes me every day, and you Tommy, you have been like a second son to me."

Tears were starting to form in Tommy's eyes as well.

"In any case, after I was given my death sentence so to speak, I hatched this, my master plan."

The Senator pulled an envelope from the inside pocket of his poplin suit.

"Here Tommy. This letter says it all. The how and the why of these killings. And it's signed by yours truly."

He handed it to Tommy.

"I just ask that you let me call my attorney before we go."

"Sure thing, sir."

Tommy just stared at the confession in his hands. It was easier than he'd thought. As he pondered its contents, the Senator was thumbing through his rolodex looking for his lawyer's home number. It was getting late and his attorney had more than likely gone home for the day. Tommy hadn't been looking in that direction, but turned when he heard the Senator scream. In a matter of moments Tommy and Susan were on their feet. The Senator was holding the side of his head.

"Sir, are you alright? Susan, call an ambulance."

Tommy knelt beside the Senator. He'd lost consciousness. He grabbed the Senator's hand. "Don't worry sir, I'm right here. Everything is going to be fine. You hang in there. I'm not going anywhere."

"The ambulance is on its way."

"Hang in there sir. Hang in there."

Chapter 28

The ambulance arrived minutes later. Tommy rode with the Senator and Susan followed closely behind in the GTO. They were pulling up to the ER entrance at St. Raphael's within fifteen minutes. As they wheeled the stretcher through the double doors, Tommy had a sinking feeling. This was the same hospital, the same ER that the Senator and Mrs. Maitland brought Maddie to twenty years ago. For some reason, Tommy knew that the Senator would likewise die at this hospital.

Susan parked the GTO illegally and ran up to Tommy.

"How's he doing?"

"It doesn't look good."

"Tommy, he's a fighter. If anyone can pull through it's him. Think about his experience in Vietnam. He made it through three years in a North Vietnamese prison camp. For a guy like him, this is nothing."

"I hope you're right."

Tommy appreciated Susan's optimism. But this wasn't nothing. In retrospect, maybe this was for the best, he thought. As the Senator had explained earlier that evening, his family had never been the same after Maddie died. At least now he and his wife and daughter would be reunited at last. Tommy and Susan sat down in the waiting room and awaited any updates on the Senator's condition. After an hour had passed, a man in green hospital scrubs appeared. Tommy saw him, and stood up. As he approached the pair, he introduced himself.

"Hello, I am Dr. Savage. Were you the ones who brought Seantor Maitland in?"

"Yes, sir we were."

"Are you members of his family?"

"I am, sort of," Tommy replied. "I've known the Senator since I was a little kid. Our families go way back."

"Well, I am sorry to be the one to break it to you, but Senator Maitland has passed away. We need to contact his next of kin. Would you be able to help us?"

"His closest living relative is his son. And he's stationed overseas. I can reach him, but it might take some time."

"Very well. Again, I just want to tell you how sorry I am. The Senator was a good man."

"Yes, yes he was," Tommy replied.

Tommy spent the next half hour trying to contact Daniel. As luck would have it, Daniel had given him a number to contact in case of an emergency. Tommy had called numerous times, but luckily there were no emergencies to report. As a police officer Tommy had broken the bad news countless times to unsuspecting family members who'd lost loved ones. He was certain this time would be the hardest. When he finally got through to Daniel, he was at a loss for words. As it turned out, Daniel's dad had told him about the diagnosis several months earlier. It seems the two had been in contact on a regular basis ever since. The Senator even flew to Iraq to be with his son for the 4th of July. Tommy felt awful for his friend. How hard it must be to be half way around the world when someone you care about dies. He told Daniel he'd take care of the arrangements. The Senator wanted to be buried in the family plot next to his wife and daughter. Tommy and he said their goodbyes and he hung up the phone.

"How'd he take it?"

"Pretty well. He knew his dad was sick. Listen, I need to get some air. Would you please excuse me?"

"Sure thing."

Tommy walked outside. What a week, he thought. As he stood by the entrance to the hospital, Tommy had a thought. When they'd left the Senator's home, he'd stuck the Senator's confession into his pocket. What did it say? He wondered. He removed the letter, and stared at the envelope. He was dying to know the rest of the story. Would it mention Arthur Townsend? Tommy walked a short distance to a nearby steel trash can. Out of his front pocket he pulled out a Zippo lighter. Tommy always carried the Zippo and a pack of smokes. He didn't smoke, but over time he obtained much information from suspects by merely offering them a cigarette. He opened the Zippo and watched the blue flame. It flickered in the light breeze. Susan had begun to make her way out to join him. As she approached, Tommy put the flame to the envelope. In a matter of seconds, the envelope and its contents were ashes floating into the trash receptacle. Susan looked stunned, but she understood.

"No good would come from releasing that letter, you know that."

"Tommy, I think the Senator suffered plenty for his crime. Although unlike most people, his punishment came first, the crime second.

Susan reached over and took Tommy in her arms. She held him until he signaled her to let go. Their embrace lasted a whole ten minutes. They walked silently to the GTO.

"What do you say that I drive you home?"

"Thanks, Susan. I don't think I'm in any shape to drive."

Susan pulled the car onto Route 34 and then onto 95. For once they took their time, since time was something the two had plenty of.

Connecticut Mourns the Loss of Two Statesmen

New Haven- In what can only be described as a tragedy of mythic proportion, the State of Connecticut has lost both its U.S. Senators in a two day period. On Saturday evening, Senator W. Arthur Townsend was murdered by an intruder while spending time at a friend's house here in the Elm City. The police speculate robbery was the motive. Senator Townsend started his career in the State Legislature before moving on to the Senate. His Colleague, Senator John Maitland was rushed to the hospital Sunday after collapsing in his Branford home. He was pronounced dead later that evening at St. Raphael's Hospital. Although the pair seldom saw eye to eye, they vigorously worked together to serve the people of Connecticut. Both men will be sorely missed.

Local Attorney and Client Perish in Explosion

The Thimble Islands- The legal community mourns the loss of one of its most esteemed litigators. Jerry Rivers and a friend and client, Bruce Damon were killed in a freak explosion at Mr. River's vacation residence in the Thimble Islands. Sources close to the story state that a propane leak on the island was the likely cause of the blast. A friend of the attorney confirmed the pair were on the island working on their strategy for an upcoming lawsuit at the time of their deaths.

Breinigsville, PA USA
10 June 2010
239514BV00003B/6/P